THE **FLOODPLAIN**

A Novel By **Anthony Robinson**

For Vici —

A wonderful
(former) student, and
a dear friend.

Terry Robinson

NOVELS BY ANTHONY ROBINSON

A Departure From the Rules

The Easy Way

Home Again, Home Again

The Whole Truth

The Member-Guest

The American Golfer

CODHILL

Codhill Press books
are published for David Appelbaum

First Edition
Printed in the United States of America
Copyright © 2012 by Anthony Robinson

ISBN 1-930337-64-7

Cover and text design by Alicia Fox

It looked as if a night of dark intent
Was coming, and not only a night, an age.
Someone had better be prepared for rage.

Once by the Pacific

—Robert Frost

■ ■ ■

"I never knew, and never shall know, a worse man than myself."

Walden

—Henry David Thoreau

For

Richard Hathaway

THE **FLOODPLAIN**

PART I

CHAPTER
1

Rick Forrester turned at the staircase in the front hall of his house and began climbing to the second floor, thinking to present his wife with a plan; really a counter-plan. He didn't like what was going on. When he reached the landing he looked through the open door of the master bedroom, watching her as she folded a pair of knee-length socks into a satchel on their bed. She had on bluejeans and a cherry turtleneck shirt, big gold loops at her ears. Shoulder-length rich brown hair. The hint of a smile, as of intimacies past or anticipated—somehow Rick didn't think with him—played on her lips.

Startled, she glanced up. "You frightened me! I thought you were hunting."

"I want to talk to you, Chloe," he said, going into the room. The flap on the pocket of his field jacket, askew, revealed shotgun shells held snugly in elasticized loops.

"Evan will be here any minute. Please, I'm packing."

"Make him wait."

Her eyes rose to the slanted part of the ceiling. The upper level of their old house was directly under the rafters. "Why are you doing this; why are you suddenly so concerned, so worried? I work with Evan every week, sometimes twice a week, here in Appleton."

In truth, he didn't like that she saw him at all. "Going away with someone is different," he said.

"Rick, this is my first time leading a group, or co-leading one. You should be proud of me."

"I am, but if I were going away with a single, attractive woman, a colleague, you'd be OK with it, I suppose." He paused for a moment. "I have a plan," he said, "hear me out. Stover

Falls is only thirty-five miles from here. Go in two cars. At the end of your evening session, you'll be able to drive home. We'll have an early breakfast with the kids and you'll get back in plenty of time to start your day."

"That's ludicrous," she said. "I'm staying in Stover Falls."

"In a quaint old inn."

"For the tenth time, we have separate rooms!"

"As if that means anything. I want you coming home at night."

"You don't own me, Rick. Now, leave me alone. Take Waldo into the woods, go shoot something!"

He stood there, remembering the night seventeen years ago—seeing a strikingly beautiful woman across the room at a party in Greenwich Village. High-bridged nose, lustrous dark hair—a wild, gypsy look. He made his way to her side, introduced himself. Rick Forrester, ex-navy officer recently home after a tour of duty in the Far East. He was at Columbia working on his doctorate. She was Chloe Cika, graduate of Long Island City High, secretary, of Turkish-Greek-Albanian extraction. Minuscule red flecks in the irises of her deep brown eyes. Rick, smitten, crazy to see her again. A man in a glittering suit coming toward her with drinks. Rick: "May I call you?" Chloe: "In the Queens directory under Raheed Cika. C-I-K-A."

Turning away from her in their bedroom, Rick went downstairs, passing the kitchen and going out to a rear deck that overlooked his backyard and, where the yard ended, a forty-foot grassy embankment—the eastern limit of the great Appleton floodplain. Fields, woods, wetlands stretched for three miles to a line of low, craggy mountains. At the foot of the embankment an oxbow lake shone in the afternoon October sun. Rick picked up the twenty-gauge Beretta he'd left on the deck and took a set of open steps down to the yard.

His brown and white springer spaniel was inside a chain-link pen, panting in anticipation. "She didn't buy it, Waldo,"

Rick said, walking over. "She called it ludicrous."

"Rrrufff!"

"My sentiments exactly."

■ ■ ■

In a big yellow field on the far side of the oxbow, shotgun resting in the crook of his arm—no way for a self-respecting hunter of game birds to carry his gun afield—Rick trudged along; clearly today he wasn't hunting. He had spared himself the agony of waiting for Evan Kendrix to come for Chloe and swoop her away in his sports car. Right about now they were probably popping along on country roads to Stover Falls on the New York/Massachusetts border, where they would be directing a weekend therapy workshop at the Bernard Institute and staying at the Stover Falls Inn. In separate rooms. Five months ago Chloe had taken off her wedding ring and Rick hadn't seen it since. He respected her espousal of the women's movement—with a single proviso: it was knocking hell out of his marriage.

With his dog, Rick entered a stand of hardwoods, then of scrubby cedars. A rabbit squirted away from a pile of brush and Waldo thought to give chase, checked himself, as if remembering he was an English springer spaniel, not a beagle. They moved on. The leaves were in full color and Rick tried to relax, to take pleasure in his favorite pastime, his favorite season; but he wasn't relaxing, he was badly preoccupied. With shadows settling across the floodplain, he whistled Waldo in and they started for home, the falling sun and Mount Chodokee, jewel of the Shagg Range, now at Rick's back.

"RrrmmMMM!"

A thunderous beating of wings, grouse swerving, gun to Rick's shoulder. *Boom!* Other barrel. *Boom!* Waldo waiting for a "fetch." Didn't get one. Nothing to fetch.

Rick broke his gun. The expended shells ejected automatically and he didn't reload. Tramping on, he kicked at a dead branch that reminded him of a divining rod. A gray squirrel jumped from a big hickory to a pine, scurried into the high branches. He no longer hunted grays. Chloe and the kids had given his squirrel dishes a couple of tries when they lived in Woodbridge five years ago, hadn't liked them—really hadn't liked the idea of eating squirrel.

He emerged from the woods. Three hundred yards away, across the yellow field, his house stood atop the embankment: white with black shutters, brick chimneys at either end of a steeply gabled roof. Originally the parsonage of the town's Reformed ministers, built in the early decades of the 19th century. About to start across the field, Rick had a sudden scare. The upstairs eyebrow windows were a fiery red. Was his house going up in flames?

No, sun's reflection. He sighed, shook his head. When they reached the oxbow, Waldo jumped right in. Rick walked along the edge until he came to his "stepping stones," little islands of matted weeds, and made his first leap, seven leaps all told (if you didn't slip and fall in). The springer, waiting for him at the foot of the embankment, gave himself a hard shake. They went up a series of steps made of embedded railroad ties that Rick had built his first year in the house. When they reached the top, Rick gave the dog praise, pulled gently on his fluffy ears, and enclosed him in his chain-link pen.

A smaller building, a combination shed and garage, sat near the house. Rick pulled at the sliding door of the shed and flipped on the fluorescent lights above his workbench. A pair of fishing waders hung on the wall, also a fisherman's vest and a wicker creel. A tangle of rusty steel traps dangled from a spike. He hadn't trapped muskrats since his early teens but had never thrown his traps out, to Chloe's annoyance. By her way of interpreting it, he didn't want to let go of his boyhood.

At his workbench, about to clean his Beretta, Rick heard

the sound of tires crunching driveway stones. Sometimes cars pulled in, then backed out and drove the other way on Elting Street. But after the crunching came the firm clunk of a closing door. He leaned the shotgun against the steep staircase leading to a loft and peered out. A dark-gray Porsche with MD plates was parked in the driveway, and striding toward the house was Evan Kendrix.

Rick felt numb with the shock of it; he hadn't escaped the agony at all.

Spotting him in the shed doorway, the psychiatrist said in a cheerful voice, "Rick, what a nice surprise! We're running late, obviously. Chloe said you were hunting."

"I was." A voice in his head saying: Here's your chance. Do something.

"Any luck?" Kendrix said. "But that's a fishing term, isn't it? How about 'any quarry?'"

"No quarry," Rick said, a sharp uptick in his heart.

Kendrix, six feet tall and powerfully built, was wearing rust-colored corduroys tucked into a pair of leather boots with a buckle at the instep, and a lined Levi jacket, unbuttoned. He had thick sandy hair that would humble any comb, and diamond-sharp hazel eyes that didn't so much look as dissect. He spotted the gun leaning against the loft steps. "Out of curiosity, Rick, what are the advantages of a shotgun with over-under barrels like yours, compared to side-by-side?"

"No advantage. It's personal preference."

"I've never hunted," Kendrix said, "but I can't think of anything more atavistically freighted than hunting, can you?"

Possibly killing someone, Rick thought.

Just then the back door to the house opened and Chloe came out. Kendrix made for the deck, taking the steps two at a time, leaving Rick in the shed like a yardman tending to the tools. He gave Chloe an embrace, within the bounds of propriety, then reached for her satchel, and they started down, Chloe first.

Over her cherry turtleneck she had on a black leather jacket.

Rick couldn't remember when, in recent years, she had looked so radiant. Halfway down the steps, she spotted him—not someone she wanted to see. But she collected herself and reminded Rick of the meals she'd prepared: pot roast tonight, Italian sauce for tomorrow. Andrew was still at the Locust Tree, the nearby golf course, and Lisa would be "needing a ride to the high school at eight o'clock for her co-rec, and don't forget to pick her up at ten."

"OK."

"Have a nice weekend with the kids," Chloe said. "See you Sunday."

"Take care, Rick," Kendrix said.

He escorted her to the Porsche. She opened the passenger-side door and got in. In no time they were speeding away.

Back in the shed, Rick set the Beretta on his workbench, his eyes tightly shut, angry at himself, disappointed. He blew out a breath, then ran a coaster-sized cotton patch, dampened with Hoppe's solvent, through the barrels, inserted dummy shells in both chambers and pulled the trigger twice—click, click—to relieve the pressure on the firing springs, and put the shotgun inside a birch cabinet. At the sound of familiar footfalls, he turned. His twelve-year-old son was walking to the shed, his hands and face filthy, lips blue, pants wet to the thighs. A bulging laundry sack was slung over his shoulder.

"Hi, Dad." He was staggering under the load. The sack hit the shed floor with a thud. "I stopped counting at a hundred. Got most in the pond on the eighth hole, also in the woods on one and nine."

Strictly speaking, balls found on a golf course belonged to the owner or the pro, depending on their arrangement. But Rick wasn't in a mood to reprimand his son and wouldn't have in any case. Hawking balls was as old as the game itself; it was like shooting gray squirrels on someone else's land or fishing posted water. As a kid growing up, here in Ulmer County, he'd done it all.

"That's quite a haul," he said.

The boy sneezed, dragged the sleeve of his shirt under his nose. "I'm set for next year."

"Great. I want you to go inside and take a long, hot shower."

"OK. Mom still here?"

"She just left," Rick said.

CHAPTER
2

Rick stood at the window in his office looking across Bliss Avenue to the college parking lot, idly observing the cars. When he arrived on campus two hours ago, he had counted five. Now there were close to fifty. With the weekend drawing to a close, it was time to get serious again at Appleton State.

He returned to his desk. His office had a ceiling-high bookcase, an easy chair, and a narrow daybed covered in red corduroy. Walls a light green, probably the same shade as twenty years ago when Grove Hall was one of the three dormitories on campus and his office was a double room. Now Appleton State had eleven new dorms, and Grove housed the English and History departments.

Spread out on his desk were 150 5" x 7" cards, a dozen books and journals, pages and pages of typescript, and an old Royal typewriter.

Rick stared at the page now on the roller. It was page 177 of still another revision of his biography of Henry David Thoreau. Ten years, seven different versions, nineteen total rejections from literary journals. A pipe with a curved stem rested in an earthen ashtray and Rick put a match to the old tobacco, getting two puffs out of it, then turned a period into a semicolon, lowercasing the first letter of the next word. A stroke of genius, certain to make an editor sit up and take notice!

His desk phone rang and Rick grabbed the receiver. "Hello."

"Hi, Daddy. Mom just called." It was his daughter.

"Where is she?"

"Evan's."

"*Evan's?*"

"It's what she said."

"She called from Evan's?"

"Daddy, yes. She'll be home in ten minutes."

"Thanks, Lisa."

Rick put the phone down. Why would they go to Evan's? Wouldn't he drop her off at Elting Street, end their weekend where it had begun? Rick pressed against his forehead as if to break his skull—and knew; all at once, he knew. Made numb with the reality of it, sickened by the pain of it, he left his office, got in his station wagon parked behind Grove, rolled by police headquarters and the Appleton Fire Department, turned left on Main Street, passed P&B's tavern, Borealis Bookstore, Manfried's Art Supplies, The Roaring Twenties, Appleton Liquor, Hobo Deli. At the minipark, where Main crossed N. Elm, he stopped for a traffic light, turned onto N. Elm, made a left on Hazel, hooked a right on Elting Street, and five houses along pulled into his own driveway.

He grabbed a rake, used it on leaves, old grass clippings by the side door of the house. Rick's hands tightened around the handle, loosened, tightened again. A car went by, then another. A heavy-set man pedaled past the house on a bicycle; two young women strolled along pushing baby carriages, chit-chatting away. Elting Street was a favorite route in Appleton for walkers, joggers, and cyclists. Then, at a distance, Rick heard the whine of a sports car.

He kept his head down, the conscientious homeowner taking care of his property. Rustle of stones, engine going dead. He propped the rake against a tree, started toward the car, thinking to confront Kendrix at once. How it would end up, he didn't know, but someone was going to get hurt. Walking toward Rick and carrying her satchel was Chloe. Parked in the driveway, the Porsche. Kendrix was nowhere to be seen.

"Hi," she said, as if coming home from one of her graduate courses at the college.

"Where is he?"

"Who?"

"Who do you think?"

"If you mean Evan, he's at his house. He let me borrow his car."

"Tell him he's a smart man."

"Rick, what's the problem?"

"You know goddamn well what it is!"

"Well, we'll talk about it later. Right now I want to see the kids." She moved away—

He reached out, grabbing her by the wrist. "Separate rooms? Did you really have separate rooms?"

"We did, yes!"

"You're a liar, a cheap fucking liar, Chloe!" His hand tightened.

"You're hurting me!"

"Am I now? Well, I'm really sorry."

He loosened his hold and she pulled away and continued to the deck stairs. Rick stood there in a fury, looking at the Porsche…saw himself behind the wheel pulling into Evan's driveway, parking, pounding on the psychiatrist's door—

The image faded, went dark. Even in a fantasy he couldn't go through with it. He had to leave, get ahold of himself. Upstairs in the house, Rick yanked down a bag, packed without thinking. On the main floor, he grabbed his briefcase and headed for the back door, passing in front of the long corridor leading to the den. Chloe was sitting with Andrew and Lisa on the daybed, telling them about her weekend, her great successes as a therapist. Rick walked on by, went out to the deck, where momentarily he stopped, his eyes spanning the floodplain.

Evergreens along the spine of the Shagg Range resembled a line of Conestoga wagons moving along in single file. Where were they going? What lay ahead? A wave of darkness and fear swept over Rick, and he thought to go back inside, to work things out with Chloe reasonably. But anger and pride overpowered his intentions, and he continued to his car.

CHAPTER
3

Just before coming to the steel bridge on her way out of the village, Chloe drove by the Appleton Hotel, a boxy three-story building with crumbling gingerbread trim, probably built in the 1920s. She didn't know who owned it but Ulmer County used it to house a number of its homeless and indigent. Rundown as it was, she loved the old place—known locally as Heartbreak Hotel—and had a plan for it: to own it one day and, with state and federal aid, turn it into The Chloe Forrester Mental Health Center.

It would be a long road but she had no doubt that she'd get there. Until then, she could never pass the rundown building without seeing it totally refurbished, inside and out, with cars bearing license plates from many different states parked out front. The view, looking across the floodplain to the Shagg Range, would add greatly to a client's experience and sense of well-being.

Chloe crossed the Walloon River, shifted into high. Rt. 289 was flat and straight, and she could nail it for two and a half miles before the road started curving, and even then she liked taking the curves fast. But more than speed, she loved going places. Rick never wanted to go anywhere. Like the quote at the start of his biography of Henry David Thoreau, Thoreau's comment about himself: "I have traveled a good deal in Concord." Certainly there were more exciting quotes than that, she'd told him years ago. Rick's reply: "That's the quote that captures Thoreau." In Chloe's opinion, it was the quote that captured Rick.

She zipped past Murello's, a large produce farm. Corn had grown there all summer, also cabbage, beets, carrots, with one great stretch just for pumpkins. Earlier this fall she, Rick, and the kids had bought pumpkins here, a traditional fall outing—but she hadn't enjoyed herself, wanting to be with Evan: canoeing on his pond, having a glass of wine, making love. She had no guilt over their affair. How could she feel guilty over something so complete, so right? Whether they would ever get married, she didn't know; it wasn't important. She just wanted to keep seeing him, working with him, enjoying life with Evan to its fullest—and have her family, too. She saw herself on the early wave of a great and growing movement—women stepping out, taking their long-overdue share of the good things in life: a fulfilling career, a wonderful lover, *and* a husband and kids at home.

Part of that equation—namely, the husband—was missing, but Chloe didn't think it would be for long. That Rick was still living out of his college office three weeks after their breakup spoke volumes about who he was. He may have walked out but he wasn't going to stray too far, stay away too long. His family, his home, were too important to him. If—not if, *when*—he came wandering back she wouldn't bar him from the house or make life difficult for him. But she didn't want to take up with Rick again as if nothing had happened. Something *had* happened, and he would have to accept it.

Chloe sped across the floodplain, now passing the Lufkin & Jenkins Orchard. People from all over the county came here to fill baskets with Golden Delicious and McIntosh apples. A yellow roadside warning sign depicted a leaping buck. Then she was by the orchard and drawing near the Shagg Range.

Her accordion-style folder skidded across the passenger's seat as she negotiated a turn. A half-mile farther on, Chodokee Road branched off Rt. 289. Chloe followed Chodokee to a rural mailbox—significantly (she always thought) marked with a bold "1"—stationed at the entrance to a long private driveway. On one side of it, in a big field, stood a number of stone sculptures seven feet tall, sensuously curved, adorned with oversized chain necklaces. Chloe continued to the end of the drive that stopped at a large shale turnaround like a stream terminating at a lake. Evan's house, a sturdy ranch stained a dark brown, was on the right. Directly in front of her, on the far side of a split-rail fence, stood a red, barn-like building.

She picked up her folder and stepped out, even as Evan, in corduroys and a boat-neck sweater, appeared in the doorway to the barn. Two neighboring posts in the fence were absent their rails, and she walked through the opening. A thin sprinkle of stone dust clung to Evan's eyebrows and Chloe smoothed it away.

They kissed; then Evan said, "Come take a look."

Two weeks had passed since she'd first seen the pinkish-gray stone, at eight feet his largest piece yet. To her surprise he had suggested she stand next to it and strike a pose. She had thought he was joking, but he had taken up a pencil and pad. Complying, she had put a hand on her hip, the other teasingly behind her head.

"Beautiful!" he had sung out.

Now she was looking at the stone again, noticing the first hints of a seductive line. That Evan had the ability to take a huge, formless chunk of rock and transform it into a work of art *and* have a successful career as a psychotherapist and writer, never failed to amaze her; but it made sense, knowing him as she did—chipping away at people's armor to get to their essence.

"Have you a name for it?"

"In my heart of hearts, 'Chloe.' What else?" he said. "But I'm calling it 'Prurience.' Don't be insulted. Think of yourself as every man's wildest fantasy."

She laughed.

Evan picked up a palm-sized remote and, pressing a button, eased the oak-and-steel dolly on which the stone rested two feet forward, simultaneously touching a tiny joystick and turning the front wheels. He (she also) now had a new perspective. Evan nodded, liking what he saw…or imagined. Then to Chloe, "Listen, go in and start a fire. I'll be right there."

"The fire is already started."

She gave him a quiet look and walked out, cutting across the shale turnaround. November afternoons, Mt. Chodokee, rising a stone's throw from the western limits of Evan's property, quickly threw the house into shadow, something she didn't like; she preferred storied houses. Evan's house did have a secure feel to it, however, while hers, dating to 1835, creaked and groaned. And there were no ghosts here, which she couldn't say of her own. Generations of Dutch Reformed clergy and their families hadn't lived and died under Evan's roof.

Inside, she turned on a couple of lamps and deposited her folder on a leather sofa in the living room. A sliding glass door opened to a small rear porch; full-length drapes were two-thirds closed, and Chloe opened them all the way. She loved the view behind the house: a stone path descending to a pond a hundred yards away. In the failing light, she saw the little dock and the green canoe lying on it, remembering her very first visit with Dr. Kendrix more than two years ago.…

■ ■ ■

She had just started her master's in psychology at Appleton State, and the name of a local psychiatrist, Evan Kendrix, kept popping up among faculty and students. A leading figure in the field of humanistic psychology and the author of *Sex and Marriage,* Dr. Kendrix—Chloe quickly learned—lived in Appleton. On impulse one day she had called him up, stated who she was, what her goals were. Did he have a moment, could they meet? Sure, come on out, he had said. How was tomorrow at two?

The next day she drove out to see him, west from Appleton,

virtually at the extreme far side of the floodplain. They had talked briefly in his office, then walked on a down-sloping path to a lovely, isolated pond and sat at the end of a small dock; a canoe lay upside down on one side of it. Thick evergreen woods encircled two-thirds of the pond. The day was warm, early September. She liked that he didn't spout erudition, didn't mention or quote Freud, Jung, Rogers, Perls, or Maslow—they just spoke about the pond and the sky, themselves, relationships, women's liberation.

That he supported the movement pleased Chloe, who had recently discovered *Ms.* magazine, read it religiously, and loved Gloria Steinem. One of the great things about the feminist movement, Evan said, was that liberating women also liberated men. Then, smiling, he said, "Name one thing about yourself that's uniquely you."

She thought about it, wanting to give a good answer.

"Chloe, say what comes to your mind."

"I'm a belly dancer."

He clapped spontaneously. "I can only hope, one day, I'll have the pleasure of seeing you perform. Would you like to go for a paddle?"

She would. Evan righted the canoe, slid it over the side of the dock and held it while Chloe got in and sat in the bow. On the stern thwart, he guided the craft out to the middle of the pond, then along the far shore and into a secluded cove, where a family of firs had allowed a few hardwoods to move in. A scattering of leaves, tinted orange and yellow, floated on the surface. Chloe trailed her hand over the side, loving the noiseless motion of the canoe. Evan said that the pond, and all the land to the east—to Elting Street itself—became a great inland sea when the Walloon River overflowed its banks after prolonged rains. How well she knew! She said she'd never forget looking out her bedroom window their first spring in Appleton after a day and a half of rain, thinking she lived on a bay instead of an oxbow.

"Do you have any lanterns?" he asked.

"Lanterns?"

"To signal the midnight paddler."

"Do I want to signal him; isn't that the question?"

"Say he was a secret lover."

"In that case…" she said with a smile, and left it there.

Making deep, smooth strokes, Evan circled the pond and soon was taking her hand as she stepped from the canoe. He invited her in for a glass of wine. On a drop-leaf table in the living room were several photographs—one, framed in brushed steel, of a small boy on a swing, a woman with strawberry-blonde hair, in dark pants and a jonquil-yellow sweater, standing beside him.

"That's Jared and my wife, Sue," Evan said.

"She's very attractive."

"We're separated. She lives in California with another woman."

Chloe could only wonder why she felt relieved; she'd known the man all of one hour.

Evan poured wine and they continued talking. Summing up, he said, "I'd like to work with you, Chloe. First in therapy, then in the role of mentor. By this time next year, with your master's degree well along, I could start referring clients to you. I have no doubt that you'll make an excellent therapist."

■ ■ ■

Chloe crossed to the fireplace in Evan's living room, set the screen to one side, then kneeled before the hearth and crumpled a couple of sheets of newspaper from a stack and laid on twigs and a trio of small logs. Whatever she knew of country living, she'd learned from Rick. Now all she needed was a match.

Usually Evan kept a box on the mantelpiece but it wasn't there and she walked into the kitchen. As she was looking in a cupboard drawer where she knew odds and ends were stored, the telephone, on the nearby counter, rang. After the third ring, his answering machine—he liked saying that he was the first person in Appleton to have one—came on. "Hello, Dr. Kendrix speaking. If this is an emergency, please call my paging service at 522-6130. Otherwise, leave your name, number, and a brief message after the beep, and I'll return your call as soon as possible. Speak in a normal tone and, again, wait for the beep. Thank you."

A female voice came on, young, hopeful. "Hi, Evan. This is Christine. Would love to go walking in the mountains with you if you're free tomorrow or the next day. Or just see you before our next session."

Chloe, pushing through steel-wool pads, ant buttons, a can of household oil, forgot what she was looking for. In her fingers was a ball of twine. That wasn't it. How about a corkscrew? Carpenter's glue? Matches?

Yes, matches.

She returned to the hearth, struck one, and touched it to the paper. The flame caught and she watched it flicker up, then ignite the kindling. *Love to go walking in the mountains with you, or just see you—*

The front door opened and Evan came in, stopped to hang his jacket in the hall, then ducked into the guest/client bathroom. Chloe went to the sofa, sat down. Soon, in the kitchen, a cupboard door opened, closed, and he walked in carrying a lacquered tray with two long-stemmed glasses of red wine and a plate of cheese and crackers. He placed the tray on the coffee table, handed her a glass.

"Great fire, Chloe." He sat beside her, popped a cheese and cracker into his mouth.

"Someone named Christine just called. She left a message."

"Christine?"

"I'm guessing a client. She mentioned her next session. She

wants to go walking in the mountains with you."

"Oh, Christine Monteleone." Evan gave his head a little shake, lifting his eyes. "College girl, smart as a whip—speech major, studying impediments—but delusional, emotionally adrift. She *believes* we'll go walking in the mountains. I gave her a roving slot."

Chloe wasn't satisfied but she didn't want to pursue it, and thought she probably shouldn't have said anything at all. Suspicion ran in her blood, something she had worked on with Evan and was still trying to control. A little gift from her mother. How vividly, to this day, Chloe saw her mother running after her father in the projects in Long Island City, shaking a condom at him, screaming, "There's nothing in it! Who you fucking, mister?" He was working fourteen hours a day to support his six kids and he had the time and energy to carry on with another woman?

"OK, let's start," Evan said. "What do you have?"

In the next hour she brought up five clients—cases she was having problems with or thought were especially interesting or enlightening. It was always the highlight of the week, to talk therapy with Evan, hear his analyses of her work, listen to his critiques. He was never judgmental of her; he would make suggestions, tell her what *he* would have said or done. And he always had anecdotes that illuminated his point, many of them humorous. He made her feel equal; when she spoke, he gave her his full, undivided attention.

"How's the Wintersteen girl?" he asked, as they were finishing up.

"Not much change. I had this impulse in my last session with her that we should pray. And we did, making up prayers as we went along. It was marvelous, very peaceful and calming. Bonnie loved it."

"I'm going to start calling you the Miracle Worker. How about Niki Nazarro?"

Chloe gathered together her papers and slipped them inside the folder. "I'm winning her confidence, letting her ramble on and on. The abuse her husband put her through is unbelievable. She's eating again, looks a hundred percent better."

"Terrific."

Chloe reached into her bag and took out an envelope, from which she removed twenty-five checks, all made out to Evan Kendrix, M.D. She had done the paperwork. He took 25% of the total and submitted statements, under his name, for insurance. To Chloe, it had always seemed unethical—the insurance company believed that the psychotherapist in these cases was Dr. Kendrix; but Evan said it wasn't unethical. He wasn't seeing the clients, but they were getting their money's worth with Chloe Forrester. Plus every week she met with him for consultation.

He looked at the bottom line, nodded approvingly, then pulled a blank check and a pen from his shirt pocket, filled it out, and put the check in her hand. They clinked glasses, finishing their wine. Then Evan said: "The divorce finally came through."

"Wonderful!"

"As for business matters," he said, "the Blair Center for Humanistic Psychology has confirmed our weekend in February. So we'll be going to New York. One of my old friends has an apartment in the Village. He's always telling me it's mine whenever I want to use it—he's never there. In March we fly to West Palm, as you know. In June the Esalen Institute in Big Sur wants me to do a five-day energy workshop. I told Phil—Phil Klein, Esalen's manager—I was interested but I have a co-therapist now, we're a team. Not a problem, he said. He's close friends with Beatrice O'Negin, the blonde woman you worked with in Stover Falls. She raved about you. So Esalen's a go. Excellent pay, all expenses. And get this—"

"Evan, slow down, I'm out of breath!"

He curved his hand around her shoulder and brought her closer in. "La Fédération Psychoanalytique Internationale, based in Geneva, wants me to conduct a series of weekend workshops this summer, the whole month of August. Would you be able to get away?"

She immediately began planning: thinking of the kids, the house. Rick's mother in Woodbridge, always devoted to her grandchildren, would take them for a couple of weeks; and Rick would probably help out. "Where will it be?"

"Corfu."

Her eyes widened. "You're putting me on, Evan."

"Why do you say that?"

"Because—because it's totally incredible!" Chloe could hardly contain herself. "When my mother was nine, her parents went to Corfu for a holiday and brought her along. My mother used to tell me stories about Corfu, what it was like, the memories she had—they were the happiest two weeks of her life! And I'd listen and dream."

She began laughing. "It's all so unreal for me. This ring—" she held up her left hand, touched the ruby in a setting of white gold, "—was bought on Corfu. My grandfather bought it for my grandmother on that same holiday. When my mother was seventeen, she came to America and her mother gave her the ring. My mother gave it to me when I turned twenty, as a gift from her heart, passing it on. I'll give it to Lisa." Tears came to her eyes. "I can't tell you what this means to me, Evan."

"Then I should answer the Fédération and say *oui*?"

"A million times *oui*!"

They embraced, kissed, then stood and went down the corridor to his bedroom. Chloe liked its absolute privacy. On those nights when Evan would come to her house she felt limited, could never express herself freely. Here she could soar.

The room had forest-green carpeting; blond mahogany dressers, one high, one low, against the far wall; projecting into the room was a magnificent king-sized bed. A plate-glass door led to a small deck, and Evan closed the drapes.

They undressed, crawled beneath the down comforter, brought each other in. Chloe was still finding it difficult to believe that she could have so much with one man—and this.

CHAPTER
4

The woman showing Rick around Orchard Hollow, a motel three miles south of Appleton recently converted into one- and two-room apartments, was giving him a sales pitch, and then some. She was pointing out the pleasures of living here: the sun coming up over the old apple trees, the singing of birds, the freshness of the air. Her name was Charlene, late thirties, dark blonde hair. If he took a suite, she was saying with her sleepy gray eyes, she would bring him coffee every morning with his favorite pastry and might even, well, linger awhile. She had Rick going, no question about it; but the place was so isolated, the rooms so new and motel-like—there was no way he could move in. He told Charlene he'd have to decline. Her eyes suddenly hardened: for all she cared he could go eat a dirt sandwich.

Rick drove away—another dead-end in his admittedly less than urgent effort to find a place, going on four weeks now. The attitude in the English Department was easygoing and his chairman hadn't said anything, if he even knew. No one was pushing him out of Grove Hall, and he wasn't feeling deprived in any physical sense. His office in the former dormitory had a pair of closets in it—students who came to Professor Forrester during office hours had no idea he bunked here. Just down the corridor was a tiled shower with a ton of hot water. His hours of walking to and fro in slippers and robe were, of course, strictly limited. Before eight and after ten.

But living in his office was getting tiresome—all his meals in coffee shops or local eateries—and he was lonely; depression was setting in. He missed his kids, the comforts of home, the pleasure of grouse hunting with Waldo. About twice a week Chloe would call in the morning, early, usually to say something about the children, and recently he'd become aware of his diminished anger toward her, far less than he'd felt when she'd pulled into the driveway in Kendrix's Porsche. If Kendrix were no longer in the picture, Rick could see himself going back to his family, working to make his life with Chloe more interesting, exciting; they would take an occasional trip....

But Kendrix *was* in the picture, and on that score Rick's emotions hadn't diminished one iota.

He had thirty minutes before his nine o'clock in freshman composition, and he thought to stop by the house for his mail, something he did every other day. Chloe would go through the delivery and drop his mail in a box inside the shed. Rick drove through the village. As he was drawing near his house, a gunmetal-gray Porsche was coming toward him on Elting Street.

Licking his lips, as if tasting the last bit of French toast and bacon he'd just had, Kendrix gave him a smile as their cars passed. *Morning, Rick. Just got out of bed with your wife, she made me a great breakfast, have a wonderful day!* In his driveway, Rick braked to an abrupt stop, pulled at the steering wheel as if to yank it from the column. It took him a couple of minutes to simmer down. His mail lay in the cardboard box. Rick grabbed the five or six pieces and went through them sitting in his station wagon. All basically junk—except for a substantial 10" x 12" envelope from the Pierpont Morgan Library in New York City. So it had finally arrived, a page-by-page photocopy of one of Thoreau's original handwritten journals. Once he would have been thrilled to have it.

■ ■ ■

Four days later he spoke to a woman at 71 N. Elm Street in the village, a Mrs. Delvecchio, who had an apartment for rent. "Maybe you like, you take a look." Rick went up two flights of stairs, the second flight steep and narrow, and pushed open the door. On first seeing the space, a large, timber-exposed room with an A-framed ceiling—an attic—he wanted to turn and run. It was filthy—trash, bags of garbage, discarded personal items everywhere. He'd seen some unattractive apartments in the past couple of weeks, but this one topped the list. A single window at the far end allowed a certain amount of light to come in, and he picked his way across the clutter to see what amazing view it offered: probably a couple of dumpsters with ill-fitting lids. The window, grimy as it was, opened to a view of the floodplain and Shagg Range even better than his view of them at home. He turned, visualized the apartment cleared, scrubbed. What was a little work? He'd have himself a place.

■ ■ ■

The next day, rubber gloves on, mouth-and-nose mask in place, Rick entered the cramped bathroom. First he nudged open the small window, then stashed everything—newspapers on the floor, a whelping/nursing blanket, a foul rubber mat in the phone-booth-sized shower—into a heavy-duty plastic bag. Then he mixed up a bucket of hot water and an all-purpose cleanser and with his new sponge-mop began scrubbing. He rinsed the mop and went at it again, and again. In the toilet bowl he shook in Ajax and swished and swirled it around with a brush. Only half the residue came off when he flushed. He shook in more of the "foaming cleanser," stirred; while it worked, he used wrench, pliers, and penetrating oil on the toilet-seat hardware, tugged and yanked and finally got the seat unbolted. He chucked it into the kitchen like a large, ugly quoit, then removed the new seat from its package and installed it. Desperate for a breath of air, Rick pulled down his mask, crammed the old seat into a trash bag, and dragged it, plus two other bags, down to ground level.

After stowing the trash in a big green barrel alongside the

house, he continued to the back yard, a haven of gliders, chaises, and lawn chairs. From the arm of a chaise a small white tag dangled. He examined it: $12.50. Old leaves and pebbles, and about three inches of murky water lay in the shallow basin of a stone birdbath. $25.00. The yard, on a larger scale, was an extension of the for-sale knickknacks in the landlady's house. In a far corner of the yard, a thin stream of smoke was rising from the metal chimney poking through the roof of a tarpaper shack. Was someone living in it?

He went back inside; on the second floor, as he was passing to his attic staircase, the light blue door to Apt. 3 opened and a young woman in chocolate cords and a rose cable-stitched sweater came out carrying a spiral notebook; her eyes were lowered, and Rick moved to one side.

She looked up. "Sorry, I wasn't paying attention."

"It's OK. I—I'm moving in upstairs."

"How is it, or shouldn't I ask?"

"It's pretty bad."

"They belonged to a cult that worshipped garbage. Evidently to take it out was a sin."

"From the evidence, I believe you," he said. "I'm Rick Forrester."

"You're an English professor at the college," she said.

"I am."

"I'm Noreen Russell. Right now on my way to class. Late as usual."

She had reddish-brown hair—auburn, if he'd ever seen auburn. Her eyes looked green, though in the dim light he couldn't say for sure. The shape of her upper lip reminded him of a gull's wings.

"Then you'd better run," Rick said.

"Welcome to the house, Professor Forrester," she said with a warm smile and started down the stairs.

In his attic, Rick finished the bathroom, washing all surfaces with a pine disinfectant, then tackled the range, though quickly he began to think it was tackling him. The lemon-scented Easy-Off was making him ill. Desperate for a break, he stripped off his rubber gloves and mask and stood at the open window in the peak, inhaling deeply, his eyes going to the Shagg Range. The image of covered wagons traveling along the rising and dipping spine of the mountains came again to Rick, as did the questions: Where were they going? Would they ever get there?

All at once so many different emotions—loneliness, anger, failure, guilt—crowded upon him that he felt close to falling to his knees here in his new godforsaken home and crying. Exhaustion had something to do with it he was sure—sleep-deprived from tossing on his office daybed, reading student essays and for the first time in his career at Appleton State assigning grades but adding no critical comments—the ultimate copout as a teacher. Rick sat on the grimy floor, stretching out his legs and resting his head against the wall. His eyes were heavy and he could feel himself drifting off. Was someone knocking on his door? He believed so.

"Yes?"

The door opened; it was the young woman from downstairs. "Were you resting? I'm sorry."

Rick blinked, then again, and got to his feet. "Please, come in."

"I thought you might want a beer." She had a six-pack in her hand.

A line ran through his head. *Is it a vision, or a waking dream?* "How nice. Thank you."

She walked across the littered floor, handed him a cold, long-necked bottle of Miller High-Life. Taking one for herself, "OK, what can I do?"

"You can drink a beer with me."

"How about the refrigerator?" She used the tail of the man's shirt she was wearing to untwist the cap.

"I appreciate your wanting to help, Noreen. I've been using oven cleaner and the fumes—"

"If I keel over, you can catch me." She lifted her bottle. "*Sláinte!*"

He repeated the word. "*Sláinte.*"

She started in, first unplugging the refrigerator, then taking out the shelves, assembling them in the sink and filling it with hot water. Rick, using a soap pad on the top of the range, asked her how her class had gone.

"Very well. Creative writing with Terry Randolph."

"He's a good friend. Is that your major?"

"No, I'm pre-law."

Lawyers dominated her family, she told Rick. She had two uncles who were lawyers and her grandfather and another uncle were lawyers in Ireland. "But I'm happiest writing," she said. "Terry wants me to stay with it."

"You can be a lawyer *and* write, can't you?"

She had a swallow of beer, went back to her task. "Law eats up your day like no other profession, especially in the first years. Once you get established, it's possible—if you have the discipline."

"How long have you been at Appleton?"

"This is my second year," she said, "and my last. I started at Sarah Lawrence, my mother's college. It was too close to home—we live in White Plains—and after two years I called it quits." Her head emerged from the refrigerator.

"And came to Appleton," he said, smiling.

Noreen went to the sink, stirred the soapy water, and began washing the shelves.

"No. I banged around for seven years—three years in New York at acting school, waiting tables, hoping to land a job. I made a few commercials, had a couple of bit parts. Went to Hawaii, worked as a bartender, for a tent and awning company, as first mate on an island tour boat. Woke up one morning at twenty-five thinking I'd had it with paradise. So I packed up the few things I owned and went to Cork, where I have family on my father's side, worked in my uncle's law firm, wrote, made a lot of friends, ending up living in the hamlet of Croghanvale, discovered one of the really great pubs in Ireland—Pharr's, where Michael Collins had his last pint. There's a wonderful B&B called Rod & Creel nearby. If I ever get married it's where I want to spend my honeymoon—fishing the Argideen in the morning, corned-beef sandwiches and a pint of Murphy's in Pharr's for lunch, then walking in the Castlebantry Hills, a breeze in your face from the Celtic Sea. Anyway, Ireland was another three years. I wasn't getting any younger. Back home again, I decided to finish college—" Noreen leaned away from the sink; sweat glistened on her forehead, her neck. "—and here I am, graduating in the spring."

"I'm still in Pharr's, having a corned-beef sandwich and a Murphy's," Rick said.

Noreen laughed. She reached for her beer, pressed the bottle to her lips. "One of my oldest friends is a student here," she said. "She also kicked around, mostly in real estate, told me I'd love Appleton. When I found out the novelist Terry Randolph taught here, that did it for me."

"Do you share the apartment?"

"With my friend, Maria. A third girl moved out. She'd had it with Mrs. Delvecchio, easy to do." Noreen rinsed a sponge under the faucet. "Maria's fiancé, Crusher, lives with us now, but he's away half the time."

"When this 'Crusher' and I meet on the landing one day, should I give him a wide berth?"

"At heart he's a pussycat, a little rough around the edges," Noreen said. "He has this goal: by age thirty to be 'Compacting King of the East.'"

"What exactly does he compact?"

"Old cars."

They kept working, talking; had another beer. "What about you, Dr. Forrester? What brings you to our house at 97 North Elm?"

"Please, call me Rick," he said. "Maybe half a year ago my wife stopped wearing her wedding ring. OK. I didn't wear one, why should she? Then she started seeing someone and I moved out, began looking for a place, saw nothing. Then by sheer accident I saw the infamous couple driving away. Mrs. Delvecchio directed me to the attic. At first glance I wanted to turn and run, but the view of the floodplain changed my mind. So I started in, beginning to think I'd tackled too much—and some kind-hearted soul appeared at my door. With ice cold beer, no less."

"Imagine that," Noreen said. Stepping away from the refrigerator, "Take a look. What do you think?"

They were both leaning down; as he peered in, her hair brushed the stubble on his face. "It gleams!"

"How about some music, Rick? The Bee Gees, Doobie Brothers. I have an album by Bruce Springsteen and his E-Street Band—"

"Terrific."

She went down to her apartment and returned with a tape player; they listened to "Space Cowboy" and "Born to Run" and other great songs, finished the kitchen area, then sat beneath the window with a second High-Life. Tomorrow, she was saying, they'd do the main room. Floors needed vacuuming and washing but except for a general dusting and pickup, there wasn't much else. Did he have furniture? Not all he needed, he said, but yes. Enough to start.

"Do you have a house in Appleton?" Noreen asked.

"On Elting Street," he said.

"Kids?"

"A girl and a boy, Lisa and Andrew."

How it happened Rick didn't know: he and Noreen were

holding hands. They continued chatting, laughing; then he pressed his face into her hair, his lips on her neck, and the next moment they kissed. He hadn't kissed a woman, besides Chloe, in any way that wasn't sororal in eighteen years; this wasn't sororal. He felt the charge through his whole body and was dying to kiss her again. At the same time he felt an inner voice telling him he shouldn't. Noreen was a student, he was a professor; but even more than that he was married, he had a wife and children. Regardless of what had happened with Chloe, the lies and the deception, he still loved her. If tomorrow she were to call and say she'd made a terrible mistake, would he say sorry, too late?

"I have an idea," Noreen said. "We'll quit for now. Come back later, I'll make us dinner."

"You've done enough. We'll go out, on me."

"Next time."

"Are you sure?" Rick said. "Because—"

"I'm sure. Maria and Crusher are away," she said, getting up. "See you at six."

CHAPTER
5

The tomato sauce was simmering. Chloe brought a spoonful to her mouth, had a taste. Maybe more oregano. She sprinkled a touch on the sauce, stirred, then turned from the range and continued making a green salad. A white apron, tied in back, protected her violet silk shirt and black pants.

Lisa was slicing a loaf of Italian bread and sprinkling garlic powder in between the slices, also adding a little butter. The kitchen table, set for four and covered with a checkered cloth, had a pair of red candles on it, as yet unlighted. It was a windy night, cold. The back door opened and Andrew came in with an armful of logs.

He kicked the door shut and went into the living room. Chloe broke off pieces of lettuce, romaine and leaf, rinsed them in cold water, and tossed them in the spinner. Then she cut up two tomatoes, a couple of carrots, and some green peppers. Lisa wrapped the bread in aluminum foil, lethargically.

"What's the problem?" Chloe said to her daughter.

"It's your party, Mom. I'm really not into it."

"Evan's having dinner with us. It's *our* party."

From the living room Andrew shouted: "God *damn!*"

"What happened?" Chloe asked.

"Nothing."

"Why did you swear?"

"I burned my finger."

"Be careful!"

"Is Evan going to spend the night?" Lisa asked.

Chloe was taking lettuce leaves from the spinner. "Why do you want to know?"

Andrew cursed again.

"What is it now?" Chloe demanded.

"It's not catching."

She went into the living room. "Andrew, you know how to make a fire. Why are you doing this?" Closer to the stove, "You've put on too many logs," she said. "Use the tongs, take one or two out."

When she returned to the kitchen, Lisa had vanished. Chloe thought of calling upstairs, telling her to come back down, but decided against it; there was enough tension in the house already. She emptied the salad into a hand-carved wooden bowl (wedding gift), stirred the sauce, had another taste. Something was still missing but she couldn't quite name it.

■ ■ ■

Evan brought over a bottle of Chianti, the dinner was a great success—"Chloe, your sauce is *magnifico!*"—and now they were sitting on the sofa, her children on the Persian carpet, a fire in the stove. Stretched out to one side of it, Waldo had his head on his paws. Outside, a cold rain was falling, sometimes coming as sleet.

The kids seemed at ease, which pleased Chloe greatly. Evan had broached the subject of school, and they were having a good time talking about it, exchanging stories and ideas. Right now Lisa was explaining why she liked art and English and saw nothing interesting in math. In art you could express yourself. That appealed to her more than finding the area of a triangle.

Chloe appreciated her daughter's comment. The evening was going well and she felt relaxed, marvelously fulfilled. One of her core beliefs was that women settled for too little, aimed too low. Only by taking risks, reaching for a star—

Andrew said, "When you find the area of a triangle you really have something. With a poem, no one ever agrees. One kid says this, another kid says that. Even the teacher doesn't know."

"To me, that's the best part," Lisa said. "Like there's no wrong answer when you read a poem. You're not going to get shot down. Plus, a poem can solve a problem for you."

"Like fix your hook or slice? I don't think so."

"It could happen," Lisa said.

"You're both making excellent points," Evan said. "I'm thinking I've just heard what the greatest philosophers, from the earliest times on, have struggled to express. There was a thinker named Baruch Spinoza. Do you know what he said God was? To define God he used mathematics."

"See?" Andrew said to his sister.

Evan's eyes shifted between the two kids. "Take a triangle," he said. "Spinoza said God was—or is—the irrefutable fact that the sum of its angles is always a hundred and eighty degrees, no matter what shape the triangle—isosceles, scalene, or equilateral. The greatest philosophers, from Aristotle on, have always loved mathematics for the rock-solid answers it gives. But times changed—which is to say, new thinkers came along. And here's where your way of looking at things, Lisa, comes in."

He paused for a moment, gave Chloe's daughter his full attention. "Because," Evan went on, "isn't it possible to know something intuitively? To sense it from a deep, inner place? A man named Rousseau, two hundred years ago in France, believed that science or math could never answer the real questions of life. In his view, dumb creatures—'dumb' doesn't mean ignorant, it means incapable of speech—had more insight into these mysteries than human beings. Then in America we had a direct offshoot of that philosophy. It was called Transcendentalism—to go beyond. There's a power, a force that transcends reason, that goes beyond scientific proofs."

"Which do you think is better?" Lisa asked.

"I don't think it's a question of comparison," Evan said. "They're points of view, after all. But as a humanist and a psychotherapist, I lean more to the nonscientific, the intuitive. When I was in college and for a time in medical school, Spinoza was my favorite philosopher. I've changed since then but math and science can't be brushed off, certainly can't be ignored. They got us to the moon."

"A poem can do that, too."

"That's a beautiful comment, Lisa," Evan said. "It certainly can."

The fire was dying and he crossed to the wicker basket, picked out a split log, and placed it on the embers. Immediately the fire sparked anew. Chloe watched him, thrilled with how he had brought Lisa and Andrew out, got them exchanging ideas. Waldo was lying near the stove and Evan reached out to give him a pat— hand lowered, fingers relaxed and slightly curved to stroke the dog's head—and what happened next startled everyone. From Waldo's throat came a deep growl; he snarled, his teeth closing down on the fleshy part of Evan's thumb. Chloe jumped up, screaming. Andrew shouted, "Waldo!" The dog's jaws loosened, let go. Evan, pale, stood up, gripping his wrist. Three, maybe four puncture wounds were in his thumb, and blood was oozing out. Andrew was kneeling beside Waldo, hand firmly on his collar.

"Get him out of here!" Chloe exploded.

Andrew took Waldo to the back door.

"What can I do?" she said, her hand on Evan's forearm.

"Do you have any peroxide?"

"Lisa, in the medicine cabinet upstairs. And the box of swabs!"

Evan sat on the sofa, keeping his injured hand elevated. Chloe went into the bathroom down the hall and grabbed the box of facial tissues on the toilet tank, her teeth clenched in fury. Stupid dog! Back in the living room, she pulled out two tissues and handed them to Evan, who soaked up the blood starting to run down his wrist. Lisa came in with a bottle of peroxide, but she couldn't find the swabs.

"They're there, they're under the sink."

"It's OK," said Evan. "No need for alarm."

He stood, walked into the kitchen and poured peroxide directly over the bite, causing each puncture wound to foam. Chloe asked him if he would like some brandy.

"No. Call up the Medical Center, would you? I should get this looked at."

She went into the alcove, checked a list of emergency numbers on the bulletin board, made the call. "Dr. Palmer's on duty," she said to Evan, coming back in. "Let me take you."

"Thanks, you stay here—it's a terrible night."

"Are you sure?"

"Positive. There's no point to both of us going," he said. "If you have some gauze and adhesive, it would help."

She went upstairs and came back with a first-aid kit that Rick always kept well-stocked and began wrapping Evan's thumb. "I can't tell you how sorry I am," she said.

"It was my fault. He was sleeping."

"The dog is neurotic, over-disciplined. Rick's idea of training." Chloe tore off a piece of adhesive, then another, taping the gauze snugly. "Will you come back?"

"Of course I'll come back." Evan slipped on his coat, gave her a kiss at the door. "The evening is young."

■ ■ ■

Upset but wanting to use the time well, Chloe sat down with a volume of Jung's *Collected Works*, trying to grasp the meaning and significance of the term "syzygy." She began reading, "On the contrary, there is every likelihood that the numinous qualities which make the mother-imago so dangerously powerful derive from the collective archetype of the anima, which is incarnated anew in every male child."

She read the sentence again, had to; Jung was tough sledding.

Especially tonight. But she had to take advantage of every free hour she had. The rain and sleet were still coming down, even a little hail. Chloe continued, "No matter how friendly and obliging a woman's Eros may be, no logic on earth can shake her if she is ridden by the animus."

Upstairs Lisa and Andrew were at it—Chloe didn't think it was over their differing philosophical outlooks. She had never heard them communicate so well; in so many ways it had been a perfect evening, and then Waldo had ended it, with a snarl and a lunge.

She shivered, pushing aside the incident, blocking out how it related to what Evan had just said about Rousseau and dumb animals. Back to Jung. So much here, so difficult to absorb. "The more civilized, the more unconscious and complicated a man is, the less he is able to follow his instincts." In the margin she wrote: "Today's world—paradoxical. Losing touch with inner self."

She came to a paragraph, the last part of which she underlined even as she read: "…these archetypes possess a fatality that can on occasion produce tragic results. They are quite literally the father and mother of all the disastrous entanglements of fate."

Chloe closed her Jung, put on a new log, stayed at the stove staring at the flames. One time when she was in grade school her mother kept her home because she'd seen a stray dog chewing on a rat on the street, and Chloe's best friend, with whom she walked every day, was hit by a car coming home later that afternoon. Her mother had seen omens in everything. Chloe sat back on the sofa, her hands pushing quietly through her hair. Then, though dimmed by weather and wall, Waldo's bark reached Chloe's ear. She went into the kitchen, peered out. Evan was crossing the deck, his whole hand, not just his thumb, bandaged. She opened the door and he came in.

"How are you?" she asked at once.

"They didn't have to amputate." He slipped out of his coat

with her help, and they went into the living room, sat down. "Dr. Palmer cauterized the bite, poked a needle in my ass. I had to sign a 'dog-bite report,' sorry to say. It goes to the police."

"Can I get you anything?"

"That brandy you were talking about? I'd love one, Chloe," he said.

CHAPTER
6

They were in the home-furnishing section of the only department store in Appleton; at the moment, however, Rick's interest wasn't in home furnishings. He glanced incredulously at his daughter. "Waldo did *what?*"

"He bit Evan," Lisa repeated. "We'd just finished dinner and were sitting in the living room." She had her hands on the handle of an Ambrose shopping wagon. In it were dish towels, pot holders, a bathroom mat, two packages of light bulbs. "We were having a pretty nice talk, actually. Evan put a new log in the stove and when he reached out to pet Waldo, Waldo went for his thumb. Mom screamed, Andrew took Waldo outside, and Evan left for the Medical Center."

"Did he come back?"

"Yes."

Rick was holding a pair of ready-made curtains. "What do you think of these?"

"It's not the right look."

"What's the right look, Lisa?"

"Something a little more kicky." She was going through the selection. "Here, like these."

"Aren't they kind of short?"

"They're café length. Red for the bathroom. Green or brown for the living room?"

"Well, the walls are wood, kind of dark—"

"Then the green."

In the shelves beneath the display Lisa picked out two boxes of curtains and put them in the cart. Rods and rings were next. For the rings, did he prefer brass or porcelain?

"Brass."

The cart was getting loaded. Rick drew an old envelope from his shirt pocket, eyed scribbled items. He and Lisa entered a new aisle. A woman, wearing a light blue employee tunic over a navy blouse, was sorting and straightening merchandise on one of the many shelves. She turned, saw Rick and Lisa, and asked if she could be of any help.

"I'm looking for sheets," Rick said.

"Size?"

"Double."

"Color, any preference?" She had blonde hair (roots showing) and small hazel eyes carefully penciled. Her skirt stopped just above her knees. Pinned to her tunic, a nametag: Fawn.

"White."

"Dad," Lisa said, "white is Dull City."

To Fawn he said: "Forget white. Something a little more… kicky."

She reached up to a high shelf. "Here you go, hon. Wamsutta, 200-count percale cotton. Blue and yellow stripe." She handed him the package. "I don't know if they're *kicky*—"

"They're perfect," Rick said.

"Pillowcases to match, hon?"

■ ■ ■

As they walked up the path to his new rooming house, carrying their packages, a stooped, gray-haired man in baggy trousers and a mismatched jacket was making a repair to one of the tinny mailboxes by the front door. "Signore Delvecchio," Rick said. "How are you?"

"I'm-a doin' all right, Professore. How-a you doin'?"

"Getting settled, finally. I'd like you to meet my daughter, Lisa."

A light in the old man's watery eyes suddenly came on. "Signorina, it is my great pleasure."

Lisa smiled. "Thank you."

"She's decorating my apartment," Rick said.

"Then I know it will be beautiful."

The old man glanced inside the foyer, as if expecting his wife to come out and reprimand him for dilly-dallying. Rick wished Signore Delvecchio a good day and went in with Lisa; they climbed the two flights to his attic. An hour later the curtains were up, his bed had designer sheets on it, colorful pot holders hung from brass cup hooks in the kitchen, a black and white dish towel fell neatly through the handle on his shiny oven door, and a red-checkered cloth covered the card table.

"Another lamp, a poster or two. But it's really nice. I think Mom's jealous," Lisa said.

"Of my apartment?"

"No. I told her about Noreen."

Rick started making a couple of grilled cheese and tomato sandwiches. "What did she say?"

"Like, is she pretty, how old is she, what color hair does she have?"

"Did you tell her?"

"I said she's very pretty and couldn't be nicer. How old *is* Noreen?"

"She'll be twenty-eight this summer."

"I said twenty-five."

Lisa was tracing one of the squares in the tablecloth with her finger. Then, looking up: "Ever since Mom and Evan started seeing each other, the kids in school say things."

"What kind of things?"

"'Your mother's a professional sex expert, I understand,' or 'Your mother and her boyfriend give classes on new ways of doing it.' It really bothers me."

Rick put the sandwiches on a hot skillet. "Lisa, they're looking to get a rise out of you. It's ignorant talk. Walk away."

"Then there's something else." She paused for a second. "When Mom and Evan are together it freaks me out."

"Like sitting together, having a drink together?"

"*Together*, Dad. At night."

"Just the idea that they're in the bedroom?"

"No, it's never in the bedroom anyway."

Rick was hearing things he didn't want to know. "Wouldn't you be in your own room, sleeping?"

"They wake me up; or she does."

He flattened the sandwiches with a flipper, perhaps more firmly than necessary. "I'll talk to your mother," he said.

■ ■ ■

A dark green sedan was parked in the driveway of the house when he pulled in thirty minutes later. Lisa kissed her father goodbye and went up the deck steps. He wanted some items for his place, but before going into the house he ducked behind the shed and let Waldo out of his pen. The dog ran down the embankment; on the frozen oxbow, he slipped, skidding along. Rick had an unexpected laugh.

Inside, he walked to the carpeted stairway. When he'd lived here, he had moved around with distinct deference whenever Chloe had a client; he hadn't tiptoed exactly but, respectful of her work, hadn't slammed doors or stomped carelessly about. Walking lightly now, he went up to the second floor, pulled down the folding ladder, and climbed into the attic. It was unfinished and if you stood up too quickly you would bang your head on the roof. Not a good move, considering that the original roofing nails protruded through. Rick stayed bent over as he searched through several boxes near the brick chimney. They had spare utensils and gadgets in them; consolidating these items, he loaded an empty box with a glass percolator, a long-handled orange squeezer, an old toaster, a couple of carving and paring knives, a cutting board, and a metal colander. Out of the attic with his claim, he closed the ladder; it was spring-assisted and the hold-string slipped out of his hand. The ladder slammed shut with a house-shaking thud.

On the main floor, going to the back door, Rick heard the sound of footsteps leading up from the basement. Chloe appeared, a look of concern on her face. "Oh, it's you. I thought one of the kids had fallen down the stairs."

"The attic ladder got away from me. Sorry."

"What did you take?"

"Stuff from Woodbridge we've never used."

"For your information," Chloe said, "your dog bit Evan. The police have a record on him."

"On Evan? It's about time."

"Go to hell. Now excuse me."

"I have something to say. It's important," Rick said. "When Evan spends the night, could you try to control yourself a little? For the sake of the children."

"I'll take it under advisement," Chloe said, and returned to her office.

Outside, on the lip of the bank, Rick spied Waldo nosing around the brush at the oxbow's edge. He whistled and the dog came running up. "I understand you're on America's 'Most-Wanted' list," he said, holding the springer's floppy ears. "Remember, anything you say may be used against you."

"Rrrufff!"

"Understood. Just don't say that in court."

CHAPTER
7

Chloe wasn't sure why she watched the evening news; it was all such bleak, depressing stuff. If she didn't adore Walter Cronkite so, she wouldn't bother. When the program ended, she clicked off the TV and left the den, in the front hallway climbed the stairs to the second floor, started a load of wash in the small laundry room, and began some ironing. She had two chapters to read in her Abnormal Psych class with Dr. Manheim and she had to push ahead with her research paper on Jung's collective unconscious. Plus the three, sometimes four clients she saw on a daily basis, and her children, and the house. Then there was Evan. Chloe couldn't remember the last time she sat down with a good book—

The telephone rang. She set the iron in an upright position and went quickly into her bedroom. On the line was a teenage girl; the next moment Lisa, on the phone in the alcove downstairs, was talking. Chloe hung up, finished her ironing, then dropped off the pressed clothes in the kids' rooms, first her son's. When she walked in, Andrew was standing in the middle of the floor with a golf club in his hands. On his bed lay an open magazine with a picture of a professional golfer swinging a club. Andrew was attempting to swing, look at the picture, and observe himself in his mirror—all at once.

"Excuse me, please. I don't wish to be killed," Chloe said.

Andrew set the club aside and she put his clothes on the bed.

"Mom, I want to show you something."

While he shuffled through papers on his desk, Chloe eyed the military medal tacked to the boy's wall. How proud she had felt telling her family that Rick Forrester, her fiancé, had won the Navy Cross in the Korean War. A jet, coming in for a crash landing on an aircraft carrier, had gone over the side and plunged into the sea, and Rick, on plane-guard duty on his destroyer, had jumped overboard as the plane was sinking—

"Read this," Andrew said. "I've written Johnny Miller, care of 'Champs Clinic' in *Golf Magazine*. What do you think?"

Her eyes dropped to the sheet of composition paper. The letter went: "Dear Johnny, I'm twelve, playing in the low 80s, and I had one 77 this year and a couple of 79s, and a hole in one too! My dream is to play on the PGA Tour. What advise can you give me to help make my dream come true? Sincerely, Andrew Forrester."

Chloe smiled, touched by the entire letter; but mostly by the word "dream." "I love it," she said, thinking "advise" should be "advice." But she didn't want to change a word. Correcting someone's English was something Rick's father had done to Rick when he was growing up. As a pre-teen, he'd had a stutter—

"I'll come and watch you play," she said.

"You will?"

"Of course. When you win the American Open, I'll be there."

"It's the *U.S.* Open, Mom."

She leaned down and kissed his eyes, as her mother had so often done to her—an old Turkish custom—delivered clothes to Lisa's room, folded the ironing board and carried it to the big closet at the top of the stairs, then picked up the receiver in her bedroom: girls still talking. She told Lisa to say goodbye to her friend; it was getting late and she was expecting a call. Then she went to the blue-upholstered wing chair in the corner of her bedroom and opened her text on Abnormal Psychology.

"Expecting," of course, was the wrong word. With Evan you couldn't expect anything. She was *hoping* for a call.

Just as she was finishing her second chapter, at nine forty-five, the phone rang. She went over to the bedside table and picked up the receiver. "Hello."

"Got your message. God, you have a sexy voice!"

Chloe sat on her bed. "Well, jump in your car."

"Wish I could but I'm wiped out," Evan said. "It's been a marathon day—three couples, two singles, three hours in the studio. How's it going?"

"I just finished my class assignment on phobias," Chloe said, "the different approaches therapists use to get to the root cause of a fear. For instance, the 'flooding' technique. What do you make of it?"

"A person is afraid of heights, so you strand him on a catwalk two hundred feet up? Come on. The idea of *gradual* exposure has merit, but I'm still skeptical. What text are you using?"

"Karl Hoss's."

"Excellent. But take these titles."

She reached for a pencil and pad on the night table. "OK."

"*Fears, Phobias and Rituals*, by Isaac Marks," Evan said. "A classic. Then a book called *Phobia's Many Faces*—written by, let me see…Joy Medved. The thing to remember about phobias, you aren't born with them. Getting someone to remember what made them afraid of dogs, water, strangers—or whatever—is the only viable treatment. Then you have a solid starting point. Listen, study well, sleep well. I'll see you tomorrow."

"Good night, Evan."

Chloe went back to her chair. Instead of the Hoss, she opened Volume 9 of Jung's collected works, *Aion, Researches into the Phenomenology of the Self*. Breathing easily, she began to read.

■ ■ ■

Shortly after Evan put down his phone, the door chime sounded and Christine Monteleone walked in—little, perhaps five foot one, with coal-black hair done in a pixielike style and powder-white skin; lots of eyeliner and shadow, full red lips; mod clothes—she loved mini-skirts. She was wearing one tonight, red like her mouth, as Evan met her in the front hall of his house.

She took off her fox jacket and had to stand on tiptoe to reach a chrome hook. Greeting her warmly, but in every regard professionally, Evan invited her into his ash-paneled office. She sat in an upholstered armchair facing Evan, who had taken his leather, brass-studded chair, at a slight angle. Christine had on ankle-height boots, with medium heels, and white scalloped socks.

For a while they were both silent. When she had first called nearly two months ago, he had agreed to see her for an interview; with his appointment book filled, he would in all likelihood refer her to Chloe. Christine was very depressed, she had told him that rainy day in early September here in his office. Sleeping with Vincent, her boyfriend, was causing her terrible feelings of guilt; feelings, she was quick to add, that had begun when her stepfather had started fooling around with her when she was fourteen.

Fooling around with her how? Evan had asked.

At first by giving her looks, watching her, Christine had answered. Then she started noticing that her underwear, as she transferred items from the hamper to the washing machine, was often sticky in the crotch.

Evan had told her to continue.

Her stepfather was a small man, a sharp dresser with manicured nails, and the idea of what he was doing sickened her, and excited her, at the same time. Christine thought of talking to her mother but kept putting it off, and next thing she knew her stepfather was asking her if she wanted to watch him ejaculate in her panties. One thing led to another and pretty soon they were having sex. Intercourse? Evan asked. Yes, all kinds. Her mother had a high-powered editorial job in New York, and Arnold—his full name was Arnold Rath; he was a

big insurance broker in White Plains where they all lived—
would come home early twice a week to be with Christine.
These meetings went on for a year, at which point her mother,
Elaine, got wind of the relationship. There was a huge family
blow-up and she divorced Arnold, who moved to Miami. To
this day she chose to blame Christine for the breakup, as if she,
her daughter, had seduced Arnold, who continued haunting
Christine with emotions of right and wrong, good and bad.
She loved going to bed with her boyfriend, she loved sex, but
the pleasure was always followed by paralyzing guilt.

Despite having planned to refer the young woman to Chloe,
Evan had squeezed her into his own crowded schedule, giving
her a variety of appointments, often at night.

"What kind of week did you have?" he asked, sitting with
her now.

"Boring. College is a drag."

"What would you rather be doing?"

"Traveling, going to Europe, living in San Francisco."

"Well, what's stopping you?"

She crossed her legs, her skirt more than halfway up her left
thigh. "Isn't it obvious?"

"I asked you a question, Christine."

"Our relationship. I don't want to say goodbye to you."

"In my opinion you're prepared, on an emotional level,
to say goodbye right now," Evan said. Displayed on the wall
behind his chair were his degrees, with several other documents
and diplomas, a few from European institutions.

"I had this horrible dream last night," Christine said. "I
was looking out a window and you were standing there and
saw me. Then I realized the window had bars on it and I kept
shaking them, wanting to break out and get to you—and you
just walked away."

"Arnold is still in your life."

"You're in my life."

"You think it's me. It isn't."

"Don't tell me who it is. I saw Vincent on Saturday. It was awful."

"What happened?"

"What happened was it wasn't you!"

"Does he know what's going on?"

"What am I supposed to say, I'm fucking my shrink? He doesn't even know I'm in therapy." Her left foot was bobbing rhythmically. "Evan, let's not talk anymore."

"All right."

In his living room, seated on the sofa, they had a half-glass of wine, a subtle (but necessary) transition between the different phases of Christine's session—the cognitive and the somatic. He had deduced from the onset that talk-therapy alone wouldn't work, wouldn't get to the core of her problem. Christine drank quickly, hardly setting her glass down. Evan had a last sip, then touched her hand and they walked down the hallway to his bedroom.

They undressed. Following his default instruction, she left her panties on—today's pair minuscule, semi-transparent, the color of an April dawn. Looking at her, his eyes lowering, he might have been viewing the veiled face of a Nigerian princess. Evan had never seen a body quite like Christine Monteleone's. Small waist, outrageous breasts, and the sweetest, roundest bottom God ever gave woman. But he mustn't digress. She was paying him to help her and he would do everything he could to effect change in her psychic makeup: to free Christine of the debilitating influence of her stepfather.

Evan never knew the form any physical session with his patient might take. He left it to instinct, to creative impulse. Bouncing around on his bed with her always produced amazing insights, and tonight's was pure brilliance. Christine was directly over him, straddling his face, hands on his knees, tendrils of jet black hair peeking from the sides of her panties.

He recognized the position they were in as a rare opportunity. "Christine, do you really want to get Arnold out of your life? Here's your chance. I'm Arnold. Snuff me out." Reaching up, he put a little pressure on her thighs.

She lowered herself, squirming, killing her step-dad with a vengeance, her pearl-pantied perfumed pussy covering his mouth, her vintage asshole making of his nose a cork. Evan couldn't breathe. He would succumb, a victim of his own blazing psychotherapeutic genius, even as she performed wondrous tricks with her lips and tongue. Mt. Chodokee began rumbling, the ground shaking, lava rising hot and fast. To live, to die? To die, to live?

Sweet Christine Monteleone!

■ ■ ■

He walked her into the hall and helped her on with her fox jacket; she had already paid him and they had an appointment for next week. Tuesday at ten thirty p.m.

"See you, Evan."

"Good night, Christine."

She went out. He returned to his office and sat at his desk, taking from the middle drawer his professional journal, a notebook with a stiff black cover, vol. 17. He wrote the date and time, then: "Christine Monteleone. Continued working on her relationship with her (ex) stepfather. Healthy transference with therapist, resulting in good associations, memories. Christine is continuing to reveal more and more of her inner self. Before college year is over, I have every confidence that she'll be a well-adjusted, independent-minded young woman."

Evan closed his journal, left his office, and walked outside. In the middle of the big turnaround he stopped, his eyes rising to Mt. Chodokee—in the language of the Black Hawk Indians who had once inhabited the region, "Powerful One." Facing the mountain, he stretched his arms high and wide, breathing in deeply of the crisp night air.

■ ■ ■

Chloe awoke abruptly, someone was moving about on the ground floor. She glanced at her clock-radio. Eleven twenty p.m. There, again; but, of course, it was Waldo. The antique kitchen clock echoed through the house—*tick-tock, tick-tock*. Waldo kept moving around. Maybe he had to go out, though once in for the night, he always stayed in. And then he was starting up the stairs.

He never came upstairs. Thump, clomp, thud—slowly, methodically. Chloe sat up in bed, body tense, eyes wide. Was it Waldo? Someone else? Whoever was out there was now on the landing, now outside her door, now coming into the room—

When she saw the familiar white blaze, her relief was tremendous; but she was still troubled, mystified. Waldo padded over to her and sat on the carpet. For the first time ever Chloe reached out, put her hand on the dog's head.

"What is it, Waldo?"

CHAPTER
8

He wasn't hunting on the floodplain today; he was in the lower Shaggs. Dusk was settling over the valley and he could make out the steeple on the Reformed Church on Elting Street and the ten-story Administration Building of the college; and he could see the steel bridge over the Walloon and tell where the river meandered because poplars followed it and he could see the poplars.

Rick moved deliberately, thumb resting on the safety; Waldo thirty-five yards ahead, nose low to the ground. This was a good area, comparable to a shaded riffle in a stream that always produced a rise. The percentages were higher in fishing; when a trout rose to your fly you had a better chance of setting the hook than of dropping a grouse when it broke cover. Waldo usually flushed a bird here. Rick held the gun diagonally across his chest, trigger finger inside the guard. Red gloves and canvas cap with ear flaps down. The land sloped away, half meadow, the rest boulders and cedars. His eyes on Waldo, dog's nubby brown tail picking up the tempo, Rick's heart following along, then: "RRrrmmMMM!"—flash of brown, gun up, safety forward, bird swerving behind trees. *Boom*! Down? Maybe. "RRrrmmMMM!" Second bird, where? There! *Boom*! Missed.

Waldo looking back, waiting. Rick pointed toward the clump of cedars. "Fetch!" He broke his gun—spent shells sailing past his hip—and lifted a pair of cartridges with 7½-size pellets from his jacket flap, slid them in. From the cedars came the fluttering of wings—it didn't last long. Waldo emerged with the bird in his mouth, trotted up, and dropped it at Rick's feet. Kneeling, he patted Waldo, giving him the only reward he wanted: praise.

Rick put the grouse, his second of the day, into his game pouch, hunted for another fifteen minutes, then stopped to field-dress the birds—making small slits with his knife and pulling out the warm entrails and organs, cleaning his hands on damp leaves and grass. Earlier he had told Noreen they might be having grouse for dinner, but that she shouldn't be disappointed with pork chops; hunting the wily bird was a far cry from bringing one home.

His station wagon was four hundred yards away, parked behind a ramshackle barn at the end of Tilson Road, but Rick decided to relax for a few minutes on a boulder. He laid his gun in the grass and Waldo sat next to him, kind of leaning against his leg. Lights sparkled on the bridge spanning the Walloon. He took his old pewter flask from the side pocket of his canvas jacket and had a nip, thinking he'd stop on his way into town and buy the few items he needed to round out the meal. What went with grouse? Wild rice, what else? String beans or spinach. Oh, bacon! Before putting a bird in the oven, you patted a few strips on its breast. For dessert, an old standby. Vanilla ice cream and strawberries.

A flock of Canada geese, maybe forty birds, was winging south in perfect formation, save two or three stragglers. And what a racket! You would think a pack of dogs was nearby, barking away. Rick had another nip, thought to head in, and saw movement at the lower end of the field. Traipsing through evergreen and boulder was a fox.

Waldo didn't see it, yet. A man's eyes were sharper than a dog's. The fox moved forward, stopped, tested the air. Suddenly, from his leaning position against Rick's leg, Waldo sat up, wired.

Under his breath Rick gave a command: "*Stay*."

The breeze, what breeze there was, blew up from the valley, and the fox didn't see man or dog or get any scent. For Rick, watching Waldo was as interesting as watching the fox, but then he realized that a whole lot of fur might soon start flying. The fox didn't appear rabid but cases of diseased animals, especially raccoons, were on the rise in Ulmer County. He didn't want Waldo tangling with a feral animal regardless, and if he so much as raised his arm, to alarm the fox, Waldo might take it as the "go" signal. Lazy red fox, now a hundred feet away, would soon be sitting in Rick's lap. He eased his hand to the dog's collar. Then Waldo—the stay command didn't have a "no barking" clause—let out a lusty yelp. In its haste to bolt, the fox's legs slid out from under it; bushy tail flying, it bounded away.

Waldo's eyes pleading with Rick. *Give me an OK, Boss!*

He gave the dog a "heel" and they started toward the old barn.

■ ■ ■

Later, in his attic, he and Noreen sat at a card table covered with a checkered cloth. Red wine in their glasses, French bread on a cutting board; wild rice, string beans, a roasted game bird on their plates. "Rick, I'm impressed. This is beautiful," she said.

He lifted his glass. "*Sláinte.*"

"*Sláinte.*"

They sipped their wine, then sliced off a piece of grouse and had their first taste. A smile came to Noreen's face. "And delicious!"

"I'm glad you like it." The next moment Rick was putting his fingers to his lips and setting something very small on the side of his plate. "Piece of shot."

"Should I be on the lookout?" Noreen asked.

"Not necessary. Your bird was winged."

"Yours was—?"

"Killed outright."

"Once they're in your jacket, how can you tell one from the other?"

"When you prepare a bird for cooking, it becomes

apparent. Your breast was—or I should say, is—perfect. Nary a blemish."

"I respond to flattery, Rick," she said, her eyes shining.

"I'm glad you warned me."

She asked him where he had grown up. He answered thirty miles to the north, in Woodbridge. Still rural now, but back then it was really rural. A kid named Dom Scileppi, a schoolmate, introduced him to hunting, fishing, and trapping. "It was how I grew up," Rick said. "My father didn't hunt or fish. He was a writer and had other interests, but if I liked hunting and fishing; that was fine. What worried him was that I was becoming a 'local kid' with no ambition and would end up working for Ulmer County on its road crew."

"He told you that?"

"He told my mother," Rick said. "I heard them talking."

"What did you think?"

"It didn't bother me. Road crews repaired bridges, plowed roads. Driving an all-wheel-drive Drift Buster in a snow storm, lights flashing. That's great stuff."

Noreen laughed; her green eyes sparkled. "So, what happened?"

"He enrolled me in one of the finest and most prestigious prep schools in the country; never asked me how I felt about it, just enrolled me. I passed an entrance exam and the next fall he put me on a train to Boston and I caught a train to Andover."

"I dated a boy at Andover once. He was a terrible snob," Noreen said.

"Do you know why he sent me?"

"I imagine to get a good education."

"Partly. He sent me to Andover because he wanted me to meet the 'top boys in America.'"

"How was it?"

"The school was too much for me, in every way," Rick said. "I was never happy there and always hated going back. I stayed the full four years."

Noreen was frowning. "Why would you stay on if you hated going back, if you weren't happy at Andover? I don't understand."

"I've been trying to answer that question all my life," he said.

"Where was your mother in all this?"

"She always deferred to my father."

Noreen pressed her lips together. "It's a wonder we grow up at all," she said, "all the 'messages' thrown at us when we're kids. When I was fifteen my mother taught me the importance of 'scanning.' She drew up a list for me: Must Qualities in a Boyfriend. She used to tell me, 'Noreen, the boy you date will be the boy you marry.' A boy had to be Catholic, white, college-educated, have parents with social standing and strong family values. It followed me into college, then one fall day it caught up with me and I ran for seven years."

"I stayed for seven years," Rick said.

"And here we are," Noreen said, with a lift of her glass.

■ ■ ■

After dinner, she helped with the cleanup, then went downstairs and returned ten minutes later in a pair of navy sweats, top and bottom, her hair brushed, socks on her feet, carrying a couple of books and a clipboard.

They sat at each end of the sofa, Rick correcting freshman compositions, then rereading parts of *The Scarlet Letter*. Noreen wrote on lined paper—erasing, scratching out—then opened a book called *Principles of Logic*. Occasionally they would look up and their eyes would meet. She would smile, and he would; or he would smile, and she would. Then back to their work.

Close to eleven, Noreen yawned. "Let's fold the tent, Rick."

"It's folded," he said, standing up, giving her his hand.

CHAPTER
9

It was Wednesday, at four, and Chloe had a last sip of tea and took the old, worn stairs down to the basement. Waiting in the fireplace room was Karen Clendenin, her first "non-Evan" referral, whom she was seeing today for only the second time. They greeted each other and went into the larger adjacent room, Chloe's office.

She settled into her chair next to a round lacquered table, her client in a chair positioned casually—they weren't facing each other directly. From Karen's first visit, Chloe saw her as structured and conventional, maybe thirty-five. Today she was wearing a beige skirt, a red blazer over a white blouse, and one-inch brown heels. Blue eyes, curly black hair. Very pretty but very controlled, structured. Wounded by the recent breakup of her marriage.

"I really like your house," Karen Clendenin said. "Everything is so—" She paused, looking for the right word, "—historic. I almost said eerie."

"Well, it's kind of eerie. Old timers say there's a tunnel in the root cellar," Chloe said.

"A tunnel?"

"Back in the last century it supposedly helped runaway slaves."

"That's exciting. Have you ever looked for it?"

"No. I don't feel compelled somehow, and my husband thinks it's apocryphal."

"How old is the house?"

"Records have it built in 1835." More to the point of their session, "How's the job search coming, Karen?"

"I'm not in a position to be choosy but so far nothing appeals to me."

Chloe's client was silent for a while, then picked up the thread of last week's session. "Ted brought back the children, finally. A whole day late. They were tired, hungry, hadn't had baths."

"What did you do?"

"I screamed at him, I was furious. He said he was going to claim custody of the kids because obviously I was an emotionally unfit mother."

"Do you feel like an emotionally unfit mother?"

"No, but it was frightening to hear him say it. As a state trooper, he knows a lot of people. Who knows what strings he could pull?"

"To me it sounds like a hollow threat. He's making you pay for what you did."

"What *I* did?" Karen cried out.

"Yes."

"I gave him a son and a daughter, had dinners waiting when he came home, kept the house looking nice, never refused him—"

Upstairs, the back door opened, loudly closed. Chloe followed the heavy footsteps from the kitchen into the front hall. Lisa moved like a gazelle, except when a client's car was parked out front; then she walked like a horse. "You did something he'll never forgive you for," Chloe said.

"You mean, kicking him out? He deserved it!"

"Tell me what Ted has now," Chloe said.

"Other than 'Beverly,' not very much. He lives with his parents."

The upstairs toilet flushed. The down-drain, concealed in the wall behind the client's chair, had insulation wrapped around it but you could still hear the sound of rushing water. Chloe had told her kids (and Rick when he'd lived here) not to flush when she had a client.

"And while he and you were together," she said to her client, "he had all the conveniences and pleasures of home *and* a girlfriend. Then you told him to get lost, and this man is supposed to like you? So who has the power here, Karen, you or Ted?"

"All right. But I'm still angry!"

"What about other men?"

A small glass pitcher and paper cups rested on the little table, and Karen poured herself some water. "I've been seeing someone in Dutcher County for a couple of months, a vice-principal at our local middle school who's cheating on his wife. A nobody kind of man. We go to bed, he does his things."

"What about sex, sex generally? How do you feel about it?" Chloe asked.

Karen Clendenin paused, her eyes drifting, losing focus; then, coming back, "To be totally frank, I never think about it. Never, just walking around or having a cup of coffee or in a store, do I ever feel—" She paused.

"Feel what, Karen?"

"I can't say the word."

"You're perfectly capable of saying it. Go ahead, I'm giving you permission."

Finally, as if responding to a dare, "Horny."

Chloe gave her a big smile. "Excellent! Was there anyone in your life, Karen, before Ted?"

"No. And I made him wait until we were married."

Chloe recalled her own girlhood, from fifteen on. She could hardly count the times, remember the boys and the men she'd slept with. At nineteen she settled down, became engaged to Maxie Hoda; and Rick Forrester came along....

"Was it difficult for you staying a virgin?"

"No. The nuns said don't have sex until you're married," Karen said. "Plus my father was a disciplinarian. He would've killed me."

"That's enough to dim anyone's ardor," Chloe agreed.

"So, what did I do wrong? I was a 'good girl.' Where did it get me?"

"You didn't do anything wrong," Chloe said. "Don't put yourself down. I'm going to give you a little homework. This coming week, no matter what you're doing, how trivial it seems, I want you to listen to your body. The mind has a way of lying, it dodges the truth. The body loves the truth and doesn't know how to lie. So listen to what it's telling you."

"I will."

"I'll want a full report. And why are you wearing your wedding ring?"

"I'm still married."

"Really?"

"It gives me a feeling of security."

"Karen, you're an attractive, intelligent woman. Start acting like one," Chloe said.

CHAPTER
10

Rick was carrying a well-stuffed backpack by its straps when Mrs. Delvecchio, their landlady, saw him and Noreen pass by the open door of her ground-floor apartment. Coming out quickly, "Professore, *uno momento*," she said. "Tomorrow if you no here, I let them in. Eleven o'clock."

"Let who in?" Rick asked.

"The people, they-a come to see the house. I show your apartment." Mrs. Delvecchio had on a shapeless, washed-out housedress, and her wispy hair was done up in a loose bun. She gave her tenant's dog a narrow glance, then spoke to Noreen. "You too, Signorina."

Noreen nodded, and they continued by. At his wagon, Rick let down the tailgate, gave Waldo a boost, and tossed in his pack. As they began driving, Noreen explained that every so often a potential buyer came around, but Mrs. Delvecchio wanted too much for the property and wouldn't budge on her price.

"Does she want to sell or doesn't she?"

"I think it's a game she plays. Her husband wants to spend his last years in Italy. She gets him enthused, then the sale falls through."

"She does that willfully?"

"Well, it's a pattern. He sleeps in the little shack behind the house, you know."

"I didn't know."

At the corner of Main and N. Elm, Rick turned right. Driving along, he glanced at the time-and-temperature display on the outside of the Ulmer County Savings Bank. 12:05p/23°. They crossed the Walloon River.

"I don't think Chloe knows you very well," Noreen said.

"Why do you say that?"

"You lack adventure, isn't that what she says?"

"She has."

"What's having a picnic on a winter day in the Shaggs if it isn't an adventure?"

"Maybe crazy."

"Doing crazy things is the height of adventure."

Soon they were going by the leafless trees of the Lufkin & Jenkins orchards. The highway started to curve; as they zipped by Chodokee Road, Rick recalled the only time he'd ever set foot in the psychiatrist's house. A small gathering, Chloe had told him. Evan had just finished a new piece and he and Susan were having a few people over for the "unveiling": drinks and dinner. As they had approached the Kendrixes' place that June evening a year and a half ago, Rick glanced at the tall stones on one side of the driveway. Of course, he'd heard about them. Chloe was always talking about the statement they made, their vision, their incredible energy. She asked him, as they drove by the sculptures toward Evan's house, what he thought.

"I think the artist harbors feelings of sexual inadequacy."

"How can you say that?"

"You asked me, Chloe. Dr. Kendrix doth protest too much."

"Stay with your dusty manuscripts, Rick. All right?"

He and Noreen swept past Chodokee. A mile farther along they turned off Rt. 289 onto a dirt road and after another mile took a deeply rutted trail, a tunnel through the trees. They bounced along, in ten minutes coming to an open, grassy area. Rick pulled in, switched off the ignition.

"Now we hike," he said.

They got out. Rick lowered the tailgate, gave Waldo an "OK"; the dog jumped down, sat. After a second "OK," he ran.

"Did you ever enter him in an obedience competition?" Noreen asked.

He shouldered his pack and they began walking. "No. I trained him for his own safety, plus hunting commands. 'Go.' 'Stay.' 'Fetch'."

"Why *two* 'OK's?"

"Because with only one," Rick said, "he'd immediately take off, not necessarily the hunter's wish. And if you're parked along the side of a road, he might run out and get hit."

Noreen had on gray wool pants and a rust-colored down jacket. "That makes sense."

"Chloe says I ruined a perfectly nice dog."

"That's absurd. I don't know where she's coming from sometimes."

As they continued trekking, a great view of the Walloon River valley opened to the east, including the town. Noreen pointed out the Administration Building of the college, Rick the old church on Elting Street. The trail started rising and soon they came to a small lake near the base of a high, sharp-faced cliff. Dark woods grew around the edge of the water.

"So this is your Walden in the Shaggs," Noreen said.

"Otherwise called Spoon Pond."

They were standing in an opening directly on the shore, arms crossed, breaths vaporizing. A turned-over rowboat lay on one side of the clearing. Inside a ring of rough stones lay old ashes. "Whose boat is it, Rick?"

"A ranger camps here on and off during the summer. The whole area is a land trust called the Chodokee Preserve, over ten thousand acres."

From his pack Rick took a small bundle of sticks wrapped in newspaper and placed paper and kindling in the stone circle. They began gathering wood, each coming back with an armful. Rick struck a match and soon had a blaze going. With Noreen's help he flipped the boat (oars were beneath it) and lugged it to a spot nearer the fire, set it on its side, and used the oars as props. Next, he chopped two saplings with a hatchet and ran them from the gunwale to the ground. From his pack he removed a lightweight nylon tarp and laid it over the framework, extending it halfway down the saplings. As the final touch he spread an old army blanket on the ground. The shelter wasn't very high and the tarp brushed their heads. But heat was gathering. He removed a pair of field glasses and a bottle of wine from his pack, setting them both aside. It was his old pewter flask he was after.

"I thought we might start with a cocktail," he said.

He produced two glasses wrapped in paper toweling. Then, uncapping the flask, he poured. "*Sláinte.*"

"*Sláinte na comharsan is go maraidh na mna go deo!*"

"Is that Gaelic?"

"Irish. It's the Irish language. 'Health to the neighbors and may the women live forever!'"

They touched glasses. Noreen had a taste of her drink, looked out at the pond, the surrounding mountains. "I have an idea," she said. "All students at Appleton State should have the option of going to the mountains with the professor of their choice; it should be part of the curriculum."

"What should we call it?"

"'Bivouacking at Spoon Pond 101'."

"That implies there's a 102?"

"Bigger manhattans in 102."

"I'll present it to Academic Senate," Rick said.

Waldo appeared on the ice at the far edge of the pond, and Rick put his fingers to his lips and whistled. The dog started across.

"Tell me something," Noreen said, unbuttoning her jacket. "Here we are in the midst of nature having cocktails. Is Thoreau rolling over in his grave?"

"On the contrary. Henry got zonked with Emerson, Bronson Alcott, and Margaret Fuller twice a week."

Noreen's light-hearted laugh skipped across the ice.

"In truth, Thoreau wouldn't even take tea," Rick said, "for fear it would alter his perceptions, dash his whole day. Water—that was his drink—straight from the pond."

"Was he ever married?"

"No. There was a girl he liked, perhaps loved," Rick said. "He took her rowing in his boat. I doubt they ever kissed."

Waldo ran up, hopeful of joining the party. Rick didn't feel like sharing the lean-to with a big panting springer spaniel, thank you. He raised his hand to a "stop," and Waldo settled for a place outside, close to the fire.

"The long and the short of their friendship," Rick said, "is Ellen Sewell rejected Thoreau because he had no 'future,' in all probability at her father's insistence—that was it for Henry's love life. He's among the famous people who died a virgin."

"Is there proof of that?"

"If you study his life, it seems clear. He made a few trips but he wasn't a big traveler. Concord was a small town. Where were the women? My feeling is he wasn't a rover in any case."

"Say he *had* married Ellen Sewell, what do you think?"

"He wouldn't have gone to Walden Pond, I know that." Rick unbuttoned his own jacket.

"And we wouldn't have *Walden*," Noreen said.

"Hard to imagine."

A hawk was gliding through the air near the face of the steep cliff and Rick drew the binoculars from their case, following its flight. "Take a look."

Noreen adjusted the glasses to her eyes. "How beautiful!" The hawk disappeared and she continued sweeping the cliffs. "I see someone."

"The area is famous for climbers."

"This person isn't climbing," she said. "He's just standing on a ledge."

She passed him the binoculars. "A little more to the right," she said. "There's a single evergreen growing in the cliff—"

"I have it now."

The man had a thick, dark beard and was wearing a tan jacket with the collar turned up. He appeared to be drinking deeply of the air; then he raised his arms, stretching them out to the valley. "I'll be damned," Rick said.

"What?"

"I know him. He's a former student, a Vietnam vet."

"What's he doing up there?"

"It's where he lives."

"Lives?"

"In a cave. So he says."

Sparks jumped from the fire and Waldo gave a start, then settled back down, head on his paws. Rick lowered the binoculars, gave his flask a shake. "Just enough for a dividend."

A snow flurry blew in from the north, giving the pond a dusting. "I was thinking the other morning, walking to class, about you and Andover," Noreen said. "Did you get anything out of it?"

"A good friend, Michael Bostwick, a classmate. We still see each other."

"That's something," Noreen said.

"Today he's a partner in the New York law firm, Pooley, Manning and Maxwell. He may have saved my life."

"How so? Can you tell me?"

"I was in a really bad place, going back to my dorm at the end of our graduation dinner, the traditional senior banquet," Rick said. "Michael caught up with me and suggested we walk into downtown Andover, where we sat at a workingman's bar and had a couple of beers. It pulled me through."

Rick was quiet for a moment, shaking his head. It was all he was going to say and she knew it. Then he said, "But here's a brighter story. Early on at Andover we discovered we were trappers. That winter—the winter of our discovery—we set three traps at Rabbit Pond on the outskirts of the campus. It was where the hockey team played. We operated in stealth, early mornings before anyone was up, and skinned the muskrats in a corner of the furnace room in Tyler Hall. Michael had a contact and we sold half-a-dozen pelts—until the fateful day the housemaster's wife found a carcass in the basement. She screamed bloody murder, thought it was a fetus, someone had performed an abortion! Likely on a girl at our sister school, Ashford. Big trouble, big investigation. In keeping with school policy, we were given a hearing. Dean of students, three masters, chaired by the headmaster himself, Charles Feuer, Cotton Mather incarnate. It didn't look good for us, but a statement Michael made at the end swayed the panel toward leniency: 'There's a little Davy Crockett in every boy.' Cotton Mather forgave us our sins and we stayed on. But no more trapping."

"Great story."

"We still talk about it," he said with a smile. "'Andover v. Bostwick and Forrester. Trial of the Century.'"

■ ■ ■

Waldo was chewing on a steak bone by the fire, now only embers. The sun wouldn't set for another hour, but with the mountain directly behind Spoon Pond, long shadows were already settling over it. Inside the lean-to, Rick and Noreen were wrapped in a blanket.

"I'm happy we met," she said, their faces touching.

"You came up the stairs with a six-pack."

"I wanted to get to know you."

"I wanted to get to know you," he said.

Another snow flurry tumbled across the pond.

"Rick."

"Yes."

"Nothing. Just Rick," she said.

CHAPTER
11

With his remote, Evan Kendrix rolled the dolly backward and turned its wheels; then, standing on the solid plank floor of his studio, he looked at, concentrated on, the work from this new perspective. No question about it, "Prurience" was coming to life; he was starting to reveal—no, *she* was starting to reveal—her soul.

He set the remote on the low table, then picked up hammer and point. Positioning his protective glasses, he climbed to the third rung of the ladder and started in. Psychotherapy was tremendously challenging and made him a fine living, but sculpting satisfied him on a deeper level. As he worked, heat built in his body and he undid a couple of buttons on his wool overshirt, even though the temperature in his studio hovered, on cold days like today, at 65°.

At two thirty, Evan laid down his tools and closed the flue to his wood-burning stove. On one of the four structural posts in his studio, serving to support the pair of heavy overhead beams, hung his sheepskin coat. He slipped it on, pushed open the door built into the barn's tall sliding door—a door within a door—and stepped out.

As he traversed the turnaround to his house, he glanced up at the hard blue sky; he hadn't heard the forecast but he wouldn't be surprised to see the bottom drop out of the thermometer before morning. Inside his house, Evan checked his answering machine, then showered, shaved, dressed; glanced at his watch. He'd be ten minutes late but that was OK. What was the director of Westgate Industries going to do, fire him? Dismiss the psychiatrist who came in every Thursday afternoon to supervise the company's evaluators? At $10.00 an hour it wasn't pay, it was pro bono; and Bernie Terwilliger knew it.

Evan grabbed his coat and entered the garage. Porsche on one side, 4-wheel-drive Blazer on the other. He opened the door to the bigger vehicle, twisted the key, and backed out; shifted gears and started down his drive. One more sculpture and the entrance to his house would be complete. "Prurience" would go…right *there*. With "Venus at Orgasm" and "Coital Dreams," it would form the apex of a glorious, quintessential delta.

The driveway hit Chodokee Road, which merged with Rt. 289. On the state thoroughfare he headed east into Appleton, crossed the steel bridge, and at the minipark turned onto N. Elm. About two miles along he came to a large barracks-like building, originally a roller-skating rink; but the business had failed and now the structure housed a piecework and components company that hired the emotionally and physically disadvantaged. The place was a halfway house to the outside world of employment; but for 60% of the people who worked for Westgate, it would remain the only job they would ever have. Evan parked near the main entrance and pushed open the heavy glass door.

In the great open space where skaters had once gone round and round to music, people sat at benches doing manual jobs of the simplest nature. Some were walking about, or standing idly, gazing at floor or ceiling. Evan ducked into the director's office.

Bernie Terwilliger was at his desk, scanning a report and biting his nails, though really he had none to bite. Out of habit, whenever he read anything he chewed at his fingertips, and he always had his head buried in a directive or an order out of Albany. He was a bald, overweight man with black-framed glasses, in his late forties; he used the sweep method to cover his naked scalp. It fooled no one but it was artfully done. "Evan!" he said, glancing up.

"Hey, Bernie."

"Three evaluators—three *candidates*, I should say—are with us today to fill Becky Shoh's position on our staff. I always thought people got *meaner* as they got older. I like all three."

Terwilliger slid a trio of file folders across his desk, sending up a small puff of dust. His office had the appearance of a storage room. Boxes containing piecework were everywhere, and individual items—bookends, shoe trees, garden rakes (minus handles)—were scattered about on steel shelving, on the floor, in the corners. "I need your help, Evan."

"That's why I'm here."

The director of Westgate Industries peeked at his watch. "I'll send the candidates in," he said. "I appreciate this, really."

Evan looked through one of the windows. A white van was parked near the front entrance and a dozen Westgate workers were shuffling toward it, ill-dressed, sorry-looking people. The van pulled away and Evan sat in Bernie's chair and glanced through the applicants' names and backgrounds. Soon the door opened and a twenty-eight-year-old woman, with maple-syrup-colored skin, entered. Her hair was cropped very short. She had a marvelously straight spine—watching her sit was inspirational. Her legs were clad in white stockings with an off-white floral design. She was bright and had a determined set to her chin—too determined, Evan seemed to think: no one was going to stop Brenda Thompson. She was currently the assistant director of the Student Aid Program at Appleton State but wasn't finding it challenging enough; she wanted a job in the private sector. After ten minutes Evan thanked the candidate, who gave him a reserved smile and got to her feet. He watched her leave. Great body, but no softness to it. Legs like steel.

The next candidate wasn't immediately showing and Evan walked to the five-gallon jug by the window, pushed the button, and filled a paper cup with water.

Through the window he saw a young woman walking on the side of Rt. 23 toward the village. Dark hair, diminutive size—was it Christine? On second glance, he decided no; but it got him thinking about her. His optimistic appraisals in his journal aside, he wasn't all that sure that Christine was making significant strides toward well-being. But he was confident it would happen. One of these evenings in their sessions together he would come up with the perfect therapeutic exercise—

"Dr. Kendrix?"

He crumpled his cup into the basket, turned. "Yes."

"I'm Karen Clendenin."

"Come in, please. Have a seat."

The woman was wearing a stylish dark blue suit, white blouse, and matching blue heels. Evan took his place at Bernie Terwilliger's desk; opened Mrs. Clendenin's folder, studied it for a few moments. "You have a Master's Degree in Social Work, I see."

"Yes."

He noticed how she was sitting—hands folded in her lap, knees touching, ankles crossed just so. "Tell me about your work at Dutcher County Welfare," Evan said.

"While I was there, I interviewed and screened clients and assigned them to individual case workers; that was my main function. In a secondary capacity I served as an intermediary between Dutcher County and the state capital—keeping the lines of communication open. Trying to, anyway. I learned a great deal about bureaucracy."

"Then this is the place for you, because we have a lot of it," Evan said with a laugh.

"I thought you might."

He glanced at her résumé. "You have children, a girl and a boy. Their father is with the state police."

"Yes." Karen shifted her ankles; in doing so, her knees separated, maybe two inches. Then touched again, quickly.

"He's in drug enforcement and interdiction."

"It's not *my* idea of how to make a living," Evan said, "but someone has to do it. How long have you lived in Appleton?"

"Not long, two months. For years we lived in Pourquoy, across the river, until the divorce."

Evan gave a little nod, liking her openness. He asked her if she had any question about Westgate Industries. She did. Could he explain his role in the organization?

"I offer advice to the evaluators," Evan said. "It's the evaluators who decide who's capable of doing what. Can a worker take on a more demanding job inside Westgate Industries or is he or she ready to enter the outside work force? I'm here to help the evaluator evaluate—simple as that."

He was speaking in a quiet, personal way, wanting her to fully relax. "Occasionally we have a worker act out: disruptive, asocial behavior," he said. "That's basically what the evaluators and I talk about—we review cases, discuss personalities. We're having a general meeting today, right after I see the next candidate. I'm sure Mr. Terwilliger would be glad to have you, and the others, sit in. If you'd like to, that is."

"I'd like it a great deal."

She was intelligent, personable, and (he suspected) dying to let her hair down; what she needed was affirmation, a little quiet coaxing. Inwardly, Evan smiled at the notion, his eyes remaining on Karen's longer than convention might allow. "Thank you, Mrs. Clendenin."

"Thank you, Dr. Kendrix."

She stood and offered her hand, which Evan politely accepted, knowing—he was never wrong on such matters— that she wanted to experience the sensation of touch. When she was gone, he made a few notes on the meeting. A knock on the door. The next interview would be pro forma. Position was taken.

CHAPTER
12

Chloe folded napkins for three places, set them on the kitchen table next to the utensils for the evening meal, and had a sip from a glass of red wine. With her Abnormal Psych class starting in forty-five minutes, she shouldn't be having wine, but she had to unwind after seeing five clients during the day, the last a mildly autistic girl she had taken on at Evan's urging last spring. Chloe loved Bonnie Wintersteen, wanted so to help her, but she didn't see that she was making any real progress with the sweet young girl, and probably never would.

She stirred the beef stew, testing the meat with a fork, then stood at the window facing west. A few lights—she counted three—flickered on the Shagg Range. Otherwise all was darkness. Lisa and Drew drifted into the kitchen and Chloe ladled out the food. The room was warm and comfortable and she sat down with her children. Lisa seemed especially quiet and Chloe asked her what was on her mind.

"Nothing."

"No, something."

"I don't feel like talking, Mom."

"Well, it's self-indulgent behavior," Chloe said.

"I don't know what that means."

"It means you're putting out negative energy."

"Mom, I'm not a client. Say something I understand."

Chloe ended it there. Possibly *she* was putting out negative energy. After a short silence, Andrew said, "I saw Dad this morning."

"Oh?"

"We were making the turn in the bus, there at the minipark. I think they'd just taken Waldo for a run."

"They?"

"Dad and his friend."

"I'm assuming Rick's made a couple of friends," Chloe said.

"The girl downstairs, who helped him clean his apartment."

"What were they doing?"

"Drinking coffee outside Hobo Deli."

"Well, how nice," Chloe said, and had a sip of wine.

■ ■ ■

The last part of Professor Manheim's lecture for the evening consisted of a few words on next week's topic: the bi-polar individual. Mood swings from feelings of invincibility to stretches of helplessness and depression. Everyone experiences days when they feel on top of the world and days when they're in a blue funk. With the bi-polar individual, those feelings are more pronounced.

Dr. Manheim paced back and forth in the front of the room. He had a mincing little step and made stiff gestures with his child-sized hands. "Is 'bi-polar' a good name for the condition?" he asked his students. "Not long ago it was called 'manic-depressive.'" The change in terminology was something he would like to take up to start next week's class.

He took a peek at his watch. "All right, that does it." Dr. Manheim opened his briefcase, which bulged at the sides like a pregnant brown dog. "Come up for your term papers, as I call your name."

Chloe wanted to believe she'd done well but part of her feared she'd hadn't. For all the inner strength, the conviction she'd gained these past few years of herself as a woman participating in a great movement, she sometimes felt that she'd never graduated from Long Island City High, that she was still engaged to Maxie Hoda, the Albanian with the snappy suits and the roll of fifties in his pocket who drove a Caddy with a gold key. An ex-navy officer working for his Ph.D. had come and taken her away, introduced her to a new life, and now a psychiatrist with Harvard degrees was rescuing her from her dependency in a dead-end marriage and guiding her to her real potential. She was a practicing therapist, her clients liked her, she was gaining a reputation, she was making money. Then why, Chloe asked herself, why so often—like right now—did she feel like she was hanging on by a thread?

Finally Dr. Manheim called her name and Chloe stood, put on her coat, and walked to the front of the room, taking the fifteen pages he handed her, at the same time giving her a little rodentlike smile. He called the next name on his roster and Chloe hurried out. Her classmate Zeke Hatalski was in the hallway, waiting for her. He was young, maybe twenty-six, tall, loose-limbed, wearing blue jeans and battered hi-top sneakers. A number of times, after class, they had gone for coffee.

"Well?" he asked.

"I haven't looked yet."

"So, look!"

"How did you do, Zeke?"

"B minus, for basic bullshit. Not even good basic bullshit."

They began walking down the hall toward the main lobby of the Koker Science Building. Chloe flipped to the last page, saw (didn't read) Manheim's comment, and at the end of it, small but cleanly stroked, was the grade. Zeke was peering over her shoulder.

"All right, Chloe!" he said, genuinely delighted. "An A! Let me buy you a beer."

They pushed through the doorway and were outside. It was a cold, clear night. A strong wind had sprung up during class; a gust almost tore the essay from her hand. "I really can't. My kids—"

"Come on, we're all meeting in P&B's."

"OK. Just one."

Her car was in the big lot across from Rick's office and Chloe looked about at the lighted paths and buildings of Appleton State, having a wonderful surge of confidence. What she really wanted to do was go home and read Dr. Manheim's comment, then call Evan.

She drove downtown and parked behind the bank, bucked the wind crossing Main Street, and went into the tavern. The place wasn't jammed, just busy—local men and women, a dozen college kids sitting and standing about. Christmas stockings were tacked to the wall behind the bar, each with a bartender's or waitress's name on it. Immediately someone was calling her and she looked over. Her classmates were sitting in the corner around a big round table, a liquid, foam-topped centerpiece in the middle of it. Chloe went over and took the empty chair next to Zeke. Her friends welcomed her and Zeke lifted the pitcher and filled her glass.

The talk continued apace. Sandy Abrams, divorced, early thirties, was talking about her paper, saying that Dr. Manheim had only given her a B and she was angry. She had presented a strong case that homosexuality wasn't a choice one made; the choice was made for the person. Her documentation was impeccable. Manheim's grade and comment only proved what everyone knew: that in the final analysis prejudice sneaked through, tainting objectivity.

Chloe agreed, but didn't say anything. Objectivity was one of the great challenges for the therapist, a point she had discussed with Evan many times. Lester Treat, a light-skinned black student who, at least once every class, smiled at Chloe, said he didn't believe anyone could ever shed their prejudices completely, even with extensive therapy.

"Prejudices and philosophy aren't the same thing," Sandy said. "A therapist has to have a point of view. Where is he coming from?"

"If it's a lousy point of view, it's prejudice," said Joel Levy, short and stocky, with red hair and a painfully thin mustache.

His quips had amused the class all semester. "What's bigotry but a twisted point of view?"

Chloe had a taste of her beer, giving herself another ten minutes with her classmates. Then Zeke was saying to her privately, "I had a weird dream the other night. I'd like your interpretation."

"This might cost you, Zeke."

He grinned. "In the dream I'm on the toilet taking a dump. When I'm done I hear this commotion in the bowl and I stand up fast. The turd is alive. It's big and has demonic eyes and sharp little teeth and it's swimming about like any second it's gonna leap up and go for me."

"Zeke, I really have to run," Chloe said.

"Listen. It's not over. I flush the toilet and it doesn't want to go down. This piece of no-good shit is fighting to stay alive! The next moment I'm awake, sweating like a pig. What do you think?"

"I'd rather not say."

"No, tell me."

Just then Gigi Pfeiffer—who Chloe believed had a lot of casual sex, not always with men—spoke up. She had a mop of tangled brown hair and a loose, sensual mouth. "Everyone," she said to the group, "this is my housemate, Christine."

Chloe glanced across the table, glad for the interruption. Settling into a chair next to Gigi was a young woman, early twenties: lips, brilliant red; skin, chalky white; hair, coal black. She didn't appear particularly joyous; something pressing was on her mind. But darling she was. A tidbit. A gumdrop!

Joel Levy asked the new arrival what her major was.

"Speech."

"Any special aspect?"

"Impediments."

"V-v-v-very interesting," Joel said. "Perhaps we c-could m-m-meet somewhere to discuss my pr-pr-problem."

Everyone laughed. The young woman said she'd think about it, then chatted privately with Gigi.

Christine, speech major, impediments.

Chloe had a sudden feeling of queasiness; she thought she might get sick. She told her classmates that the weather was getting pretty bad and she had to get home to her family. As she ran across Main Street, dark clouds, low in the western sky, resembled a tidal wave rolling in.

■ ■ ■

After checking on her children Chloe got ready for bed, slid under the covers, and read Dr. Manheim's critique. "One of the most sensitive, thoughtful, and astute papers I've read in a long time." Then the grade. "A." She wanted to dial Evan's number but fought the temptation. What would she say? I met Christine Monteleone. Of course you gave her a roving slot!

Stop it, Chloe thought. *You're not your mother.*

The wind slammed the house, locust branches scratching at the roof like a clawed, frenzied animal wanting in. Then, at an extra strong blast, she sat upright, startled by a great crashing sound as if a tree or branch had just fallen and hit a corner of the deck.

Please help me, God, Chloe thought.

CHAPTER
13

Walking with Waldo early in the day, Rick saw the street people assembled in the minipark on the corner of Main Street and N. Elm. Greg Horboychuk, a former student of Rick's—dour-looking with his black beard, deep-set eyes, and sloping shoulders—was dragging on a cigarette. Next to him stood Jean-Jean the Artist, thin and raptorlike, who never seemed to stand so much as perch. Holding his staff, the Good Shepherd appeared asleep on his feet, his vaporizing breath forming vague halos above his head. Rick gave a "stay" command to Waldo and went up the steps of Hobo Deli, buying, once inside, a paper and a container of coffee. When he came back out, Greg Horboychuk was crouching beside the dog, patting his head.

He looked up. "Rick. How are you, man?"

"I'm OK, Greg. How about yourself?"

"I met the Great Death, stared him straight in the fucking eye."

"Were you sick?"

"Starving! We're all starving! Let Jean-Jean the Artist do your portrait. Thirty bucks. He's a great painter."

"I'm sure he is." Rick brought the coffee to his lips.

Greg got to his feet and looked at him beseechingly. "Can you give me a hand?"

"I can give you a few dollars to buy yourself breakfast."

"I'm talking work, not breakfast. You got any work?"

"I live in an attic. What work?"

"God-damn society! Man has a college degree, graduated top in his class—fought for his country in Nam—and there's nothing for him! Look at Jean-Jean over there. He's an artist of the beautiful, and he's dying." Greg came a step closer.

"Ever since that day you walked into the classroom and started rapping about Thoreau, I've loved you, man."

"If there was anything I could do—" Rick stopped, then said, "I might have something."

Greg's crow-black eyes brightened.

"At my house on Elting Street we had wind damage in that last storm—locust tree smashed the end of the deck. I want you to clear and cut the limb, stack the wood, sweep the deck. Then start on the trees below the house; three or four got blown down. I'll pay you $6.00 an hour. When can you start?"

The Good Shepherd and Jean-Jean the Artist were looking over. "I'm ready right now."

"Let me arrange a few things. Make it tomorrow morning." He took three dollars out of his wallet. "Here, have breakfast."

"God bless you, man!"

With Waldo at heel, Rick headed back to his place, thinking he'd give Chloe a call—let her know one of his former students would be coming out tomorrow.

■ ■ ■

Books, journals, manuscript pages of his biography were scattered all over the floor of his attic apartment, and stacked underneath the window were additional books, close to forty, taken from his college office, the library, and his house. In his lap, as Rick sat in the old leather easy chair with cracked leather arms and cushion, was the photocopy of one of Thoreau's original journals. Open on the small adjacent table lay a dark, hard-covered book. He would read a few of the scribbly words in the photocopy, then match them against the book, same exact date, hoping to discover omissions or changes that the editor of the published work of Thoreau's journals had made, intentionally or unintentionally.

Rick made a note on a yellow pad. Nothing—just another instance of William Bradford Torrey "standardizing" Thoreau's punctuation. The morning sun, slanting across the floodplain, gave the thin layer of snow a rose tint. The attic was comfortably warm and very quiet, perfect for working. He lighted the tobacco in his pipe—Barking Dog, Never Bites—had a few puffs, smoke curling lazily, then set the pipe down and continued his comparison. His eyes began closing. How long Rick stayed in a quiet half-sleep, he didn't know; but something cool and moist in his palm brought him to consciousness. Waldo was at his chair.

Rick brought his face close to the dog's. "'Tr-r-r-oonk, tr-r-r-oonk,'" he said. "Do you know what that is, Waldo? That's how Thoreau described the sound of a bullfrog. What do you think? Is it accurate? Listen again: 'Tr-r-r-oonk.'"

"Rrrufff."

"You don't think a bullfrog sounds like that? So, give me your impression."

"Rrrufff!"

"Well, if you say so. But it's a funny-sounding bullfrog to me." Rick got to his feet. "Come on, let's go for a run."

■ ■ ■

As always, Karen Clendenin was nicely dressed, today in a red blazer and pleated skirt, as she took her chair in Chloe's office. What Chloe noticed particularly, however, was a brightness in her client's eyes and a general aura of well-being not evident on earlier visits.

"You look terrific, Karen. If I were to see you on the street—" Chloe was smiling, "—I'd say now there's a woman who's in love!"

"Not quite." She gave an easy laugh. "But something did happen."

"Oh? Tell me!"

"Remember how I said I never felt the urge during the course of an ordinary day, like I wanted to have sex? Well, last week

I met someone and I wanted to make love with him then and there! I'm really embarrassed to say this, Chloe. When I got home, for the first time in my life—" She didn't go on.

"Your body spoke to you and you listened to it," Chloe said. "That is so great, Karen." Then, with a cajoling ring in her voice, "Where did you meet him? Come on, I want the details. Will you see him again?"

"It happened during an interview, so if I get the job I'll see him. Probably not—that way. We definitely clicked, but I'm sure he's spoken for."

"Whatever happens, I'm delighted," Chloe said. Sometimes all someone needed was an OK.

"It's like I've been asleep all these years," Karen said, happy with herself. "But my priority is getting the job."

"After an interview like that, I'd say you have it," Chloe said. "Where would it be?"

"I applied for a position at Westgate Industries, as an evaluator," Karen said. "I didn't think my interview with the director went that well. Then I met the man who supervises the evaluators, Dr. Kendrix. That was when it happened."

Chloe felt a sudden rush of heat to her face; her eyes went into staring mode. Quickly, willfully, she regained her composure.

"Then something else occurred this week, nonsexual but related. Can I run it by you?" Karen said.

It took Chloe a couple of seconds to say, "Yes, of course."

Karen began—something about a visitation with her children and their father—but Chloe was finding it impossible to follow along, preoccupied with a more pressing issue. How could she continue seeing Karen Clendenin as a client? Ethics demanded that she say Dr. Kendrix and she were a couple. Karen would be embarrassed, humiliated, but you have to tell her, Chloe, a voice was saying. *Now. Right now.* Then another voice, more sinister, barged in. You want to find out about Evan, don't you? You're already skeptical, nervous, threatened. Here's a way to find out who he really is. With weekly updates.

"Do you think it's significant?" Karen asked.

Did she think *what* was significant? Protecting herself, Chloe retreated to a standard therapist's response. "Do *you* think it is?"

"I do, I really do," Karen said. "I felt strong, in charge—and he was standing right there in the doorway of my apartment!"

"Dr. Kendrix?"

Karen frowned. "Ted, my ex."

"Right. Of course," Chloe said.

CHAPTER
14

He imagined he could "eyeball" the bookcase he was in the process of making, but why not take out the guesswork? He needed his level—plus some finishing nails and a couple of chisels. Rick set aside his saw and propped the six-foot length of pine next to three similar pieces against the wall.

He grabbed his coat, left his apartment with Waldo, and soon was pulling into his driveway. Knowing he'd only be two minutes, he drew up to the rear bumper of a client's car and got out. Waldo waited for an "OK" (didn't get one) and Rick circled the green Buick, his eyes darting, once he was in the shed, to the peg that always held the level: not there. That same moment the side door to the house opened and a woman in her mid-thirties, trim, wearing a belted gray coat, came out and walked toward the sedan, then stopped, seeing the station wagon blocking her in.

"I'm sorry," Rick said, stepping from the shed. "It's mine, I'll move it."

"Thank you."

He went to his car parked on the far side of the driveway. As the woman backed out, she smiled and gave him a wave of thanks. Rick smiled in return and walked to the deck steps, thinking to inquire about his level inside. Andrew sometimes used his tools and left them lying around. As he crossed the deck, he noticed that the locust limb and all evidence that it had fallen were gone from the far end. Greg had also made inroads on the downed trees near the oxbow. Pleased with his former student's work, Rick entered the house just as Chloe was coming up from the basement.

"Oh!" she said.

"Have you seen my level?"

"No."

"Is Andrew home?"

"I've been working. I don't know."

He gave her a closer look, detecting a kind of frantic, fractured expression on her face. "Are you all right?" he asked.

"Sit with me, Rick."

"Excuse me?"

"Stay with me for a minute."

He sat down at the round oak table without taking off his coat. "What is it?"

"Did you see someone, just now, leaving by the side door?"

He thought for a moment, then said, "I saw a woman in a gray coat."

"What did you think?"

"I didn't think anything. I was blocking her and had to move."

"Did you find her attractive?"

"Moderately, I suppose. I wasn't really—"

"Would you sleep with her?"

"What in hell are you talking about, Chloe?"

She smoothed her eyebrows with her thumb and fingers— harder, it seemed to him, than necessary.

"Are you OK?" he asked.

"Hold me, Rick."

"I have to run."

"Just for a second."

He put his arms around her, awkwardly, then stood and went to the door just as the buzzer, which he'd installed to alert Chloe to a client, sounded. A gray Plymouth had taken the place of the Buick in the driveway. Searching in the shed, Rick spotted his level among random golf clubs and garden tools in the corner; found chisels, nails—

Behind the wheel of his station wagon, he glanced at the

house. Waldo sat close and Rick stroked the dog's shoulder; then, as much to scatter his thoughts as to start the engine, he turned the key.

■ ■ ■

The bus for high-school students stopped at the corner of Hazel and N. Elm, and Lisa Forrester got off with two other kids, a boy and a girl, who lived in a boxy brown house on the corner of Hazel and Elting. The boy was close friends with Andrew; they played golf together. Donnie Malone had a lot of jokes and a friendly manner, if you could take his loud, annoying laugh. Eleanor, his sister, wore nice clothes but had zero personality. She and Lisa never talked as they walked up Hazel, and they didn't talk today. Lisa started along Elting by herself.

It was a quiet street. She liked the view of the floodplain and Shagg Mountains, and she liked their house. It had a lot of rooms, plenty of space, and had a mysteriousness about it, a romantic quality, dating back as it did so many years. Still, she missed Woodbridge, where they had lived until five years ago when her father had commuted to the college. It had nothing to do with houses or towns. In Woodbridge they were a family.

She walked on. In all likelihood, a car would be in the driveway, which meant her mother would be with a client. She would have to tiptoe about or else Chloe would come running up from her office to say things like, "Why are you doing this to me, Lisa?" or "Why are you punishing me?"

She opened their rural mailbox, reached in, and took out three or four envelopes, a couple of flyers, and her brother's magazine, *Golf*. She liked getting the mail; nothing was ever for her, but she still liked bringing it in. She walked around to the back of the house passing a silvery-gray car in the driveway. About to go up the deck stairs, she heard someone sawing wood near the oxbow. So he was here again. He had smiled at her one day last week as she was coming home from school. Now she went to the lip of the embankment—and there he was, in a flannel shirt and combat boots, with his thick black beard and dense black hair, cutting a limb propped on a sawhorse, his arms moving rhythmically, pushing, pulling on the saw.

Lisa took the rough steps down, though a voice in her head—her mother's—told her not to. Suddenly he stopped sawing, looked up; his chest was heaving. About twenty feet away from him, Lisa stopped.

"Hi," he said. He smiled; his teeth were white, strong. "What's your name?"

"Lisa.

"*Mona Lisa.* I'm Greg."

She sensed he was a kind person and went a little closer. "Where do you live?"

He wiped his face with a neckerchief; wood chips clung to his beard. "In a castle."

Lisa laughed. "A castle?"

He pointed across the floodplain. "In the Shaggs."

"There's a castle in the Shaggs?"

He took a few pushes on the saw; the log fell. "Castlegregory stands on the edge of the world. Maybe one day I could take you there, Lisa."

She could hear her own breathing, as if *she* had just used the saw. "Maybe. Well, see you."

Lisa moved away. Crossing the deck she glanced down. Greg stopped his work to wave; she waved back. Then she was inside, depositing the mail on the secretary and walking to the stairs, though as she thought about it she wasn't walking at all. She was floating.

No way would her mother come running up today.

CHAPTER
15

With Chloe away—she and Evan were in New York co-directing a therapy workshop—the kids spent the weekend with Rick in his apartment. Friday night he took them to the movies in Ambrose Plaza, the next morning to the college gym, and then to his mother's house in Woodbridge, where they were now having lunch, though, as Lisa had already said, it wasn't lunch—it was a feast! Baked chicken pieces with a crusty lemon glaze, fresh string beans, a rice pilaf with almonds, creamed onions, and a big tossed salad.

"That's amazing. Forty laps!" Margaret Forrester said to her granddaughter. "How about you, Andrew? How many laps did you swim?"

"None. Dad talked to the golf coach, Mr. Sheridan. I got to hit balls."

Margi indicated to Rick that he should pour her a little more wine. To her grandson, "In this weather?"

"Inside."

"Isn't that dangerous? Golf balls bouncing off the walls, my goodness!"

"Margi, you hit into a big net," Andrew explained. "The balls hit the net and drop."

Margaret smiled proudly. "Well, what a wonderful weekend you're having."

"This is still the best part," Lisa said.

"Let me give you more; anyone who swims forty laps needs to eat."

Lisa held out her plate. "We haven't seen food like this in weeks."

Margi gave her a second helping of everything, looked at her grandson. "Andrew?"

"Just a piece of chicken."

"Have a little rice also."

After taking care of her grandson, Margi spoke to Lisa, asking her if she was doing any cooking.

"Not really."

"I thought your mother was teaching you."

"She was."

"I remember when you lived in Woodbridge, Chloe was always teaching you something. Ballet. Painting. Are you sewing?"

"No."

Margi sighed, placed a lid on the rice pilaf serving dish. "It's all a mystery to me," she said to her son. "When you were first married, Chloe used to say, 'A man's house is his castle, and Rick is king.'"

"I remember."

"It isn't right what she did—taking up with that man, then getting the house."

"Margi, Chloe is not 'getting the house,'" Rick said. "She's living in it with our children."

"While you're living in an attic."

"It's really quite comfortable."

"I think she's taking advantage of you, Rick. We don't have dowries in America but what did she have, what did she bring? A glass of swizzle sticks."

"I married Chloe because I loved her," Rick said.

"She's beautiful, I'm not saying she isn't beautiful; but you rescued her, you know you rescued her. Your father used to say from the street and an untimely death."

"Didn't my father rescue you?" Rick said, not sharply but right at her.

"He gave me a new life and I didn't run out on him and have affairs," Margi said.

Rick sat quietly, not wanting to go any further with it. His kids were focusing on their plates.

"I'm hoping you and Chloe will have a reconciliation," Margi said to her son. "That's my deepest wish—for you, the children, for everyone. Now, dessert. I have a peach upside-down cake. Lisa, start whipping the cream. Andrew, clear the table. Rick, why don't you make some coffee for us?"

■ ■ ■

It was later that same day, and they were in his attic—Lisa on the bed with a paperback novel, Andrew studying the latest issue of *Golf,* and Rick on his way out the door. Noreen was having a party downstairs. "Be nice to each other," he said.

"Dad, can I go out for a while?" Lisa asked.

"Out where for a while?"

"In town."

"No."

"All the kids my age—"

"The answer is no."

"Just for half an hour."

"Talk to your mother," Rick said. "But the answer, right now, is no."

He took the steps down, knocked on the light blue door. Opening it was a man in his late twenties in designer jeans, a silk lavender shirt, and a chef's apron emblazoned with the words: "I Got My Crabs on the Jersey Shore." "Rick! Good to see yuh," he said enthusiastically. "How yuh doin'? Come in, come in."

"Not too bad, Crusher. How about yourself?"

"I'm cookin' up a big pot of chili. 'Crusher's Own'." He was a short man, all muscle, with a doll-like face; stick him behind a booth at a county fair, you'd throw baseballs at him.

"Sounds good," Rick said.

Crusher looked right and left, then spoke in a low, confidential voice. "Remember that deal I was telling yuh about? Get this. It'll be puttin' four-hundred grand in my pocket. I should be in Dover right now, working on it."

"Dover, England?"

"Delaware."

"Then why aren't you? That's big money."

"Never appear eager."

"True." He could learn from this man.

Crusher came a half-step closer; they were standing between kitchen and living room. "What are we gonna be havin' more 'n more of down the line?"

"Crime?"

"Garbage. And I'm gonna to be the guy pickin' it up. In two years they'll be calling me the Refuse King of the East."

"You're the future Compacting King of the East," Rick said.

"With this deal I'll be both. The Dover package—"

Just then someone shouted his name from the kitchen.

"Rick, talk to yuh later. Oh, Nory just stepped out, she'll be right back."

Rick spied a keg in the center of the living room and walked over to it. Twelve, maybe fifteen people were standing about, socializing, listening to the Steve Miller Band, "Space Cowboy." Rick grabbed a paper cup from a card table, depressed the thumb lever on the keg's dispenser. Looked around. College kids. He had a swallow of beer. Across the room, on the maple-framed sofa beneath a bubbling fish tank, he recognized Noreen's roommate, Maria, who was sitting with a young man and woman, talking to them in an earnest way, as if offering her opinion on a personal matter. Rick found himself interested, involved, mostly because the young woman was so striking in appearance, her face like a mask in its whiteness, raven-black hair, full red lips. Maria spoke for a short while, the man said something in reply; then she got up and left.

Rick looked about hoping to spot Noreen, didn't see her,

and gave his attention, once again, to the couple on the sofa. The man did most of the talking, with intense feeling; the young woman said little. Rick, suddenly aware he was staring, made to turn away, but just then the man looked over, his eyes keen, penetrating, as if saying to Rick, *You have a problem with something?* In that brief moment, Rick sensed a connection, a link with the young man, imponderable to name or define. He turned away just as Noreen pushed into the apartment with a couple of paper bags.

She set the bags down and came over in a flared denim skirt and a light-gray cashmere sweater. "I had to run to Hobo at the last minute," she said. "Have you talked with anyone?"

"Just Crusher. He gave me the lowdown on his entrepreneurial ventures."

"This morning when I woke up and you weren't there, it was awful," Noreen said.

"Don't remind me. Who's the couple on the sofa?"

She glanced into the living room. "Oh. That's Christine, she used to live with us. And her boyfriend, Vincent."

"They don't seem too happy."

"It's a sad story. I'll tell you about it, but not now. How are your kids doing?"

"We're having a good time."

Noreen smiled, kissed him on the lips. "Tomorrow let's all of us have lunch together."

■ ■ ■

The next afternoon, Rick, Lisa, and Andrew were sitting around his apartment waiting for Chloe; at five o'clock from the second-floor landing she shouted his name.

Waldo barked. Andrew went to the door; opening it, he shouted down, "One more flight, Mom!"

They heard her footsteps coming up and, next thing, Chloe walked in, greeting her kids with a big smile and full hugs, and a hug for Rick as well. She looked tired, shadows on her face, especially under her eyes, but she seemed in high spirits.

It was her first visit to his place. "You've finally got your garret, Rick," she said. "I like it. Café curtains. One of Margi's braided rugs, I see. You've made a little home out of it."

"Friday night we saw *Star Wars*," Lisa said.

"I got to hit golf balls in the college gym," Andrew said.

"Wonderful."

"How was the workshop?" Lisa asked.

"Very successful." Chloe sat down on the sofa with her children, resting her leather bag on the floor. "Most of the group were professional therapists. Half of them expressed interest in coming to Appleton."

"To see the town?" Lisa asked.

"To see me! To work with me professionally. *And* I have a big fat check!"

Rick half-expected her to reach into her bag, take it out and wave it. "Remember that little club we used to go to on 9th Avenue and 25th Street?" she said to her husband.

"Port Said."

Taking in Lisa and Andrew, she continued, "After the evening session on Saturday, I had this urge for stuffed grape leaves. When Evan and I walked in, a woman in a flowing gown and veil was doing a belly dance on the little stage, or attempting to. She came back out in a sweater and a skirt, sat at a table, and another woman was announced. Better, still not good. The maître d' asked if there were any other 'contestants.' On impulse I raised my hand. Backstage, an older woman made up my eyes, dressed me in silk. She reminded me of my mother, dark hair just like Efet's, lovely smooth skin. Then I went out. One of my favorite selections from *Scheherazade* was playing."

"Did you win?" Andrew asked.

"It was by applause," Chloe said, "and no one else was even close. The maitre d' brought over champagne and a bouquet of roses."

Dying as he was to see Noreen, Rick couldn't help feeling a twinge of jealousy. "Sounds like you had a really good weekend," he said.

"It was, it was very nice." She leaned back against the sofa as if settling in but then, almost at once, "Come on, kids. Time to go," she said, and got to her feet.

Goodbyes at his door. Hugs. Rick listened to the diminishing sound of their footsteps, waited a couple of minutes, then reached for his phone. The telephone directly below rang once; then he put down the receiver. A minute later he was out the door, going down the stairs—as she was starting up. They didn't meet so much as collide, arms outstretched. They kissed, kept kissing, all the while stumbling into Noreen's apartment, into her room, onto her bed….

CHAPTER
16

It was Saturday, just before noon, and Lisa had told her mother she'd be spending the afternoon with her friend, Muriel Lewis. She didn't like lying, but what else could she do? Tell her she was going hiking in the Shaggs with Greg Horboychuk?

Now she and Greg were in the backseat of a rattle-trap car that had stopped for them on Rt. 289, a half-mile west of the Walloon. Empty boxes of Kentucky Fried Chicken, dented cans of Pepsi, and an assortment of candy wrappers lay on the floor. It was like getting a lift in a Dempsey Dumpster. Her hand casually over her nose and mouth, Lisa was grateful when they reached the foothills and Greg said to the driver, "Just ahead, on your right."

The driver had a raw, bony face. He pulled over. "You guys have a great day."

"Thank you, man."

They got out, the car chugged away, and they started down an unpaved road, Greg with an army rucksack on his shoulders and Lisa breathing in the fresh mountain air. Three inches of snow covered the ground. The road ran between thick woods, mostly evergreen. No houses, no sign of people. After a mile Greg branched off onto a rising footpath. He helped Lisa along, where necessary, taking her by the hand or arm. They continued walking, always going up, and soon a view opened to the east—the great floodplain of the Walloon River.

"Not much further," Greg said.

They trudged on for another twenty minutes, then Greg stopped and stood, taking in the view. "There's the old church on Elting Street!" Lisa cried out.

"Lisa's Street, I call it."

"What happens when it snows, really snows?"

"I'll find a room somewhere."

He dipped his head, bringing his lips level with hers. She had worried about what his beard would feel like if or when they kissed, but it was kind of nice, actually—it tickled a little. They walked on, always climbing, and after a while came to a rock-strewn but level area, a small plateau.

"This is it," Greg said.

He walked up to the lip of the plateau and raised his arms. Then he turned and reached out his hand; hesitantly she went closer, inching forward, and when she reached his side he wrapped his arm around her shoulders and they stood there, gazing out, two feet shy of the drop-off. A small wind whirred and moaned behind them in the trees and rocks.

"What do you think, Lisa?"

"It's beautiful!"

"As Princess of Castlegregory, the mountains, the fields, the air—they're all yours."

Hundreds of feet beneath them lay great jagged rocks and, off to the right, a snow-covered pond. Greg kissed her forehead. "Are you afraid?"

"A little."

"Don't be."

"I'm getting kind of cold."

"I'll make a fire."

They turned, moved back from the edge. Lisa almost asked, "Where's the castle?" But then, suddenly, she realized she was looking at it. The rocky cliffs resembled the front of a huge cathedral. A fireplace, made of crude stones, and a couple of old wooden chairs were close to the cliff; hanging down, like a curtain, was an olive drab blanket. Greg tossed it aside, revealing the mouth of a cave. The inside was deep but not very high; a small person would just be able to stand. On one side the ground was strewn with evergreen boughs; on the boughs lay a sleeping bag. A table and chair, both roughly made, were toward the rear, and on a large flat stone, also toward the back, rested cups, plates, and pots. The only appliance she saw was a small round heater, the kind people used in tents. Her father had one. Greg lighted it, then picked up some twigs outside. He stirred up the ashes in the fireplace and laid the twigs on the glowing coals. Soon a small blaze was going. He put a couple of small logs on top. Lisa sat in one of the chairs, grateful for the heat.

Greg unpacked his basket. He had a slab of bacon which he cut with a hunting knife, then cooked up thick cheese and bacon sandwiches in a black skillet. Did she want a beer? Sure. He talked about Vietnam, the horrors and stupidity of the war, while they ate the sandwiches. He had saved the life of a little Vietnamese girl wounded in a battle; both her parents were killed. He had wanted to bring her home with him but the bureaucracy was too great, too difficult.

"One day I'll go back, I know the village," Greg said.

Lisa smiled. She liked the way he spoke, the things he said. She told him about the year they spent in Paris while her father was on leave from the college. They had had a wonderful apartment near the Palais Royal. She and Andrew both went to French schools not knowing a word of the language. She had studied ballet and still loved it, wanted to take it up again.

"I bet you're a wonderful dancer."

Greg reached out and held her hand and kissed her lightly on the cheek. She wondered if he was making a move. She didn't mind, she wanted him to, but she was nervous about it. At the back of her mind was what her mother had told her about the problem of becoming pregnant. One day she would have sex. It was the way of life, of nature. Lisa just had to be careful, very careful, Chloe said. She had to make sure the man used protection.

"I love you, Lisa. From the first moment I ever saw you,"

Greg said.

"I—I don't want—anything to happen."

"Don't worry."

"Do you have—?"

"Yes, trust me." He took her by the arm. "Our castle awaits us, Lisa."

■ ■ ■

Evan Kendrix was eating rice, steamed carrots, and a piece of baked haddock at his kitchen counter, dressed in his sculpting clothes, when the telephone rang. Instead of answering it, he waited—first for his message, then the caller's. A woman, Sheila Liccori: her husband of twenty-five years had called her two days ago from work saying he wouldn't be "going the distance" with her. She wasn't trusting herself. In tears, she left her number.

Evan speared a piece of carrot. Chloe to the rescue. As he was finishing his meal, the phone rang again. His message. Then the caller: "Evan, I'm coming east on business and I was thinking—"

He reached for the receiver. "Sue, hello."

"Well, *himself.*"

"You're coming east," Evan said.

"Next month, with Jared. Dr. Blizzard says seeing his father, sleeping in his old bed, will allay his anxieties. He's calling it E.U.S., 'Environmental Uprootedness Syndrome.' Jared's been acting out. The other day in McDonald's—"

"How long will you be staying?"

"One night, part of the next day."

"Just let me know. How's Nadine?"

"It's not working. I'll call with my itinerary," she said, and hung up.

He sat for a couple of moments, then walked through the house to his room and stripped off his clothes. In his bath he showered away the sweat and stone dust, rinsed thoroughly, grabbed a thick maroon towel and began drying himself before the big mirror: chest, arms, thighs. He dried his scrotum and penis, then held both in his hand, cupping them, cock dozing serenely between plum-sized balls.

Was that a package, or what?

Then why was he still haunted by a memory? Why, after years of psychoanalysis, did it linger in his mind? He was just sixteen at the time, still a virgin, but determined to change that status with the first willing female. He and his parents were in Maine, on a two-week vacation in Kennebunkport. Their waitress at the hotel was an eighteen-year-old girl from York named Beverly—small, not great looking but she had wonderful breasts; it didn't take long for her and Evan to start looking at each other. He had a junior license, and one overcast day after lunch he asked her if she wanted to go for a drive. She said yes, but soon suggested they park. Parking was more fun than driving. She directed him to a deserted road canopied with drooping hemlock boughs. Quiet, private. They got in the backseat of his parents' big Olds 98, began kissing, petting. He unhooked her bra, held her tits: pure, inexpressible delight. Put his face between them, ran his tongue over her nipples. Beverly was breathing hard, squirming, and then she was taking off her panties and he was kicking off his pants. He moved between her legs...and that was as far as he got. He swore under his breath. It was over; he was done.

"That's it? You call that fucking?" she cried out.

He didn't answer, too humiliated to speak.

"You got a tissue?"

"No."

"Jerk-off artist, take me back! Fucking rich kid!"

On the way to the hotel he fantasized stopping along the rock-framed Maine coast and pushing her over the edge. At the employees' entrance, Beverly got out and slammed the door.

That night at their table they had a new waitress, a forty-seven-year-old peroxide blond who worked the Fort Lauderdale-Coral Springs-Boca Raton circuit in winter.

Evan shaved, patted on English Leather, put on easy-fit corduroys, a blue shirt, and slip-on shoes. The front-door chime sounded and he went out. In the hallway, hanging up her fox jacket on tiptoes, was Christine.

They talked for no more than twenty minutes but he still believed their cognitive therapy was effective, served a distinct purpose. Nor would he bypass the wine, so helpful in transitioning from one form of therapy to another. They had their last sip and repaired to his alternative office. The drapes were open and Evan left them open; against the night, the plate glass became a perfect mirror.

Christine undressed, taking off everything except her eggshell-white bikini panties dotted with violets. As always, Evan gave free rein to his unconscious, believing in its incisiveness and power. They rolled about, kissing, playing. Pleasurable as it was, Evan never forgot his goal—to help Christine, to free her from the deep, debilitating pain—the pain of guilt—that so dominated her psyche. She was on her knees, he directly behind her. *Pain.* Yes, of course. She must win her battle with pain. Only then would Christine know peace.

Evan removed her panties, drawing them down; they landed on the floor like a tossed bouquet. He dampened the tip of his erection with Christine's own sweet juices, realigned himself slightly, and gave a small but firm shove—and Christine shrieked.

He didn't go any farther, spoke in reassuring tones. She wouldn't stop crying out. Her head was raised and he reached forward and rubbed her shoulders, her neck.

"Evan—it hurts!"

"By overcoming pain, we gain freedom—"

"You're killing me!"

"—from those who have hurt us."

"*You're* hurting me!"

"There's power in surrender, Christine. Say, 'I surrender.'"

"Fuck you, Evan! You son-of-a-bitch!"

In increments, with infinite tenderness, he pushed fully in. She was still screaming but, by degrees, no longer in agony alone. How well he knew the nuances of a woman's cries.

"Christine, I want you to accept the pain Arnold caused you. Say, 'I accept the pain.'"

"I—I—"

"Say it."

"I accept the—"

"Pain. Say it."

"The pain."

"Say, 'I forgive you, Arnold.'"

"I—I forgive you—Arnold."

"Beautiful, Christine."

She was now moving against him in little backward thrusts. Evan slid his hands upward on her back, then, lowering them, cupped her full, rolling breasts. His eyes drifted to the dark window. "This is your night, Christine," he said, watching. "Arnold will never hurt you again."

CHAPTER
17

When the session ended, Chloe walked her client through the fireplace room/waiting room to the side door. "I never thought I'd live to see this day," Niki Nazarro said before going out. She was very thin, hollow cheeks, with long straight hair.

"Well, you have, and it's only the beginning."

"I wake up every morning blessed that I know you, that you're here, Chloe."

"Niki, I feel blessed knowing you. See you next week."

They embraced warmly, and Chloe went up the steps to the front hall and continued to the second floor. The washer and dryer were tucked into a small space at one end of the landing, with a single eyebrow window looking west. She removed a white wash, stuffing sheets, pillowcases, t-shirts, and underwear into the dryer. Straightening back up, she peeked out to see what kind of afternoon it was. A dark-bearded man was working in the lower yard, near the oxbow, cutting and stacking wood.

It wasn't the first time Chloe had seen him on the property; he had done a good job clearing the deck of the locust limb, and if Rick wanted to keep giving him work, and pay him for it, fine. He had described Greg Horboychuk as one of his former (and best) students. He had graduated from Appleton State, was an army veteran, a latter-day Henry David Thoreau. Whoever he was, the first glimpse of him on any given day always gave Chloe a start.

She went into Andrew's room; it was cluttered with golf paraphernalia. She quickly made the bed, hung a windbreaker in his closet, picked up a pair of dirty pants and two shirts and dropped them into the washing machine. Once again she looked out the narrow window.

He was a strong man, handsome, though she didn't like his dour expression. And why was a college graduate doing yard work? Typical of Rick, who befriended the down-and-out, the indigent. Chloe turned away from the window—then turned immediately back to it. Going down the embankment steps, her school backpack hanging from one shoulder, was Lisa. She went over to the worker, up close—too close. As if they might kiss! They didn't but she was obviously flirting with him, acting coy—perhaps even seductive—and the "latter-day Thoreau" wasn't discouraging her!

Chloe would have thrown the window open and yelled at her daughter, but there was also a storm window to contend with, so really all she could do was watch. Just then her office buzzer sounded. She'd certainly call Rick and give him an earful and lay the law down to Lisa. Man was twice her age!

■ ■ ■

Her client, wearing a green crepe dress and dark green heels, had come straight from her new position at Westgate Industries. "Yesterday I was driving home from my job and caught a glimpse of your house," Karen Clendenin was saying. "There's a stretch where you can see it from Rt. 23. I so wanted to stop by and tell you what happened."

"So, tell me now."

"I have to say I'm a little embarrassed."

"Come on, Karen. You're over that," Chloe said.

"To a degree, not entirely. Anyway, it involves Dr. Kendrix. We were in bed—"

"You and Dr. Kendrix?"

"No. Ralph, the man I'm seeing."

Chloe poured herself a cup of water. "Go ahead."

"I've never had any pleasure from intercourse," Karen said. "I've never had—another word I can't say but here goes—an orgasm. Ralph paws at me, undresses me—that's the extent of it. Nothing ever happens." Her lips formed a little smile. "But the other evening—well, it was no different to start with. Then, suddenly, it wasn't Ralph in bed with me. It was Dr. Kendrix."

"In your mind," Chloe managed to say.

"Yes, of course. And suddenly I felt pleasure, honest-to-goodness sexual pleasure. My body was saying, 'Let yourself go! Let it happen!' Then it got really wild. We were no longer in bed. Dr. Kendrix had me on the edge of Mr. Terwilliger's desk at Westgate. My skirt is up and my underwear's nudged to one side—and he's driving at me and I'm going crazy, the pleasure keeps mounting and mounting—and then it just crashes. Chloe, it was so wonderful I screamed."

"Who—" saliva like glue in Chloe's throat, she had to start again, "—who do you think brought the orgasm on? Ralph or—or Dr. Kendrix?"

"Oh, Dr. Kendrix!"

"Did you say anything to Ralph?"

"No. He was proud as a peacock. How could I?"

Chloe was struggling to maintain a professional attitude. "Sexual fantasies are normal, Karen, and exciting; but we have to keep in mind that we live in a real world. Your sex with Dr. Kendrix was a dream. It's OK to have a fantasy but living in a 'fantasy world' isn't healthy."

"My fantasy only told me what I really want," Karen said, "and it isn't Ralph."

Chloe sensed her objectivity leaving her; in its place was a general sense of disorientation. "Karen, I think I'm coming down with something. Suddenly I'm feeling dizzy." She was surprised at how calm her voice sounded.

"I'm sorry. Can I do anything?"

You can leave, Chloe thought. "I'll be all right. I won't charge you for the session."

"That isn't necessary."

"I think I've helped you as much as I can, Karen."

"What are you saying? Every time I see you I learn something. God, the doors you've opened for me!"

"It's best if we end it now."

Karen looked confused, hurt. "What have I done?"

"It's not you, Karen. Please go."

Her client stood, struggled to hold back tears, and walked out. For a good while afterward Chloe sat at the little round table, remembering the day she and Rick had bought it in a used-furniture store in Woodbridge, shortly after they left New York, and she had refinished it and painted sweetheart roses around its edge....

■ ■ ■

Mr. Delvecchio was dragging a chock-full trash barrel to the curb, struggling with it, as Rick walked up the path to his rooming house, a bag of groceries in his arm. He set the bag on the steps and hurried over, taking one of the handles.

"*Grazie mille*, Professore."

Together they lugged the barrel to the street. Walking back, Rick asked the old man if someone had bought the house; the sign was gone. "No, the college boys, they take."

"Well, maybe one of these days," Rick said.

"Last people they offer a good price but she say no. Nine years now she say no."

"Suppose she said yes?"

"Ah, then we go back. It is my one dream, Professore."

Rick looked at the man's lined, weary face. "Where is your village, Signor Delvecchio?"

"On the Adriatic. Salvuccia, it is heaven on earth!" His watery eyes brightened, then quickly dimmed. "But she never sell."

"Why leave it up to her? It's your house too."

The old man gestured toward the backyard. "There's-a

my house, Professore." He hobbled around the corner of the building.

Rick looked after him, feeling a remote kinship, then went in and took the flight of stairs up to the second floor. Outside Apt. 3 he stopped and knocked. When the door opened he saw a worried expression on Noreen's face and spotted someone at her kitchen table. "I'll drop by later," he said.

"No, come in."

He set the bag on the counter. Sitting at the enamel-topped table was the young woman he'd seen at Noreen's party.

"Rick, this is Christine," Noreen said.

"Hello, Christine."

Her eyes lifted slowly. "Hi."

Rick produced a six-pack of Miller and deposited it on the counter, then picked up the bag, still with several items in it, and told Noreen he'd see her later. She followed him out to the landing.

"What's going on?" he asked.

"It's not good. I'll tell you about it."

She kissed him and he went to his stairs, climbed to the next landing. Before reaching it he heard a couple of excited barks.

■ ■ ■

After stowing his supplies, Rick re-buttoned his fleece-lined jacket and gave Waldo a whistle. They went out. As they drew near the minipark, he saw Greg Horboychuk standing with Jean-Jean the Artist and the Good Shepherd; they were looking down Main Street, out across the steel bridge. Rick stopped at the corner to let traffic pass, and Greg ambled over.

"I finished the work, Rick. Cutting those trees and stacking the logs in the lower yard."

"I noticed. It looks good."

"I'd like to start with the repairs to the deck."

"Greg, I won't be needing you anymore," Rick said.

"Anything wrong? I'm not doing a good job?"

"It's not that."

Greg wasn't angry; he seemed genuinely confused. "What is it, man?"

"My wife saw you talking with Lisa."

"We're friends," Greg said.

"I believe you—but that's it for working at the house."

"You want me to stop talking to her, I'll stop," Greg said, becoming agitated. "I need the money, it's keeping me alive."

A huge Freightliner, hauling a flatbed loaded with lumber and pallets of stone, rolled by. "I'm not living there, Greg. What Chloe says, goes."

"You talk to a girl, people right away get ideas."

"Just to be clear, Lisa's mother isn't 'people,'" Rick said.

"I really like working for you, man. Have a heart!"

"I'm sorry, Greg. What do I owe you?"

"I've got seven hours on the books."

He slid three twenties from his wallet. "Thanks for your help. Just keep away from Lisa."

With Waldo at heel, Rick went west on Main, turned on Wirth, crossed the railroad track on River Road and, on entering the stretch of desolate land, gave the dog an "OK." Waldo took off and Rick made his way to the banks of the Walloon River. Three homeless men were huddled around a campfire. Rick stayed clear of their circle, looked down at the water: frozen, one shore to the other, except along the bank where the ice was thin, like a veil covering deep, ebony eyes. Rick kicked loose a stone; it tumbled down the bank, crashed through, disappeared. In the west, a thick gray curtain of snow was blanketing the Shaggs.

CHAPTER
18

On the second-floor landing, when he returned with Waldo, Rick heard sobs and moans inside Noreen's apartment; her friend, Christine, was in a scary place. Upset, feeling bad for both of them, he continued by.

After feeding Waldo, then making dinner for himself, he sat down with Thoreau's *Journal*—the photocopy of the original—thinking to keep on with the slow, painstaking comparison: reading a line written in Thoreau's own hand and checking it against the published version. Again and again and again. It was brutally boring work and, he was coming to think, pointless.

He read and compared for an hour and a half, got up and stretched, had a glass of water, and went back to his task. About to set aside his project for the evening, he came to a section in the hand-written pages, dated November 5, 1843, that didn't compare, even remotely, to the printed pages. What was this? The section in the photocopy was headed: "Prom. Desmo." An abbreviation for *Prometheus Bound,* the great drama by Aeschylus written about 500 B.C. Rick checked and double-checked the published edition. Nothing there. According to the editor, the published journals included everything except "occasional lists of flora and fauna." And here were four full pages Mr. Torrey had decided to leave out. How could that be? Scholars knew Thoreau had translated the work—the first ever translation into English—but no one had ever made anything of it except to say the translation pointed out Thoreau's superb intellect and knowledge of Greek.

Who *was* Prometheus? In mythology, he was a Titan, whom Zeus had given the task of creating man out of clay and water, which Prometheus did. Liking his creation more than Zeus had anticipated, Prometheus brought mankind a gift: fire. This angered Zeus, whose intentions were to keep men weak, powerless. Prometheus was the great benefactor of mankind, and for his efforts he was punished by Zeus, who had him chained to a huge rock, the Scythian rock, where vultures daily attacked his liver. All Zeus wanted was an apology from this upstart and the great father would undo his chains. The apology never came.

Rick sat back in his chair, astounded by the similarities between Prometheus and Thoreau that sprang quickly to mind. Hadn't Thoreau gone to jail rather than pay taxes levied by a pro-slavery government? Thoreau/Prometheus—both nonconformists, standing up to authority. And certainly—speaking of gifts—wasn't *Walden* a gift to mankind, a book of hope and enlightenment to lift, to fire the spirit?

There was a knock, the door opened, and Noreen came in with a couple of books, dressed in navy blue warm-up pants and a loose-fitting top. "I heard the moans," he said, standing, going over. "How are you? What's going on?"

"I'm beat."

"Can I get you anything, a drink?"

"No. Just sit with me." Noreen laid her books on the table before the sofa. "I don't know what to do for her, Rick."

"Off hand, how about suggesting she see a therapist?"

"She's seeing one. That's the whole problem."

"Why is that a problem?"

"Because it's not therapy she's having so much as a relationship," Noreen said, "and it's not going well. For her. He's helping her, supposedly, to get over her former stepfather, who induced her into an affair when she was fifteen. But the stepfather is no longer the problem; the problem is her therapist. Christine has fallen wildly in love with him and there's no future in it and he's using her, having all kinds of kinky sex with her, ostensibly as therapy. I hate the man with a passion, murderously hate him. Rick, I've changed my mind about a drink."

He went into the kitchen and made two rum and Cokes, brought them back, and sat down with Noreen on the sofa. "Who's the therapist?"

"I promised Christine I wouldn't say."

"Is he local?"

"I shouldn't comment, Rick."

"It sounds to me like you're describing Evan Kendrix." She had taken a swallow of her drink and began to cough. Rick slapped her back.

"Do—do you know him?' Noreen asked.

"I do."

"Please say he's not a friend of yours."

"He broke up my marriage—with help from my wife. You decide."

"*Chloe and Evan*—?"

"—travel about conducting weekend therapy workshops," Rick said. "They're a team."

"This is just too bizarre." Noreen gave her head a bewildered shake. "Are you going to say anything?"

"No."

"Most jilted husbands would jump at the opportunity."

"It's tempting but it wouldn't be a smart thing," Rick said. "For a woman who seems so stable, on top of things, Chloe can fly off the handle. When we were living in Woodbridge, a woman I'd met at an MLA meeting in Chicago sent me a Christmas card. Some harmless message on it. Chloe saw the card and threw a one-pound Yule candle at me. It whizzed past my ear."

"Sounds to me like you're protecting Evan."

Rick laughed. "Hardly. It's the kids, the family. Why stir up trouble? What does Christine's boyfriend say about Evan?"

"Vincent. He doesn't know about Evan. Doesn't even know

Christine's in therapy."

"He gave me a pretty harsh look at your party. Pretty territorial about Christine, I have to say. What kind of guy is he?"

"I've known him since we were teenagers," Noreen said. "Yonkers High School—White Plains High. We went out for a while but I didn't want to get involved, with him or with anyone. When I left for Hawaii he drove me to the airport, and all those years I was away we wrote letters, cards, have always stayed in touch. Vincent Ciccarelli is true blue. I don't know how else to say it. Of note, he's going to the Olympics this summer in Montreal."

"As a spectator?"

"As a member of the U.S. Team. He's—" she lifted her arms, swung them back and forth, "—a skeet shooter."

"Really."

Noreen pressed her lips together, closed her eyes. Then, looking up, inhaling, "When I came in you looked really excited."

"I did? Oh, right." Suddenly it seemed irrelevant. "I'd just made a discovery in Thoreau's *Journal*."

Noreen had a sip of her rum and Coke. "Tell me about it."

■ ■ ■

After breakfast the next day Noreen left for the campus and Rick settled down to the serious work of restructuring his biography: namely, selecting places in it where the Promethean thread could best be woven. He was excited, hadn't felt such a rush of energy since the early years in Woodbridge. At ten fifteen his phone rang; it rested on an old overturned nail box close to the bed and he walked over and answered it.

"Hello."

"Good morning, Rick."

"Chloe?"

"You seem surprised."

"Well, maybe a little." What he knew was burning in his brain. "What's up?"

"A workshop just opened up for Evan and me in Albany," Chloe said. "Not for a month yet, but it's my weekend, which is why I'm calling. Would you be able to take the kids?"

"Sure."

"Thank you, Rick. How are you?"

"I'm doing all right," he said. "How about yourself?"

"I'm OK."

Something told him she really didn't mean it.

■ ■ ■

Lisa hoped she would be able to pay for everything she was taking from the shelves in Hobo Deli. She had twenty dollars on her and had already spent seventeen, roughly; then she picked up—at $1.99—a pound of bacon.

The checkout boy was a local kid and they didn't speak in high school and didn't speak now; his name was Chuck and sometimes she would see him on Main Street, smoking. He was a big smoker. The way he lifted the cigarette to his mouth, then dropped his hand, then raised the cigarette for another drag, made it seem like a puppeteer was controlling his arm. He rang up the package of baloney, the Cheez Whiz, coffee, Ritz crackers, dozen eggs, loaf of bread, peanut butter, bacon, and jar of strawberry jam, then hit the "total" key. $21.10.

Lisa reached into the back pocket of her jeans and pulled out the two crumpled bills. "This is all I have."

"Don't worry about it, stuff here is overpriced."

He packed the groceries and Lisa gave him a smile and walked out and stood on the stone steps in front of the deli. So far she'd been lucky, but one of these days her mother or father would come driving down Main Street and see her and ask her what she was doing with the groceries. She had an answer ready but she hoped she wouldn't have to use it. At least not on Chloe, who would say she was lying. Rick would probably buy it.

The Good Shepherd was under the elm, staff in hand and carpet over his shoulders. Next to him, hands in the pockets of his thin jacket, stood Jean-Jean the Artist. Both of them frightened Lisa, the way they stared at her whenever she walked by. Greg had told her not to mind them, they were jealous; he had the Princess of Castlegregory and what did they have?

The Good Shepherd twisted his head to see her hurrying along with her groceries, but Jean-Jean the Artist couldn't move his head. She always thought of him as having a rusty neck. He had to turn his whole body to look anywhere, and it gave her the creeps.

She walked quickly along. By the clock on the front of the bank it was 5:14 and 37°. Main Street slanted downward, everything in Appleton sloped toward the river. Lisa crossed Main and continued on it toward the bridge, and ahead of her was Heartbreak Hotel. Greg told her it had once served as a dormitory and recitation building for students at Appleton Normal, one of the first teachers' colleges in the country. Appleton State had started right here, over 120 years ago.

She liked when Greg told her interesting things, it added to the history of a place. Sometimes when she walked into the hotel she thought of herself as a student back then, studying to be a teacher. Lisa didn't know what she wanted to be, but she knew what she didn't want to be—she didn't want to be a psychotherapist!

The front door to the hotel wasn't locked and she went in. The lobby had no desk and no furniture in it, just huge windows and worn grayish-blue linoleum on the floor. She took wide steps to the second floor and could smell marijuana in the hallway. Greg's room was on the top floor and she went up another flight. The community bathroom was ajar and Freda, a woman of thirty-five who lived here, was sitting on the toilet, leaning forward, underwear at her ankles; she was absolutely still and her eyes were closed.

Lisa continued by. It was kind of scary in Heartbreak Hotel but there was a feeling here of family—people sharing, helping each other out. Freda was nice to her, almost like a mother. She gave a knock on Greg's door, #37, and went in.

The room was small, nothing more than a cubicle; what she liked about it was how the bed was. It didn't take up any floor space because it was built into the wall, recessed. She had never traveled in a Pullman but she'd seen movies that showed people on trains in their berths, and this was something like that.

Greg was in his berth now and he rolled over and put out his arms and Lisa set down the groceries, took off her bomber jacket and went over and lay beside him and he called her his Princess. It was what he always called her. A man and woman in love ruled all, he said.

Here wasn't like the mountain where you could see forever and the world was yours; here you smelled cooking and marijuana and you could hear people through the walls. But she liked it here. Greg kissed her lips. It wouldn't be long now, he was saying. They would return to Castlegregory and live in harmony with nature and one day—one day, Lisa—they would have a child and start the whole world anew.

She was happy in his arms. It was everyone's dream, he said, to return to the Garden. They would be the first couple to really do it. My princess, he was saying, his bearded face soft on her cheek. Lisa of Castlegregory, beautiful princess of a brave new world.

CHAPTER
19

Once across the steel bridge spanning the Walloon, Chloe shifted into third but not into high. Tip from Rick when conditions were bad—stay in third, better control. Actually Rt. 289 was fairly clear but the snow banks on either side were high and gusts kept buffeting them and blowing snow across the road.

It was a cold day, with a wind-chill that made it feel like five below. To say she was looking forward to her workshop with Evan next month at the Oikos Institute in West Palm—and the two extra days they were taking to soak up some rays in Key West—was putting it mildly. Chloe came to a bend in the road and down-shifted instead of using her brakes. Right about here she always felt the excitement, the anticipation of seeing Evan, start to build. Troubling as it was to discover that Christine Monteleone was a young, luscious sweetheart and to hear Karen Clendenin tell of her wild-sex dreams with Evan, Chloe had come to accept that the problem wasn't Christine or Karen or, for that matter, Evan. People saw in others what they knew about themselves. Was she a faithful woman? An honest woman? How many times had she told Rick that she and Evan would have separate rooms at Stover Falls? God, she had so many aspects of herself to work on! To think that she had actually used Karen to satisfy her own sick needs. In many ways it was more egregious than deceiving Rick. But what bothered Chloe most was her failure to practice what she so tried to instill in the women who came to see her. The world was filled with teachers, emissaries, leaders who said one thing and did another. She did not want to be one of them, but she was afraid she was.

Chloe turned onto Evan's private drive, his sculptures gowned majestically in white. She drove to the end and parked next to his winter car, whose stance reminded her of its owner: power in all wheels. The snow, cleared from the turnaround, was piled in great hills around the sides. A path led to his house; she walked to the front door, pushed the chime, and walked in. Evan was on the phone in his office; he waved to her, then covered the receiver: "Go in and warm up, I'll only be a minute."

He looked so handsome, so masculine, sitting in his big leather chair in a collarless green-and-black shirt and loose-fitting rust-colored corduroys, that she wanted to remove the phone from his hand and lead him to his daybed. Chloe hooked her coat in the front hall and continued into the living room.

A blaze was going in the hearth and she stood looking down at the burning logs. Soon Evan came in; he put his hands deeply—but so lightly—into her hair. "Today, let's not delay gratification."

Chloe turned. "You read my mind."

"I read your eyes."

■ ■ ■

Afterward, they showered, then dried with big towels, each doing the other's back. Sitting on the edge of his bed, she began dressing, but as she was pulling on her knee-length socks Evan was suddenly holding her again, caressing her arms, her breasts, nuzzling her ear. Whatever Chloe had already put on, she quickly took off; forget the socks....

In the living room, afterward, Chloe settled into the sofa, and Evan brought in two glasses and a bottle of burgundy. Emily, Niki, Beatrice, Franny, Stella—in all, they discussed five cases in depth and ran through another six quickly. Sometimes she took notes on what he said or suggested, but she spoke as his equal; it wasn't a lecture, and he was quick to give her credit and praise.

"Anyone else?" he asked.

"That does it."

Classical music was on his record player, the fire was crackling, and Chloe felt perfectly relaxed and free of tension. They did their paperwork; he gave her what her gross came to, minus 25%. That done, he asked, as he frequently did, after her kids.

"What's the latest on Lisa and the Vietnam vet?"

"Who knows? I have a clock on her, so to speak."

"Well, be kind to her, she's something special," Evan said. "Lovely, bright—takes after her mother." He reached out, smiling, squeezed Chloe's hand. "Listen, I'll pick you up tomorrow at five. I know a restaurant in Albany, Quintessence. Their scampi's out of this world. We'll kick off the workshop at seven." He paused for a second. "Oh, there's something I want to tell you. I almost forgot."

Something about his tone, the offhanded nature of the comment, made her think he hadn't forgotten at all; in fact she knew he hadn't. "What is it?"

"Speaking of problems with children," Evan went on, "Sue has her hands full with Jared. She's called me a couple of times— he isn't making friends, he's lethargic. The term going around is 'Environmental Uprootedness Syndrome.' Jared's psychologist thinks the boy needs to reconnect with his father, sleep in his old bed again, play with his old toys. Sue will deliver him here, then she'll head for her parents' place in Cold Spring."

"Why are you telling me this?"

"It's something you should know."

"I mean now, as I'm leaving."

"It's relatively unimportant. An afterthought."

"Something tells me you're dissembling."

"My ex-wife, a lesbian, is coming by to drop off our son. What's there to dissemble?"

Chloe gathered together her papers, pulled on her coat. He

kissed her at the door and she went out, on her drive home turning over and over again what had just taken place. Evan had made his comment about Sue and Jared seem like a P.S. when clearly it wasn't, except in one very important way. The P.S. in a letter was really where the most revealing thing was said. As for Sue, Chloe remembered the first time she'd ever seen a picture of Evan's wife, thinking how drop-dead gorgeous she was. It was hard for Chloe to believe the woman was a lesbian, though she knew that physical appearances did not define sexual orientation. Chloe knew this, but from the start she'd doubted that Sue Kendrix preferred women. And now she was coming east for a little visit, leaving her faux partner on the Coast, and nothing was going to happen when she walked through the door into her old house, with Evan welcoming her with a big hug, her breasts smack on his chest? No, not much.

There's something I want to tell you, I almost forgot.

Fuck, I know what I know! thought Chloe, nailing it on the floodplain.

■ ■ ■

Andrew was watching television when he heard the back door open. It was his mother. She put her coat on a hook, saw him sitting on the daybed in the den. "Is Lisa home?"

"No."

"Did she call?"

"No."

A few moments later Andrew heard a loud, crashing sound in the kitchen. He rushed in. His mother was standing at the counter. On the floor against the far wall lay fragments of a white pitcher. "Mom, what's the matter?"

She didn't say. He didn't like the expression on her face; it frightened him. Then Lisa was coming up the deck stairs with fast steps and when she opened the door the cold followed her in, because she stood in the doorway staring at her mother.

For a moment Andrew didn't think Chloe knew Lisa had even come in and he tried telling his sister to get up to her room by head-signals; but Chloe knew.

She spun around. "You're late!"

"I'm here, I'm home! What's five minutes?"

"It's five minutes too many. What have you been doing?"

"What have *you* been doing, Mom?"

Chloe, going toward Lisa, made to slap her face, but the girl stepped back and Chloe's hand caught her shoulder. She went after her daughter again and Andrew stepped between them, doing what he could to restrain his mother while yelling at Lisa to shut up and get upstairs. Chloe was bigger than he was and stronger too, she could twist and bend. But if he didn't hold her she'd kill Lisa and things were bad enough without having a dead sister on the floor. He just wouldn't let go of his mother, no matter what, and he kept shouting at Lisa, and finally she got the idea and left the kitchen and went up to her room.

His mother sat down at the oak table and they were both winded but she seemed calmer. "Will you make me a cup of tea?" she asked him. He put on a kettle, found a tea bag, and when the water boiled he poured it in and after a while poured in a little milk; the sugar was already on the table.

"Thank you, Andrew. I want you to go to your room and study. I never see you studying anymore."

"I'm doing fine, don't worry. You're worrying too much, Mom."

"What about the window in the front hall?"

"I fixed it."

"You shouldn't be throwing snowballs at the house."

"I wasn't, I was throwing at Lisa."

She sipped her tea, then pressed her lips together tightly, but not because she'd scalded them. Something was tearing her up and he didn't think it was just Lisa coming home late. He hated seeing his mother unhappy. Life wasn't any fun when your mother was unhappy.

■ ■ ■

It was later now. Lisa and his mother were sleeping and Andrew came downstairs, in the alcove dialing his father's number. It rang, and rang. Andrew held onto the receiver, wanting to hear his father say, "Hello" so he could tell him what had happened, how he'd kept Lisa and Chloe apart—just barely. Mom would've killed her, Dad! But his father wasn't answering.

Andrew hung up, feeling alone and scared in the big old house, and angry too. *He* wasn't the father, *he* wasn't the husband! And it wasn't just today. It went back to the Sunday last fall when his father had walked out, had let Evan come breezing in like the place was his. Had let Evan sit with them at the table and tell stories and make his mother laugh and walk with her down by the oxbow.

From the alcove, Andrew looked out at the dark kitchen. His father was a hero, winner of the Navy Cross, he'd rescued a pilot when his jet had crashed coming for a landing; had jumped from his ship into the ocean and saved the man's life. How could he have let Evan come in like that, so easy, without a fight? Is that what a hero did? Is that who a hero was?

CHAPTER
20

After embracing Emily Abbot goodbye at the door to her basement office, Chloe climbed the stairs to the kitchen, warmed a half-cup of coffee, and took it into the alcove where she reached for the phone. She dialed; he didn't pick up and she resented his recording: "Hello, Dr. Kendrix speaking. If this is an emergency—"

After the beep she said: "Evan, I don't feel up to the Albany weekend. Last night I went through a bad scene with Lisa, then with myself. This morning I don't feel any better. I'd be a hindrance rather than a help. It's best if I stay home...."

Chloe hung up, immediately trying to reconstruct what she'd just said. Evan's answering machine had given her nothing but headaches since he'd installed it six months ago. She went into the kitchen and set her cup on the counter, sipped from it while she loaded the dishwasher. The phone rang.

But it wasn't Evan. It was a woman, a friend of Karen Clendenin; her name was Josephine Ziegler and she called Chloe *Dr.* Forrester. Her husband had left her five months ago and was now begging her to take him back, but she was involved with a new man. The kids wanted their father home again and she was going crazy trying to decide what to do. Could she make an appointment for a visit?

Chloe didn't respond immediately. How could she think she could help this woman, could help anyone, when she herself was so scattered? But then, amazing herself by her audacity, she said, "How would four o'clock be for you this afternoon?"

"That would be wonderful," Josephine said.

Chloe put a few more plates in the dishwasher—and the phone rang again. This time it was Evan. He didn't pressure her; she had to follow her inclination, he said. If she didn't feel positive about doing the workshop, she should definitely stay home. He'd miss her and the workshop would be the less without her. He suggested they spend their next meeting discussing her decision.

"It never changes. Everywhere I look I feel threatened."

"Chloe, it's a path, it's not an easy path. It's strewn with obstacles. But we have to stay on it."

"I can't talk anymore," she said.

"Don't give up on yourself."

She put down the phone, sat there twisting her ring—her Corfu ruby—around and around on her finger.

The unexamined life.

■ ■ ■

The back door opened, clunked shut. Then, "Mom?"

Chloe loved hearing Andrew's voice when he came in from school; Lisa's also but they weren't speaking now, except to yell at each other. "Upstairs."

He came in, saw her resting on her bed. "Aren't you going away today?"

"I was, something came up—do me a favor and call your father. Tell him thanks, anyway."

"All right." He made to leave.

"Stay with me for a minute," Chloe said.

He went over and sat beside her on the bed. "I was wondering, Andrew, what is it you like about golf?"

"A lot of things."

"Tell me one."

"Well, if there's no one around to play with, you can still play. It's always there for you."

"I like that." She smiled, loving his looks, the thick dark hair, the nose less high-bridged than hers. "Have you got a reply to your letter yet?"

"What letter?"

"The one you wrote to Johnny Miller."

"No. He gets hundreds."

"He'll answer it," she said, and drawing her son in, kissed his eyes.

■ ■ ■

Chloe awoke with a start. What was that? A distinct pinging sound from downstairs. Lying in the darkness, thinking, listening. There was an odd, musical quality to it. As if someone were tapping a pipe in the basement, playing a tune. Odd, but not alarming. Nothing to worry about.

"Ping." Again. Then again.

It was almost sleep-inducing, like a chime....

When she opened her eyes again, at the reasonable hour of seven forty-five, Chloe went downstairs. The kitchen seemed colder than normal when she walked in; she always turned the heat down at night to 60°, so she knew what 60° felt like—and this wasn't it. This was closer to 40°! How about her office and fireplace room?

Chloe took the stairs down; the temperature was cool, not ice cold. Something was very strange. Thinking to warm up the basement and let the heat rise, she set her office thermostat to 75°. Back in the kitchen, she made coffee.

When the old percolator finally finished gasping, Chloe filled her mug. The furnace was going full blast. She decided, before calling Appleton Home Heating, she'd let it run for an hour. Back in bed, she sipped her coffee, reflecting on her session yesterday with Josephine Ziegler, a woman nearing forty with lovely graying hair and sad hazel eyes. If Chloe didn't know her personally, in her heart she knew Josephine, a woman caught in a trap of indecision. What to do, *what to do?* It was almost as if Chloe were looking at herself, sitting across from the woman at the little table wreathed in roses. Josephine, she said, I can't tell you to take your husband back, I can't tell you to stay with the man you're now involved with. But "involvement" is short-lived. Affairs blow up. Maybe your husband was rotten to you, maybe your lover is a prince! I don't know. But if your husband wasn't rotten, what matters goes beyond what the soma—our body, our flesh and bone—clamors for. The body doesn't lie but it only cares about itself. It has an agenda—future generations at any cost! Josephine, I'm beginning to think that indulging the body is like deferring to a spoiled, selfish child. No good comes from it, and in the end you pay—

Lisa, shouting to her from downstairs, broke her train of thought. No ordinary shout. Chloe got out of bed and went to her door.

"Yes?"

"Come quickly!"

She grabbed her robe, pulled on slippers, and hurried down. The main floor was still cold. "Where are you?"

"In the basement!"

Chloe started down the steps, immediately feeling heat on her face and wondering if she had turned up the thermostat too high. Was there a fire? She reached the basement level, looked into her office. From five or six places in the ceiling, water was flowing, pouring over the furniture, over her books and papers. From the water collecting on the floor, steam was rising. She stood in the doorway, horrified, feeling a terrible helplessness—

"I came down for a glass of o. j. The kitchen was ice cold," Lisa said. "Then all at once I heard this sound in the basement, like rushing wind."

"Go call a plumber!"

"*Any* plumber?"

"Clyde Kellerer. His number's on the board!"

Lisa went upstairs and Chloe splashed across her office, snatched her appointment book from the lacquered table, and opened the door to her clients' bathroom. Pushing aside the folding screen, she looked at all the valves and pipes servicing the three floors of the house. Which was which? What did what? Would turning the wrong valve blow up the boiler pounding insanely away? From the furnace-room doorway Chloe looked out at her chair, the little round table, her client's chair. Papers floating about on the floor, ceiling collapsing—

"Mom, Clyde isn't answering!" Lisa shouted from the main floor.

Chloe splashed across her office, ran up the stairs. By the pendulum clock, it was eight twenty. In the alcove she dialed Rick's number. After three rings, he answered.

"Rick, you have to come over! The basement is flooding!"

"Call Clyde."

"He's not in."

"Well, I'm having breakfast."

He didn't mean a bowl of raisin bran by himself. "Rick, it's an emergency! My office has six inches of water on the floor!"

"Go into the root cellar," he said. "Just to the right of the cistern you'll see the village water-inlet valve. It's a blue wheel about the size of a saucer. Crank it shut."

"I won't see it, I'll never do it. Please, come over."

A pause. Chloe heard a woman's voice faintly in the background. Then Rick was saying, "OK. I'll be there in ten minutes."

She hung up, walked about nervously, peered at the thermometer attached to the outside kitchen window frame: eleven below zero.

■ ■ ■

She and the kids were all waiting for him in the kitchen when he opened the door. Without stopping, without saying a word, Rick went down to the basement. He could hear the water pouring out, splashing on the floor of Chloe's office. In the fireplace room/waiting room he crossed to the narrow door leading into the old root cellar, flipped the light switch on the door frame, and lifted a brass hook. The door squeaked when he opened it. Rick went in, down an additional three steps; on its own the door creaked shut. There was no floor, just plain dirt.

The space was now used for storage but not much was in it. A couple of metal lawn chairs badly pitted, several cans of waterbase paint on a wobbly table, tools he seldom used. Dominating the near wall was a brick-and-mortar cistern. Rick angled past the seven-foot-high holding tank (empty now for seventy-five years), pushed aside a stubby wooden ladder lying at its base, and grabbed hold of the blue valve, twisting it all the way to the right. The sound of rushing water immediately ceased. Overhead, a naked bulb, screwed into an ancient porcelain base, flickered.

He went out, kicked loose dirt from his shoes on the top step, passed in front of the fireplace, and stood in the doorway to Chloe's office. Water was still coming through the ceiling but in drips only. The ceiling was wrecked. New sheetrock and insulation would be easy enough to reinstall; and if the heat were left on—he reduced the thermostat to 68—the floor and carpet would be dry in a week to ten days. Whether Chloe's books and papers could be salvaged was something he couldn't answer.

The dripping overhead ran along the junction of the east wall and ceiling—directly beneath the baseboard units in the living room. Heat was circulating in the upstairs bedrooms and here in the basement, but not on the main floor. A section of main-floor pipe, obviously, had frozen; in freezing it had ruptured; then when the pipe had thawed….

Chloe and the kids were at the top of the stairs, in the front hall. Rick said he'd stopped the flooding. What he wanted to find out was why the pipes had frozen in the first place. At the front door, he kneeled, touched the baseboard unit. Ice cold, as he had expected. But what was the icy draft he felt on his neck? Glancing up he saw that one of the small windows, framing the door on both sides and on top, was shattered; someone had "repaired" it with a piece of cardboard. The bottom edge of the cardboard was loose, however, and frigid air, sneaking in, had done its work.

Rick pointed. "Who did this?"

Silence.

"Who broke this window?"

"I thought I'd fixed it," Andrew said.

"Well, you didn't. OK, here's what we're going to do," Rick said. "We have to heat this place up. Andrew, make a fire in the wood stove. Lisa, put on gloves and a coat—go out to the shed and grab the kerosene heater underneath the steps. Bring it in."

The children left and Chloe said she'd make a pot of coffee. When she went to draw water, the tap sputtered, and she looked at Rick. He reminded her that he had cut off the supply. But there were a couple of gallon jugs in the pantry. He got one. Andrew came in with kindling and logs, and Lisa trudged up the deck steps lugging the kerosene heater by its bail. Rick took it from her and set it on the floor next to the oak table. After dusting it off, he struck a match and lighted the wick.

"How long will it burn?" Chloe asked.

"Ten to twelve hours."

"After that, what?"

"By then Clyde should be here."

He went into the living room to see how Andrew was coming along. The fire was catching, starting to grow. Chloe brought in a steaming mug. The coffee hit the spot but he only had three sips of it before saying he had to run. "Andrew, keep feeding the fire. Lisa, check the yellow pages. Call every plumber between here and Kingsley-on-Hudson."

"A morning like this," Chloe said, "we'll never get one. It'll be days."

"Then call Evan. Isn't he your man?"

"What can he do?"

"This is a fine time to ask!"

"Rick, help us, please."

He bowed his head, gave it a shake with his eyes closed. Then, looking up, he told Andrew to go out and get his stepladder from the shed; bring it into Chloe's office. Lisa should bring in his fishing boots, also in the shed—not the waders, the boots. They would be ice cold so she should take her hair dryer, put it on low heat, and warm them up. From the inside.

The kids left. Rick finished his coffee.

"Would you like a little more?" Chloe asked.

"No, thanks."

Andrew walked in and said the ladder was set up. Rick told him to get the wrecking bar and hammer from his tool bench; also trash barrels. There was a coil of garden hose hanging on the shed wall. He should bring it in with a couple of buckets.

"What's the hose for?" Chloe asked.

"I have to purge the system."

"What system?"

"The heating system. Most likely I'll be soldering. So we have to drain the pipes—it's called 'purging'."

Lisa came in with his boots, nicely warmed. He dragged them on, letting them flop over at the knees. She said he looked like a fireman. In the basement, the first thing Rick did was locate the valve on the furnace for the main-floor loop, closing it; then, using the length of hose, he drained the water in the loop, letting it run into a bucket; each time it was full, Andrew emptied it into the toilet.

"OK, now we can start," he said.

■ ■ ■

He had located seven splits in the copper tubing in the ceiling—each split had caused a ping—had repaired six, and now, on the ladder, was examining the last one. Chloe, Lisa, and Andrew were all watching. Damaged sheetrock and soaked insulation filled the barrels. Like the other ruptures, this one was about an inch long and a sixteenth of an inch across. First Rick steel-wooled the split until the copper shone; then, using a vise-grip pliers, he applied pressure, bringing the two edges of the split together. Next came the flux, applied to the scar like a dressing.

"Torch."

Lisa was in charge of it; she lighted it with a spark-making mechanism, then handed it to her father. With his other hand, Rick took the roll of solder from Andrew. Applying the pinpoint of fire to the tubing, on and about the rupture, he waited until the copper was sufficiently hot, then ran the solder over the split. It was drawn in, making a smooth, silvery bead. Rick backed down the ladder, turned off the torch.

"OK, moment of truth," he said.

In the furnace room, he opened the valve for the main-floor zone; water rushed in and every repair held—no leaks; but in the far corner, extending beyond repair seven, water started spurting. Chloe groaned and Lisa cried, "Oh, no!"

Rick closed the valve on the furnace and came back out.

"Now what?" said Chloe, fingers pressed together.

"I must have missed one. We have to re-purge the system."

■ ■ ■

By the time the last rupture was repaired, the carpet lifted off the floor with milk crates and fireplace logs, and a double-thick square of cardboard installed in the broken pane in the front hall, it was five thirty-five. The furnace was humming away, the main floor warming nicely. Rick was standing in the kitchen with Chloe.

"I have a beef stew all made, ready to heat," she said. "Have dinner with us."

"I really can't."

"Then a drink, at least. You've been going nonstop."

"Thanks, I have to run."

He said good night to the kids and pulled on his coat, and Chloe went with him to the door. "You're a good man, Charlie Brown."

It was a sweetness, an intimate expression she used to say to him for getting them home in a snowstorm or repairing a leaking roof or bringing in extra logs on a cold winter day. He paid no heed to it, said he was glad to have helped, and soon was parking in front of 97 N. Elm. Inside, he knocked on Noreen's door, Waldo barked, and he went in. She was on the sofa in the living room reading a book. He patted the dog, asked Noreen if she'd like a drink.

"Are you having one?"

"I am, yes."

"Then whatever you're having."

He made two bourbons, gave her one, and sat beside her on the sofa. "There were eight ruptures in one length of copper tubing," he said. "It took forever."

"How's Chloe?"

Rick had a taste of his drink, settled back. "Appreciative."

"I would think. It's nice having a husband around."

"I'm sorry, I should've called you. I didn't stop once."

"I thought you were probably staying for dinner with her and the kids."

"No," Rick said, drinking again from his glass.

CHAPTER
21

When his front door chimed at five fifteen p.m., Evan walked into the hall to welcome his ex-wife and their son, who were coming in; their taxi was just driving away. He hugged and kissed the six-year-old boy, marveling at how he'd grown since he'd seen him last. Hanging Jared's coat first, he then helped Susan with hers. From its silk lining, an evocative fragrance filled his nostrils.

They all walked into the living room, where a fire was going in the hearth. "How are your folks?" Evan asked Susan.

"Fine. Dad won the over-fifty squash tournament at the Racquet Club."

"Which was the first thing you heard when you walked in, right?"

"Second."

"You've lost some weight."

"Fifteen pounds. What do you think?"

"It's becoming. Nothing upstairs, nice to see. Jared, how about a Coke?"

"Sure."

"Sue, anything?"

"I'd love a Scotch."

In the kitchen Evan busied himself preparing the drinks. Glancing up, he saw Sue and Jared in front of the flickering fireplace. She had on smooth-fitting black pants, a twilight shirt and a pair of silvery-gray heels. Her body had lost a certain fullness but not disadvantageously. Evan brought in the Scotch and the soft drink, returning quickly with a glass of wine for himself and sitting down with his ex-wife and son.

"How do you like Sausalito, Jared?"

"It's OK."

Evan said, "Your mother told me you have a new bicycle."

Jared nodded; his long blond bangs kept falling into his eyes.

"Do you still have the training wheels on?"

"No."

"So you're actually riding!"

The child had a slurp of Coke. "Sometimes I fall."

"That's part of having a bike, isn't it?" Evan gave his son's head a gentle pat.

"Would you like to play with your Lego blocks?" Susan asked; then to Evan, "I'm guessing they're still in his room."

"Nothing's changed. They're on the shelf."

Susan and Jared walked into the corridor. When they came back out, she set the boy up with his blocks, a good distance from the sofa; it was clear she wanted to talk. He liked the way she was squatting on the floor as she snapped three or four pieces together, to get Jared started; it had always been one of her favorite positions. She had a nice way of whacking him alongside the head with her breasts, no little back-and-forth brushes. She would batter him mercilessly, and he'd always felt, if he were to have a choice in the matter, that getting clobbered with Sue's tits would be how he'd like to go. She also liked having sex standing up, and for them, unlike most couples, it wasn't a difficult union to attain. He would have to bend his knees just slightly, then, by standing to full height, he'd be home.

"Jared's usually very talkative," Susan said, sitting with Evan again. "He's tired; also shy, I think."

"Understandably." He lowered his voice. "How, exactly, is he acting out? Still fighting with his classmates?"

"The other day he bit a child on his arm. The teacher reprimanded him, whereupon he kicked her in the shins."

"What did Dr. Blizzard say?"

"It's all part of the same pattern. E.U.S manifests itself in many ways." Susan had the first taste of her drink. "Like sometimes Jared will stop in the middle of what he's doing and begin masturbating."

"Some kids start young," Evan said.

"I don't care when they start, but to do it in McDonald's? It's embarrassing."

"Did you ask him to stop?"

"I did, at first—tried restraining his hand—and he wailed and screamed. Dr. Blizzard helped me along."

"Compared to biting, it's harmless," Evan said.

"I think it's Nadine."

"How so?"

"The tension, the fights we're having. Jared's picking up on it." Sue had herself a healthy taste of Scotch. "I've been having second thoughts."

"You should've listened to me. I never thought you were a lesbian."

"Listen to you? Always looking to shove a boner up my ass!"

"We never had a sex problem," Evan said.

"I beg to differ, and in my mind Nadine was the answer to it. When we were in college she was always saying we'd be perfect for each other. I used to laugh at her. One time we kissed just for the fun of it. I pretended that nothing happened but a lot happened." Susan was doing a good job on her drink. "You and I got married, had Jared. About then we started having those stupid fights, really going at each other. One day I called her up. That started something. It was great; I found what I needed, what I wanted. No one understands a woman like another woman. But after a while the blush went off the rose, something was missing; and then one night I had a dream." She held out her glass. "Make me another."

In the kitchen he poured the Scotch, looking over the

counter at his son who was building a kind of airplane; at least it appeared to have wings. He was concerned about Jared. Biting was definitely *out*. As for the other thing, he had started early himself—not Jared's age, more like ten, intrigued by how his penis would suddenly stand up like a soldier. So he decided to salute it, and saluting it, he discovered, was great fun. It became his favorite game.

Evan added ice to Susan's glass and went back to the sofa. "Tell me the dream," he said.

Susan lifted the glass to her lips. "How many times when we were married—this isn't the dream—would one of us start groping the other in our sleep? Then we'd wake up and fuck like mad. Anyway, I was in bed with Nadine, dreaming it was you, maybe six months ago. I was rubbing your thigh, then reached between your legs, and in my mind I began screaming, 'Your cock is gone! Evan, Evan, where's your cock?' I wanted to suck on it, I wanted it in me, fucking me, pounding me! I woke up in tears and Nadine woke up, and I told her the dream. She took it personally; she wasn't exciting me anymore, she said. So she went out and bought a dildo and strapped it on. It got me off but why would I want a dildo when I could have the real thing? Does a dildo grow, expand? I could always tell with you when your cock began getting really big and hard that any second it was going to explode. Can an ersatz hard-on explode? A woman loves it when a man blasts off inside her, and it got worse and worse—I mean, with Nadine. More toys, devices from India and China—she'd do anything to make me happy. I never felt guilty when we were together, I was never ashamed—like I'm a fucking dyke. Never! I just began thinking it wasn't me."

Susan pulled down the finely crafted zipper on her shirt several inches. "Fire's making me hot."

"Fires will do that," Evan said.

"Do you mind if I take my shoes off?"

"Why should I mind?"

"It's polite to ask when you're in someone else's house."

She slipped off her pumps; only now she sat closer, toying with her hair, leaning in, her fragrant breasts pressing against his arm and chest. "It's so weird," she said, "I'm here but I'm not, I'm in my old house but I have to knock on the door, I think you're an egomaniacal asshole but I can't wait to fuck you." She nibbled on his ear. "Let's conduct the acid test, Evan. Am I or am I not? Help me decide."

"What about men on the Coast? You've never—?"

"I had an affair with a real-estate agent from San Rafael and a publicist in Berkeley. West Coast men are creeps. Both times I went screaming back to Nadine."

"I never thought you were a lesbian, you know that," Evan said. "But one roll won't settle it."

She took hold of his erection through his pants, throttling it, as if trying to subdue a copperhead. "I say it will."

"What about Jared?"

"Let me turn on the TV for him."

Just then the door chime sounded.

"You don't have to answer it," Sue said.

"It's not locked. I have to."

Evan stood, straightened his shirt, gave his hard-on a harsh downward push. He walked to the front hall as his visitor pressed the latch and came in. "Well, Chloe, what a lovely surprise," he said, embracing her but not fully. "How are you?"

"We have to talk, Evan."

"I understand. But right now—well, Sue and Jared are here."

Chloe's eyes were drawn to the end of the hall. Standing there in black pants, cleavage showing, shoeless and drink in hand, was Susan Kendrix.

"You remember Chloe," Evan said to his ex.

"Of course. Hello, Chloe. We're having dinner in half an

hour," Susan said. "Will you join us?"

"Great idea," Evan said to Chloe. "I'll get you a glass of wine."

"Don't bother."

Sue Kendrix retreated, and Evan said, "I told you they were coming."

"Is that why you're wearing Chanel No. 5?"

"I greeted her with a hug."

"That's more than you gave me."

"Chloe, be reasonable, please. They're visiting, we're trying to make plans."

"I'm sure you are." She looked at him as if seeing him, seeing through him, for the first time, then slapped him hard across the face. She turned, went to the door, and walked out.

Evan stayed for a long second, then closed the door, locking it, and went back to the living room. Seated languidly on the sofa, his ex-wife said, "What gives?"

"She has issues."

"I used to think Chloe Forrester was a very beautiful woman," Susan Kendrix said.

CHAPTER
22

The lights on the bridge spanning the Walloon River were glimmering in the dusk as Rick and Noreen drove into Appleton; crowded in the back seat of her VW were Lisa and Andrew. They had spent the afternoon visiting Mountain View Thoroughbreds, a horse farm in nearby Gardner, then had stopped by a roadside Italian restaurant.

Noreen was telling Rick she had a big test tomorrow in her pre-law course on torts, and Terry Randolph was bugging her for a new story, but she wasn't in the mood for studying or writing. It was the perfect night for a movie. *Rocky* was playing in the Ambrose Plaza Cinema and they should all go. Cries of delight from the kids. Rick said he had nineteen freshman compositions to correct and *Sister Carrie* to brush up on for his senior seminar. Plus he was sure Lisa and Andrew had homework. They insisted they didn't.

"I've heard that before," Rick said.

"If we make the early show we'll be home by nine."

"Lisa, it's a school night. Sorry."

Rick, who was driving, found himself suddenly peering ahead, squinting. Was that smoke rising on the village side of the river? He kept looking, then saw orange streaks spurting upward.

"Guys, there's a fire in downtown Appleton!"

"Where, can you tell?" Noreen said.

"It could be the lumber yard."

"No, it's closer to Main Street," Andrew said, leaning forward. They drove on, now moving slowly; traffic was backed up at the bridge. "It looks like the old hotel."

Lisa's hands went to her mouth, eyes going wide. "Oh, God,"

she moaned.

An Appleton policeman was stationed on the east side of the bridge detouring traffic onto Elting Street. Rick would have taken Elting anyway to drop off the kids, though he would've made it to the house in three minutes. Now, with the crush of cars and trucks on the narrow tree-lined street, it took fifteen.

■ ■ ■

Lisa rushed in before her brother, immediately took the stairs down to the basement, waited for Rick and Noreen to drive away, then went out the side door used by her mother's clients. On Elting Street she ran to the corner, down Hazel to N. Elm, then ran/walked into the village, staying on the far side of the street when she passed her father's rooming house. At the minipark hundreds of people were milling about, their attention riveted on the burning hotel. Lisa pushed through the crowd. Everywhere red lights revolved atop cars and trucks; a never-ending screech of sirens tore at the air.

A policeman yelled at her but she went closer. A ladder from one of the trucks was fully extended and a fireman was on it, trying to reach someone trapped on the third floor. Or several people. Shouting, flashing lights, water shooting up, flames raging inside, cries for help, sparks rising high above the old building where Appleton State had had its start. Was he up there? Was that Greg at the window, reaching for the ladder? Was he in his bunk that seemed like a berth in a train, overcome by the heat, the smoke? The man at the window fell, his clothes on fire; people screamed, and another person at the window extended her arms to the fireman.

Then she saw Greg. He was running from the building carrying a woman to safety. Even in the confusion, Lisa recognized her as Freda, good-hearted Freda. He delivered her to a paramedic, and Lisa shouted his name.

He glanced over, his face smudged with soot and a gash on

his forehead, eyebrows singed; she ran to him, threw her arms around him. His chest was soaking wet and she smelled sweat and marijuana and booze on his body, in his beard. It didn't bother her; she loved his smells.

"Greg!"

"You shouldn't be here, Lisa."

"Are you all right?"

"Don't worry."

"Where will you be staying?"

"Somewhere."

"Come out to the house. You can stay in the loft."

The sky was a bright orange-red, streaked with gray. A policeman was shouting at Lisa to leave.

"You'd better go," Greg said.

"Be careful!"

She ran, stopping at the street and turning back. Was that Greg silhouetted against the building, moving toward the flames?

■ ■ ■

Rick finished grading the last composition in the recent batch, gave it a comment and a grade (B minus), then stood, pulled on his lined jacket, and went out with Waldo. At Noreen's door he heard the clicking of her typewriter and continued by.

Outside they crossed Main at the minipark, weaved through the back streets until they reached River Road, and soon they were at the wash-out. While Waldo ran, Rick walked to the river. A half-moon hung in the southern sky. A cloudless night, crowded with stars. Cold but no longer mid-winter cold. Spring was a day closer. He gave a whistle and Waldo came running up. Instead of weaving through the back streets, Rick decided to stay on River Road, wanting to have a look at the burned-down hotel.

He saw no reason to put Waldo at heel, and the dog ran

ahead. On Rick's left, tucked alongside the railroad track, was a string of dingy huts; every town had its slum. Two hundred yards farther along he came to Appleton Lumberyard. Great open sheds, in daylight a deep green, were filled with 2x4's and 2x6's and stacks of plywood, all manner of moldings and trim. At this point, River Road rose, bending, and as he walked on, the air, quite suddenly, was thick with the odor of smoldering wood.

Then he was at the site. Orange police ribbon encircled the property. A bathtub, probably from an upper story, had fallen and lay near the base of a brick chimney. With its feet sticking up, it resembled a dead steer. In addition to the chimney, only the foundation and a section of western wall were standing. A few firemen, still at the scene, sprayed hot spots. Rick looked about for Waldo, spotting him up ahead. Someone, obscured in the shadows, was kneeling on the side of the road stroking the dog's head.

Curious, Rick drew closer. It wasn't like Waldo to go up to a stranger. Then Rick recognized the person—she was anything but a stranger. "Chloe, what are you doing here?"

She stood and came toward him, arms clasped over her chest, in jeans and a thin shirt. "It's gone."

"There are other places," he said.

"Evan didn't want me to have it." She pointed at the smoking ruin.

Rick slipped off his jacket, put it around her shoulders. "He had nothing to do with this. Someone was smoking in bed, there was bad wiring—"

"No, it was Evan!"

Rick gave her a long, slow look; she was becoming more and more difficult to reach. "For your sake, the kids' sake, you have to get away from him," he said. "Evan Kendrix preys on women. A friend of Noreen's—a young woman I know—sees him professionally. He has sex with her during their sessions, calls it therapy, and it's ruining her life."

She was staring at Rick, like someone snapping to, becoming suddenly sober. "Who is she?"

"Chloe, it makes no difference who she is; it's who *Evan* is."

"Tell me!"

"It's unimportant. I'm just trying to convince you—"

"Who is she?"

The hell with it, he thought. "Christine Monteleone."

Chloe let out a low, excruciating cry, hands pressing against her abdomen. Then, at once, she spun around and ran, Rick's jacket sliding from her shoulders. Waldo, muzzle lifted to the sky, gave a full-throated howl; his eyes had a yellow glow. Rick looked at the dog, startled, then ran after Chloe. When he reached the crest in River Road, she was almost at her car, parked on lower Main.

He shouted her name but she got in, pulled the door shut, and gunned it over the bridge, racing without headlights across the floodplain. The dog raised his muzzle and howled again.

"Waldo, knock it off! *Heel!*"

They started back. His jacket, ahead, resembled an ink blot on the road.

■ ■ ■

She was driving, at the same time watching herself from the passenger's seat; and the *passenger* Chloe was saying to the *driver* Chloe, Nothing good can come from this. And the *driver* Chloe was saying, I know what I'm doing. Nothing has ever been clearer in my mind! *Passenger:* You're not in a good place. *Driver:* I've never been in a better place!

A car was coming at her, its headlights flashing, horn blaring. Then she was spinning up Chodokee Road. At Evan's mailbox she turned, tore by tall figures standing ominously about.

Passenger: Be smart about this. You have responsibilities!

Driver: I know. To myself.

The house was dark.

She got out of her car, tried the front door. Locked. Rang the chime, waited, rang it again.

Nothing.

Chloe angled across the turnaround to Evan's studio. The door within a door was open and she went in, fumbled for the light switch, flipped it on. Springing before her was a pinkish-gray stone, gargantuan in form and size. Rusty iron bands cinched the middle; spikes, similarly oxidized, angled out from the top. It was the ugliest, most demeaning, most vengeful creative work she had ever seen.

"Strike a pose, Chloe."

She went up to the stone, shoved it with her hands; it was like pushing at the side of a monument. On the squat table, among points and chisels, she saw a hammer. As she reached for it, her hand became still; also on the table was the black remote.

Chloe snatched it up, jabbed one of the buttons and the dolly jerked forward; touched another button and it reversed— the stone teetered. Again she stabbed the first button, then the second, simultaneously pressing the tiny joystick. But "Prurience" held on. Determinedly, Chloe kept at it. "Fall, damn it, fall!" But it wouldn't go. Just as she was about to hurl the remote, the dolly collided with one of the heavy posts supporting the roof. The vehicle stopped abruptly, jolting the stone. Chloe sent the dolly forward and the sculpture was caught in a precarious balance. She gave the reverse button one last jab and pressed the tiny joystick—and the stone went over, crushing the cast-iron stove and breaking into several huge pieces. One of the spikes, hurtling away, rammed through the side window.

"That's for all of us, Evan," Chloe said, "for every Christine in this world, and every Niki, and every Chloe too!"

She threw the remote at the pile of debris, pushed open

the door within a door, and ran to her car; started it, turned on her headlights, and drove away, doing sixty on Rt. 289 heading east. Tomorrow she'd make inquiries at a local real-estate agency into properties for sale. Heartbreak Hotel wasn't the only place. There were other places available, even better. It would be a huge undertaking but she could do it, and one day the Chloe Forrester Mental Health Center would open its doors. A journey of a thousand miles....

She rolled down her window and let the cold air race in. She had taken back the power and would never again give it up. Chloe began yelling into the night air stinging her face. "I don't need you, Evan! You're out of my life. Fuck you, Evan!"

Ahead, a large deer sprang from the apple orchard. Chloe jammed on her brakes. The deer was at her window, eyes staring into hers—she knew those eyes! At the last instant, the huge animal leapt, skimming the car, one hoof piercing the vinyl top and coming down like a sword thrust, missing her by inches and rending the passenger's seat. Car out of control, swerving, spinning, and finally coming to a ragged stop.

Chloe gripped the steering wheel, hyperventilating, her foot jumping uncontrollably. She didn't recognize the road she saw through the windshield, didn't know where she was. Then at once it came to her. She was on the floodplain road but... silhouetted against the night sky loomed Mt. Chodokee with its axe-like face. A scream started building in Chloe's chest, then broke loose.

CHAPTER
23

The Appleton police notified Rick, calling him while he was having dinner with Noreen in his apartment. He drove to the site, brought Chloe to the house—no physical injuries, just badly shaken—and made sure she was comfortable in bed. He would have her car brought back, he told her; not to worry, just rest. She thanked him, holding his hand, wanting him to stay, but after a few minutes he said good night to her and the kids and left the house. Lisa and Andrew stayed with their mother for a good while, then went to their own rooms and Chloe was alone in the darkness. She felt a core essence of herself, too remote, too nebulous to identify, slipping away.

■ ■ ■

The fireplace room, ever since the water damage in the basement, had served as Chloe's office, and she was sitting with a client now, telling Niki Nazarro in soft, emotional tones that she was closing her door.

"What are you saying?"

"I'm quitting my practice."

"Why, Chloe?"

It was hard to answer the question, even to herself. "I've lost something, Niki."

Tears were filling the woman's eyes. "You'll find it, I know you will."

"You're doing so well, you don't need me anymore."

"We all need you, that's just it!"

A wan smile touched Chloe's lips. Niki circled the table. Kneeling, she rested her head on Chloe's lap, wrapping her arms around her knees.

■ ■ ■

She was sitting in the kitchen thirty minutes later drinking a cup of coffee when the phone rang. Her heart began to race. Chloe went and picked up the phone.

"Hello."

"What the hell were you thinking?" It was Evan.

"About what?"

"About destroying 'Prurience', you bitch!"

"I destroyed it because it was a misogynistic piece of shit, and I'm glad I did it."

"There will be consequences, Chloe. I want you to know that."

The phone went dead. She went back to the table and picked up the coffee cup, her hand shaking.

■ ■ ■

It took a week and a half to tell all her clients, and now she was making a last farewell—holding little Bonnie Wintersteen in her arms, kissing the child's eyes, watching as she walked out to her mother. Chloe closed the side door to the house, locking it, then went upstairs and continued to the second floor and the security of her bedroom. She took off her shoes and got under the covers, pressing against her ears to silence the scream still echoing in her head.

■ ■ ■

Tick-tock, tick-tock.

The kitchen clock sounded extraordinarily close, as if it were here in her bedroom. She dozed, woke. *Tick-tock, tick-tock.* Dozed, woke—this time with a start. Listening, her senses keyed. Someone was moving around on the deck! She glanced at the clock on her night table. Three twenty-seven a.m. There, again! Chloe sat up. Panicking, she reached for the phone, dialed—

Groggily, "Hello."

"Rick, you have to come over!"

"Chloe?"

"Someone's moving around on the deck!"

"You're having a bad dream."

"It's not a dream!"

"Well, if you're worried, call the police."

"Bring Waldo."

"No, you handle it!"

He hung up and Chloe put down the phone—waiting, listening. There, again! Without hesitating she dialed the Appleton police. A man answered: "Headquarters, Patrolman Rizzi."

"Someone's moving around on my deck, send someone over. 135 Elting Street!"

She stayed at the side bedroom window overlooking the driveway. Soon a squad car pulled up and two officers got out with flashlights. Ten minutes later the front-door knocker clacked and she went down in robe and slippers. The officers were standing on the small porch. The older of the two, a sergeant with a bushy mustache, said they had searched high and low, no sign of anyone.

"I heard noises!"

"There's no one around, Mrs. Forrester."

She didn't believe them; they were lying. Chloe went back upstairs, got into bed. The lights from the departing car slid ghostlike along her bedroom wall.

Tick-tock. Tick-tock.

Trying to calm herself, she started taking deep breaths. Inhale, hold, exhale. Inhale, hold—

Sounds, again! Except now, instead of outside, the noises were *in* the house, low, in the basement. Of course, the root cellar! Chloe reached for the phone. This time he wouldn't say no; she wouldn't let him. His college girlfriend would just have to live with it.

■ ■ ■

He was sitting on the edge of his bed, phone in hand, hearing the terror in his wife's voice. The police had come, had seen nothing, she was saying. Whoever was walking about wasn't outside, he was *inside*. She could hear him moving around in the basement.

"No one is there, Chloe," he said, fingers tight on the receiver.

"Hurry, Rick! Please! We could all be killed."

After an agonizing moment, "All right." He put down the phone.

"Are you going?" Noreen asked, sitting up in bed.

"I have to."

"Did she call the police?"

"They didn't see anything. Someone is in the house, she says."

"She says."

He started pulling on his clothes. "If anything happened, I'd never forgive myself."

"Don't you see what she's doing?"

"She's a frightened woman, Noreen. Try to understand. I'll be back in an hour." Rick whistled to his dog and they left.

■ ■ ■

He pulled into his driveway and grabbed a flashlight from the glove compartment of his car. With his dog at heel, they walked toward the deck stairs. When they passed the shed, Waldo seemed distracted and Rick gave him an "OK". Immediately Waldo began sniffing the ground at the sliding door. Rick opened it, snapped on the fluorescent light over his workbench, his eyes going to the stairs leading up to the loft. Uneasy about this whole business, he started climbing, kicked open the door at top. In the corner, someone was huddled in a sleeping bag.

Without getting up, hardly stirring, the person spoke. "Rick, I love you, man."

"What are you doing here?"

"Sleeping, I'm sleeping."

"Get your stuff and get out."

"I'll go in the morning. Give me a break."

"I'll give you two minutes, Greg."

"Have a heart. You used to have a heart!"

"I remember. Now beat it!"

His former student pulled on his boots. Using his light, Rick saw a Coleman stove at the side window. Empty cans kicking about, mostly beer. Two chairs were pulled up to an old card table, and draped over the back of one was a denim jacket, way too small for the army vet.

Greg crossed the room, floor swaying under his weight, and descended the stairs.

As he passed Waldo, who was sitting at the shed door, he reached out to pat the dog's head. "Waldo, how are you?"

"Greg, listen to me," Rick said. "Don't set foot on this property again. Next time you'll pay."

He watched Greg shuffle away, favoring his left leg. When his former student was well down the street, Rick slid the shed door closed and attached the padlock. With Waldo, he went up the deck steps and inside.

Chloe was sitting up, a couple of pillows behind her back, when he walked in with the dog. "Greg Horboychuk was in the loft," he said. "He's gone. I warned him not to come back."

"What was he doing?"

"Sleeping."

"Has Lisa been seeing him there?"

Evidence said yes. But this was hardly the time to tell her mother. "Don't know. But now you know what you've been hearing."

"No, you're wrong. Listen!"

He indulged her for several seconds. "All I hear is the clock."

"Someone is in the tunnel."

He gave her a long slow look. "What?"

"I want the door to the root cellar boarded up."

"Chloe, that's crazy."

"He's in the tunnel!"

Rick sat on the edge of the bed, took hold of her hands. "Let's get this straight. The 'tunnel' we've heard about—it isn't a real tunnel."

"Of course it is!"

"Chloe," he explained, "this house was part of the network set up by the anti-slavery movement called the Underground Railroad; but it wasn't an actual railroad. Runaway slaves knew of it, or were told about it—when you get to Appleton, New York, go to the parsonage out on Elting Street." Rick was speaking slowly, calmly. "It was all done in secret, because it was illegal. Why would there be a tunnel? What purpose would it serve?"

"The oxbow was once the river," Chloe said. "Isn't that right?"

"Yes."

"It's all so clear! The Walloon flows north. That made it very convenient for the slaves. For added security, a tunnel led to the river."

"Even if there were a tunnel back then," Rick said, "would it be passable today?"

"Then what am I hearing?"

"Who knows? It's that time of year. Animals—"

"This is heavy—a scraping, clawing sound!"

"Then it's a heavy animal." Rick glanced at the clock. Four eleven.

Suddenly Chloe brought her finger to her lips. "Shhhhh!"

"What?"

"Do you hear it?"

"No."

"There!"

Then, well aware of the power of suggestion, Rick did pick up a sound—dull, muffled—coming from the depths of the house. He dipped his head, heard it again. Rick gave Waldo a glance. He was lying by the side of the bed, eyes closed. "Well, I hear something."

"Go look!"

His first impulse was to say, "Excuse me?" But he inhaled, made a hand gesture to his dog; the springer spaniel followed him down to the basement. They went into the fireplace room and crossed to the door leading into the root cellar. Rick stood in front of it, hesitant to flip the brass hook. Was there a chance, any chance at all, that someone, slogging through a "tunnel" 130 years old, was waiting to greet him when he walked in? Rick snapped on the light and unhooked the door. It creaked open. "Go," he said to Waldo, then, under his breath, "you first."

The dog went in and sniffed around in a lackadaisical manner. Rick took the pair of hollowed steps down to the dirt floor. On his left, the cistern; on his right, the wall separating the root cellar from Chloe's office—her damaged office—and, because the root cellar was lower than her office, access to a crawl area existed all along the base of the wall. Rick kneeled, bent down, and shone his light into the low, gloomy space.

The earth had a fine, powdery appearance, untouched all these years; he spotted thick lengths of adzed timber—floor joists—and the brick and stone footing for the fireplace. But nothing that resembled a tunnel, or some fuliginous figure emerging from one. It was a cursory scan but what was he going to do, crawl in on his stomach and investigate every corner? Rick stood, brushed off his knees.

"What do you think, Waldo? Anyone here?"

Rick saw nothing in the dog's attitude to suggest alarm, even curiosity. They went back out. Chloe was still in bed, in the same sitting position, when they entered the room. "We went in," Rick said. "I looked in the crawl space. Waldo sniffed around. Nothing."

"You heard it yourself!"

"Chloe, there's no one in or near this house."

"Did you look in the cistern?"

"No."

"That's where he's hiding!"

Rick ran his hand back through his hair. "The only access to the cistern is a hole for rainwater, roughly the size of a saucer; it's been closed off, plugged, for fifty years. Now try to get some sleep."

"Rick, stay with me."

She was wearing him down. "I'm sorry. No."

"Then bring me your gun."

"What do you want with it?"

"Protection! What do you think?"

"A gun doesn't 'protect' unless you know what you're doing."

"All those times we shot clay pigeons in Woodbridge, I know what I'm doing!"

"Shooting targets on a bright October day isn't the same as facing an intruder," Rick said. "We have children. Mistakes happen."

"As if I'll shoot blindly!"

"People have. Forget it. No."

"Goddamn you, Rick. If one day you come home and find me dead on the floor—"

"Chloe, stop the dramatics."

"He's coming for me!"

"No one is coming for you."

"Evan is! The night of the fire, when the hotel burned down,

I drove to his house—"

"You told me he wasn't home."

"He wasn't. I went into his workspace. His newest sculpture, 'Prurience'—for the first time I saw it for what it was, an ugly gargantuan depiction of a woman in chains! I wheeled it around on a dolly until it fell and broke into huge chunks."

"Does he know you did it?"

"Yes, he does, because he called me the next day. I wanted him to know, the son-of-a-bitch!"

Rick was struck by her story. Whether Kendrix would settle the score by doing Chloe harm, he doubted. But who knew? Destroy an artist's work, you'd hear about it; one way or another, you'd pay. "I'll bring in my gun," he said.

Rick went out to the shed and took his Beretta from the cabinet, removed the dummy shells, grabbed two loose shells from the handy box and went back inside. Upstairs in their bedroom, he tucked the gun in her closet and placed the live rounds on the top shelf. For a second as he stood there, a thought, so terrible he could not articulate it, raced through his mind, then vanished.

"There," he said. going over to Chloe.

"Is it loaded?"

"No. If you need shells, they're on the left side of your shelf."

"Thank you, Rick."

"Sleep well."

He went quickly out, down the stairs, helped Waldo in, and drove away.

CHAPTER
24

They talked for ten minutes in his office, if you could call it talk. Christine cried and carried on when Evan said—drew to her attention—that their sessions were over. He had prepared her in advance, and now this was it, a parting. He hoped she would finish her degree at Appleton State, and he had every confidence that she would make a name for herself in speech therapy—and find the right man to share her life with.

She used a couple of tissues, dropped them into a handy basket, then took a check from her saddle-stitched bag. He told her to keep it and they walked out together. Under a starless sky he gave her a hug and she drove away, swerving at the end of the driveway, almost to find herself in a ditch. But she kept on. Evan let out a great sigh when her taillights finally disappeared.

Inside, he sat at his deck and opened his journal, dating the entry. He thought for a moment, finally writing: "Christine Monteleone's last session. Free of the toxicity of her relationship with her (ex) stepfather, she leaves my office a fulfilled young woman. It is my firm belief that Christine is now capable of loving with an open heart, her stated goal when we started. I am very proud of her and the great strides she has made, and will continue to make, on the path to self-knowledge."

■ ■ ■

Sitting on the edge of the bed in his apartment, Rick kicked off his shoes, thinking to lie down for thirty minutes. Noreen's last class today started at four thirty, so he wouldn't be seeing her until six, and a little mid-day nap would be very nice. But just as his head touched the pillow, his phone rang. Rick reached over the side of his bed and grabbed the receiver. His son was on the line.

"Dad, Lisa didn't come home on the bus."

"Maybe she had to stay over. Did she call home?"

"Mom says no."

"When she left this morning, was anything different?"

"Nothing I saw."

Rick exhaled loudly, closed his eyes. Then, pulling himself together, "I'll pick you up in fifteen minutes. Put on warm clothes and wear boots."

"I was just heading out the door to play golf with Donnie. It's our first day."

"Your sister comes before golf, Andrew. Get ready."

■ ■ ■

Left front wheel broke through a frozen pothole—*kerplunk*—jolting father and son and everything else, unfastened, in the station wagon. "Hang on, Andrew. Beats golf, doesn't it?" No comment from the boy. Two hundred yards farther on, Rick pulled off the old wood road into an unpaved parking area, yanked on the emergency brake, and opened his door. He and Andrew got out and began walking on a narrow trail. Here and there, on both sides of it, snowdrops were coming up. After a fifteen-minute trek they came to Spoon Pond, covered with soft, opaque ice. The ranger's boat lay turned over, just as he and Noreen had left it.

"What do we do now?" Andrew asked impatiently.

"See that single evergreen on the side of the cliff?" Rick pointed. "Just above it is a ledge."

At first Andrew didn't see the tree. He wasn't looking high enough. Then, "OK. So?"

"That's where she is. I think."

"Dad, there's no way—"

"We'll find a way."

They tramped around the edge of the pond, pushing through trees and brush. As they drew nearer the escarpment, the ground began rising. Rick reached back and extended his hand, helping his son negotiate a tight squeeze between a boulder and a hemlock big around as a wagon wheel. Finally they reached the cliff. Rocks and rubble were strewn along its base; both breathing heavily, they stopped for a rest.

"We're looking for an access route—" Rick pointed over their heads, a couple of hundred feet up, "—to that shelf or ledge. Just so you know."

They were moving again, picking their way over and through big rocks. It was darker, colder, close to the steep face, and slippery too. Andrew pulled his hat from his pocket and put it on. They stopped for a moment to look at the remains of a shack tucked among trees and boulders, flush against the face of the cliff. Roof smashed in, floor rotted away. Artifacts by the score—cups, bottles, a rusted-out frying pan—lying about.

"Who lived here do you think?"

"Maybe a hermit," Rick said, "or a trapper."

They kept going. Making their way over the rocky terrain was arduous, and Rick saw the strain in Andrew's face. They were now directly beneath the solitary evergreen. The only positive sign, as Rick saw, was the ledge itself. It sloped downward like a mildly pitched ramp. But darkness was setting in, and the temperature was dropping.

They clambered over more stones and boulders, hiked on. Above them, the ledge continued slanting downward, more sharply now, and at the place where the slant terminated altogether they both saw a shoe print in a patch of mountain snow. Then others—some large, others smaller.

"We're on their trail," Rick said.

The shelf, about twenty feet wide, rose gradually; there was no danger of falling off but the going was slick and rocky, no casual stroll on a forest path. Rick estimated they had about three hundred yards to the evergreen—or the spot directly above it—and his adrenaline was rising, even as he told himself, repeatedly, to stay calm. Far across the floodplain, in Appleton, lights were sparkling in the early evening.

They kept on, the face of the cliff at this point slightly convex, and as they moved along Rick suddenly saw his daughter and Greg about 150 feet ahead. They were walking across the ledge, hand in hand, and Rick had the excruciating thought that they weren't going to stop; they had just made a pact. His heart exploded in panic.

"Lisa!"

She snapped her head around, staring in disbelief as her father and brother approached. No such reaction from Greg. He seemed delighted to see his ex-professor and his ex-professor's son. When they were thirty feet away, he said in a bright voice, "Rick, Andrew, welcome to Castlegregory!"

"Lisa, we're taking you home," Rick said.

"I'm not going with you, Dad." She stood beside Greg in her bomber jacket and bluejeans. Early stars in a gray sky seemed to be resting on her shoulders.

"Lisa, one way or the other you're coming back with us. So make it easy on yourself."

"Give us your blessing," Greg said. "We're starting a new life here, Rick."

Now, face to face with his daughter and the veteran, Rick reached out and grabbed Lisa by the wrist. She struggled, trying to pull loose. "Let go of me!"

"Rick, I don't want anyone getting hurt," Greg said.

"Then stay out of this."

Greg came in a step. Rick didn't know what chance he'd have against a jungle-hardened Green Beret, but he couldn't worry about it. He handed Lisa to her brother. "Don't let her go, Andrew, no matter what." The next moment he and Greg were grappling, falling to the ground. No way was he stronger or better trained, but Rick didn't feel overpowered, outmaneuvered. It was almost as if Greg wasn't really fighting. Stones poked at Rick's legs, punishing his hips and shoulders. From Lisa and Andrew came cries of internecine struggle. Then Rick and Greg were at the lip of the cliff. In a top position, Rick picked up a rock—

"You want to—kill me, man? Smash my—brains out?" Greg was looking up, unafraid.

"Just—stay away—from Lisa!"

"Didn't you always tell us—find your own Walden? This is it, Rick. I've found—my own Walden."

"Good. I didn't say—with my—daughter!"

"I love you, man."

Rick tossed the rock over the edge and the crash didn't come at once. He stood, his eyes fixed on Greg as he backed away; then he was looking at his children. Andrew's hands were full trying to contain Lisa, and he really wasn't succeeding. He was a compact kid, but Lisa had her mother's quick, lean body. She was kicking, clawing; then one of her kicks caught her brother square on his hip, and stumbling sideways Andrew fell on the rough ground, crying out in pain. Lisa tried to go back to Greg but Rick caught her by the arm.

"Stop it, Lisa! *Stop!*"

"I'm staying!"

"You're not, you're coming home!"

His son was on the ground, groaning, writhing about, tears running down his cheeks.

"Andrew, are you all right?" Rick said.

He didn't answer. Rick glanced at Greg, who was standing near the edge watching his professor and the kids but not coming any closer. Taking advantage of her father's lapse, Lisa tried yanking away, almost succeeding. Rick clamped down harder on her forearm.

"I hate you, Dad!"

"Well, Greg loves me—so we're all square." He spoke to Andrew. "Can you get up?"

"I think—maybe. I'm not sure."

Andrew struggled to his feet. A dark stain extended all along his thigh to his knee.

"OK, slow and easy now," Rick said.

They began moving away, his hand locked on Lisa's wrist. Several times she glanced back, straining to break loose. Greg stayed at the cave, watching them go. Finally he disappeared from their view, and eventually they arrived at the place where Rick and Andrew had first seen footprints. It would be impossible—considering the boy's condition, the failing light, Lisa's recalcitrance—to renegotiate the boulder-route back to Spoon Pond. Rick decided to keep on the path and asked Lisa where it led.

No answer, but he found out soon enough. Two hundred yards on, it merged with an unpaved road. Andrew said he had to rest. Rick was afraid that resting might stiffen the boy's leg, and the falling thermometer wouldn't help; but he said OK, for a minute.

Andrew sat down on the side of the road on a fallen tree. Lisa wasn't talking. Rick felt as if he were lost behind enemy lines with two POWs he was attempting to bring in. His own body was sore, aching. "We have to start moving again," he said.

"My leg's killing me, Dad."

"Andrew, we have to keep going."

Just then Rick heard the sound of a car. He stepped into the middle of the road with Lisa, and when the vehicle came into view he waved it down. It was a full-size pickup. The driver rolled down his window, and Rick, his hand tight on Lisa's wrist, said they needed a lift into Appleton—

"Rick, that you?"

"Nolan!"

"I'm just heading into town. Pile in."

"My son needs a hand. He had an accident."

The big Ulmer County journeyman, in a red-checkered lumber jacket, swung down from his truck. Rick knew Nolan Schrade from P&B's; on numerous occasions, through the years, they had talked at the bar, bought each other beers. The bed of his truck was wavy with logs, the handle of a chain saw sticking up like a yellow buoy.

"What do we have here?" he said to Andrew, going over, helping him stand.

Rick directed Lisa to get in first, then slid beside her and held Andrew on his lap. Nolan released his emergency brake, and they were moving along.

"We have to get to the Medical Center," Rick said.

■ ■ ■

Nolan waited with Rick's daughter while Rick and his son were in seeing the doctor. "She'll run on you," Rick had told him, like maybe her carburetion was faulty. "Watch her." Nolan had tried talking with the girl but she wasn't into it, so he just sat there with her waiting for Rick and the boy. Something was going on but he didn't know what. She sure was a pretty girl but ornery, he could see. Sometimes he thought about having a wife and kids, what it would be like, but each year less and less; you got used to being alone. The girl set down her magazine and looked like she might be getting ready to bolt, then Rick came out with the boy and settled up at the desk and they all went back out to the parking lot. Rick said it was a bad contusion and bruise. Now they had to keep it clean and change the dressing twice a day. Nolan said he was glad it was nothin' worse. A few minutes later they were on Elting Street, and he was pulling up in front of Rick's house.

"See you at seven tomorrow morning," he said. "We'll get your wagon."

"Thanks for everything, Nolan."

"Glad I come along. So long, kids."

Nolan drove off, turned onto Hazel Street. He'd had a good day—hauled out three truckloads of wood, good seasoned stuff, then helped out a friend. Soon he'd be putting down a few Buds in P&B's. What more could a man want or ask for?

■ ■ ■

When they were inside, Rick told Lisa and Andrew to wash up thoroughly. He would call them for supper in about thirty minutes. He looked into the refrigerator to see what he might warm up, if anything—and heard loud noises. Like someone using a hammer in the basement.

What now?

Going down the hollowed-out steps he saw Chloe at the root-cellar door, holding a slat with one hand and nailing it to the door frame with the other. Several random pieces of wood leaned against the wall and a box of nails rested on the floor.

"Chloe, what are you doing?"

"He's in the tunnel!"

She was still in her nightgown, with one of his chamois-cloth shirts over it and a pair of upland boots on her feet, unlaced, her hair wildly mussed. After a moment he said, "We found Lisa."

She kept missing the nail; when she did connect, it barely went in.

"Andrew hurt his leg. Dr. Palmer looked at it. It's a bad scrape—"

Chloe missed again and he relieved her of the hammer. "Come on, I'll take you upstairs."

"No! Nail it for me!"

He nailed the board across the doorway, not driving the nails all the way in.

"That wouldn't stop anyone, Rick!"

Chloe handed him a new board, and another. As he was

nailing the third, a shout came from upstairs. "Dad, Lisa just left!"

He set the hammer on the windowsill, dashed out the side door, and saw his daughter as she was disappearing down Elting Street. He ran after her, not sure he'd catch her, but at the corner of Hazel he just managed to, shoving her up against a big catalpa tree, pressing his forearm across her upper chest.

"I've had it with you, Lisa!"

He should be scaring the hell out of her, right? Father coming down the street foaming at the mouth, wouldn't that throw a sixteen-year-old girl into a panic? She looked at him icily. He pressed harder with his forearm. "Are you going to stop?" He was raging at her, his face close to hers. "*Are you?*"

She was going pale. Rick took away his arm. Breathing raggedly, she used her fingers to wipe her cheeks. Not of tears.

"We'll see," Rick said. "We'll see who wins here, Lisa." He pointed back down the street. "Start walking."

■ ■ ■

It was eight forty-five by the time he made dinner, brought a tray to Chloe in her bedroom, and sat down with his kids at the kitchen table; no one was interested in his tuna casserole—Lisa was too upset to eat, Andrew too uncomfortable. Rick had a few forkfuls, suggested to Andrew he should turn in, and enlisted the help of a steaming-mad girl for doing the dishes. When they were finished, Rick told her to go to her room and don't make the mistake of trying anything—no repeat performances, thank you. Also, from here on she was grounded. He'd be driving her to the high school every day and then picking her up.

He went upstairs, banister assisting him—his entire body in pain—and looked in on Chloe. She was in bed, lying on her side looking at Waldo, her lips moving quietly. Rick thought to say, "Excuse me for interrupting," but held off, saying, "I just wanted to tell you I'll be spending the night."

He seemed to think she was pleased with the news.

"I'm setting up a cot at the foot of the stairs. Oh, I've grounded Lisa."

In the landing closet he found his old cot, also a blanket and a pillow, and took them down to the front hall; unfolded the cot and tossed on the bedding, such as it was. When the house became still, he went into the alcove, dialed a number. Noreen picked up on the first ring, concerned, wanting to know where he was. Was he all right?

"I'm at the house. I'm OK, but we're having problems."

"Like what?"

He told her everything, starting with the mission to track down Lisa, finally finding her in the Shaggs with a Vietnam vet. He and the vet had fought, rolling to the edge of a precipice. Andrew had fallen and injured his leg but they managed to get Lisa home, only to find Chloe boarding up the door to the root cellar. Lisa tried running away and he had to chase after her down Elting Street.

"I'm all aches and pains—"

"Then come over," Noreen said. "What you need is a hot shower and a good massage."

"That's true." It was heaven just thinking about it. Then he said, "I'm spending the night."

"I *hope* you're spending the night," Noreen said.

"Here."

"At your house?"

"If I leave, Lisa will split. Andrew needs care, doctor's orders. And Chloe's more of a problem than the kids."

Noreen said tonelessly, "Family comes first. I forgot."

"I'll see you tomorrow, early. We'll go to breakfast."

"Don't bother, Rick. Clearly your hands are full."

"My family needs me, I have to be here," he said. "I'm sleeping on an old cot—"

"Good night, Rick." After a short silence, she hung up her

phone.

He sat for a minute in the alcove pressing shut his eyes as if to black out the entire day. Then he went to his bar and positioned a glass, tilted a bottle of bourbon, and dropped in ice cubes in the kitchen; walked into the living room and sat down in the wing-back chair in the corner. Sitting there alone, in the quiet, he heard the first drops of rain....

One time, maybe eight years ago, they were camping at a site in the Catskills—their fourth or fifth outing since he'd bought the tent the previous summer. It had come with an 8' by 10' fly, which you could either put up as part of the tent or leave in the car. Rick always put it up, in case of rain. It had never rained, until that night. Chloe, Lisa, and Andrew were all inside the tent, sleeping, and he sat under the fly as the rain fell, thinking it was the happiest moment of his life.

He finished his drink, set the glass down, at the foot of the stairs took off his boots and pants. Grimacing, he slid beneath the blanket on the cot.

CHAPTER
25

Weeks went by—taxiing Lisa to and from school, tending to Chloe, preparing meals for his kids, teaching classes; and spending time with Noreen. Rick was determined to keep the flame alive but despite his efforts he saw it fluttering. On his last three visits they hadn't got anywhere near her bed.

Now, heading down Main Street during a noon break at the college, on his way to Noreen's, Rick thought to make a stop at Hobo Deli. He found a parking spot in front of The Roaring Twenties, pressed a nickel into the meter—sated, its tongue disappeared—and walked toward the corner. A narrow alley ran between Appleton Liquor and Homestead Tavern. As if by habit he glanced in. Two shadowy forms were crouched in the alley passing something tiny back and forth, held in their fingertips. Rick seemed to recognize the stiff, creaky movements of Jean-Jean the Artist; opposite him was someone Rick couldn't identify, but in all likelihood the Good Shepherd was taking a break from his guardian duties.

In Hobo, Rick bought a few necessaries for the house; for Noreen a couple of oranges and a box of Earl Grey teabags. As he was walking back to his wagon, Jean-Jean the Artist (sure enough) was just coming out of the alley with—not the Good Shepherd. At his side was a young woman, petite, jet-black hair, chalk-white skin. Rick did a double take. Christine? She was so altogether wasted he wasn't sure. As they passed on the sidewalk, their eyes met. Hers, once so fiery-dark, had a dull, lifeless glare.

Rick looked after her, terribly upset, then continued to his car, drove down Main, and was soon parking in front of his boarding house on N. Elm. Rick grabbed the things for Noreen, climbed the stairs, and tapped on her door. No response.

He went in, set the paper bag on the kitchen counter, then walked into the living room; from her bedroom he heard the clicking of a typewriter. "Hi, Noreen," he said.

The clicking stopped and she came out, her hair in something of a tangle. "Hi."

"How's it going?"

"I've developed writer's block."

"I heard you typing."

"Words, nonsense. Anything to break out of it."

They sat on the sofa beneath the fish tank. "I just saw Christine," Rick said.

"Where? How is she?"

"Coming out of an alley with Jean-Jean the Artist. She looked wasted."

Noreen lowered her head, pressing against her eyebrow. "Poor lost girl. God, I hate Evan Kendrix. What he's done, the wrong, the harm!"

She began crying. A box of tissues lay on an end table and she reached for one. They didn't speak for a while and he sensed she wanted to say something, was having a hard time saying it; and then she came out and said it. "This isn't working, Rick."

"What isn't?"

"Us. You and me."

"You're not allowing it to work. I don't know what more I can do."

"You can tell Chloe you're leaving, you have another life. Say goodbye to her the way she said goodbye to you!"

"She's an ill woman, incapable of taking care of herself," Rick said.

"That's the way you see it."

"Then enlighten me. How do you see it?"

"How? By putting an antic disposition on—first to bring you back, now to keep you home. Wives have their ways." Noreen pulled another tissue, pressed it against her eyes. "We've had our day in the sun, Rick," she said. "I want you to go. It's over."

■ ■ ■

At Westgate Industries on his regular weekly stint, Evan sat behind the director's desk listening to Sid Glickman's tale of woe. Evidently the infamous Rosie Roppenecker had told Sid to "stick it up your ass and mind your own fucking business" when he had reprimanded her for using abusive language in the cafeteria. "What did you do then?" Evan inquired, thinking the weekly, mind-boggling tedium of the job was starting to take a toll. He had wanted to give something back to Appleton, and he had—but the time was fast approaching to bid Westgate farewell.

"I told her I'd write a T-17 on her unless she watched her mouth," Glickman said, "and she said the same thing again, only louder, and everyone laughed."

With his pointy eyebrows and soft chin, Sid reminded Evan of a snail. Evan told him to write the T-17 on Rosie, he'd personally back him up on it. But Sid had to strengthen his leadership skills. It wasn't done by yelling at people but by example. Sid thanked his supervisor and walked out. Evan checked his watch—four twenty-five. Maybe Karen Clendenin wasn't coming in for her customary one-on-one. For the past three weeks she'd stopped by for a chat, and they were getting to know each other. He finished off his day in conference with Bernie Terwilliger, going over the problems the evaluators had encountered during the week. Was it at all possible, Evan asked, to give Sid a new billet, Assistant to the Director of Westgate, and hire someone to take his place as an evaluator? The man wasn't all that good with people, actually he was poor with people; but he had a brilliant mind for administration.

"Evan, the state doesn't want me to hire, they want me to cut!" Bernie interjected. "Budget overruns, it's all you hear out of Albany these days."

Ten minutes later Evan left the old roller-skating rink. Going out just ahead of him—he couldn't have planned it better; then again, maybe he wasn't the one who'd planned it—was Karen. In the parking lot, he called her name. She stopped; it was a windy, chilly day, and she was wearing her coat snugly belted.

"Oh, Evan," she said, as if surprised.

He walked up to her, stopping six or seven feet away. Going too close, too soon, was disrespectful; you never wanted to invade someone's space, especially a woman's. "How about a cup of coffee?"

"Love one."

It was agreed they would take their separate cars and meet at the diner in Ambrose Plaza. Evan led the way out of the Westgate parking lot, heading toward the center of town. At the corner of Main Street and N. Elm, he stopped for a traffic light, making a left when it changed. Karen followed along.

Passing P&B's he slowed—it was a busy intersection with no traffic signal—and glancing in his rearview mirror, Evan caught her reflection. She had a certain allure—a conventional, level-headed woman who had suppressed her sexuality all of her adult life and was now dying to let go. At this point, post Chloe, just what he wanted. Crazy fucking Albanian belly dancer! The savagery of her attack on "Prurience," the devastation, had stunned him. He had called her the next day and his instinct was right. She said she had done it. His immediate impulse was retaliation: pure, unadulterated, physical; but a saner part of him had stepped in. There were better ways to get back, safer ways, like bringing charges. Then why wasn't he bringing them?

Evan came back to more pleasurable pursuits. His eyes again went to the rearview mirror, and he lifted his hand and waved. Smiling, Karen waved back. In a couple of days he'd invite her to supper, tell her to bring the kids. Best way he knew to build trust, confidence in a woman. Next time, they'd have dinner out, then sip a brandy at the house to Debussy's *L'Après-midi d'un Faune*. They were at the Ambrose Plaza and Evan turned on his directional signal. Final thought on the topic. If Karen was as ready to kick her rigid Catholic lifestyle as eagerly as he imagined—did he really have any doubts?—he might just ask her to accompany him to Corfu.

CHAPTER
26

The rain was coming down hard as Rick and Lisa, home from the high school, ran to the house one afternoon in late March. Great sheets of water were sweeping in from the west. Once inside, Lisa continued upstairs. Rick took off his raincoat, then tore off two sections of paper toweling in the kitchen and dried his hair and face.

"Will it ever stop?" Chloe asked from the living room.

"Later tonight, they're saying."

"Bring me a glass of wine, would you?"

"Sure."

He poured wine, made himself a bourbon, and went in, handing her a long-stemmed glass. Lying by her chair was Waldo. Rick put his drink on the mantel and began the makings of a fire. "How was your day?"

"Not good," Chloe replied. "The rain frightens me."

"It happens every year, and I don't think this is a bad one." He carried his glass to the sofa. "Besides, you like rain. Remember in Woodbridge when we ran around naked in a downpour? The kids were little. They were laughing, we all were—"

"Rachel called."

She was the older of his two sisters. "Oh?"

"She wants me to come out for a visit. She'd pay for the ticket."

"That might be a good thing, a change of scenery." Rick had a taste of his drink.

"I'm not going," Chloe said.

"Why not? Chicago's a great city."

"I'm just not up to it."

The fire was starting to catch. "Well, we're safe here," Rick said. "There's nothing to worry about."

■ ■ ■

At ten that evening he wrote his comment on a student's analysis of Whitman's poem "When Lilacs Last in the Dooryard Bloom'd," and closed his briefcase. Eleven papers, enough for one night; it was amazing he'd got through three. He went into the kitchen. Even standing next to the pendulum clock, he could barely hear the ticking. He looked out at the rain-laden night, trying to bring back his earlier confidence. Right now he had the sensation of being on a rudderless ship, a derelict on the high seas.

He went upstairs, saw light in his son's room but not his daughter's, and he opened her door. She was in bed, sleeping— at least something resembling a body was beneath the blanket. Rick went in, saw (in fact) it was Lisa. He left her room, knocked on his son's door.

At his desk, Andrew was cutting 4"x5" rectangles from a large piece of cardboard. He was in the process of producing golf cards, similar in many ways to baseball cards. Scattered all over his desk were photos of Hogan, Sarazan, Byron Nelson, Nicklaus, Watson, Johnny Miller, Hagen, Vardon, Bobby Jones, Sneed, Palmer. The boy's motives weren't a mere love of the game and its legendary players; he wanted to make money, so when he was old enough to play on the PGA Tour he'd have financial backing. Where his son got his entrepreneurial flair, Rick didn't know—certainly not from him.

"You're coming right along, it looks great," he said. "But it's time to turn in."

"OK."

"Good night, Andrew."

On the landing Rick saw a light under the master-bedroom door; he tapped and went in. Chloe was in bed, arms crossed over her chest, trembling, as if she were having a chill. Rick went over to her, sat on the edge of the bed, and put his hand on her upper arm. "What is it?"

"Stay with me, Rick."

"You know where I am, just give a shout." He straightened her blankets. "See you in the morning."

He gave the hunting dog-cum-psychotherapist a glance and went out. On the main floor he washed up, took off his shoes and pants, and crawled under the blanket on his cot. He lay on his back staring at the ceiling, hearing the rain as it came down, doubtful he'd fall asleep....

■ ■ ■

But eventually he did, and somewhere in the early hours, Rick awakened. That sound, what was it? Then he knew: it was the absence of sound. What he was hearing was silence. Grateful the storm was over, he tried a new position hoping to get comfortable, but his mind immediately began working, telling him to go upstairs. Rick rolled out his feet, wincing as he pulled on his trousers—the cot was killing his back—and climbed to the second floor.

The door to her room was open and, glancing in, he was alarmed to see Chloe at the window, barefoot, in her thin gown, arms clasped over her chest. He went over to her, saying her name.

She spun about, a terrified look in her eyes. "Don't light any lanterns!"

He had a lantern in the shed he hadn't used in fifteen years. "All right."

"He's out there," Chloe said.

"Who is?"

"The midnight paddler!"

Indulging her, he looked out the narrow window. Clouds thinning rapidly, full moon unfurling a gold sash across the inundated land. "I don't see anyone."

"Stay with me, Rick. Here, in bed with me."

Tired of refusing her, and sleep-deprived in any case, he led her away from the window, slipped off his pants, and got under the covers. They didn't talk, and in time her breathing became steady and he seemed to think she was asleep. He fell asleep also. When he awoke at dawn, Chloe was close to him, her hand on his chest, eyes open.

"Good morning, Rick."

"Good morning."

And she began kissing him.

■ ■ ■

At seven thirty he dragged on pants and a flannel shirt and went downstairs, put on coffee, and let Waldo out, watching him give chase to a muskrat on the floodwaters, once the oxbow. Dog was a great swimmer but no match for this glossy-coated fellow with the swooshing tail who could do amazing things like, well, disappear. Rick sat down to breakfast with his children who complained about the two-hour delay. School should be canceled, they said. What about the kids who lived across the river? Rick said he didn't know. There were alternate routes to get into Appleton. It was a town on a hill, and rain delays were scarce. In the years they had lived here, only one that he recalled.

He brought Chloe a tray, coffee and toast. She thanked him and he went back down and reread the final chapters in *Walden,* sent Andrew out the door to catch his bus, and told Lisa he'd be driving her to the high school in twenty minutes. Upstairs, Rick showered and shaved, then went into the bedroom. Chloe was in a half-sitting position, her eyes partially closed. She'd had a couple of bites of toast, drunk a third of her coffee. He began dressing, tucked his shirt into a pair of trousers, and grabbed a sports jacket from his closet.

Stopping by the bed on the way out, he spoke to her quietly.

"I'll be home by four thirty."

Smiling faintly, "See you then."

"What are you going to do today?" he asked.

"Nothing special, rest, catch up on some sleep."

"Sounds good. Do you want to keep your tray?"

"Put it aside for now, would you?"

Rick set it on her nightstand. Her hands were folded on her stomach, and it was then he noticed the ring, her wedding band, on the same finger as her Corfu ruby. Deep, powerful feelings stirred in his chest. He kissed Chloe and left for the day.

CHAPTER
27

Entering his third-floor classroom in the Humanities Building a few minutes before three, Professor Rick Forrester crossed to one of its tall windows and viewed the land west of Appleton, or the great body of water it had become—recalling, as he stood there, how he had awakened in the middle of the night to see his wife at their bedroom window shivering in a thin gown. Alarmed, but not surprised—nothing Chloe did surprised him anymore—he had gone to her side, only to have her turn on him and command: "Don't light any lanterns! He's out there!" What was out there was a pounding March rain and impenetrable darkness, and taking her by the arm Rick led her back to bed.

He remembered how he had awakened at dawn, realizing where he was. Chloe's hand was on his chest and she reached up and touched his lips, kissed his ear. He didn't know, he really couldn't say, as they held each other there in the early light, if it presaged a new beginning for her, for them. He hoped, he wanted to believe it did. Now, he was about to start his last class of the day at Appleton State.

All of his students had come in and he broke away from his thoughts and moved to the loose circle of chairs in the room. "Today we're finishing *Walden*," he began, talking to the eleven young men and women in his seminar in Great American Writers. "This morning as I was reviewing the final chapters I came upon the line where Thoreau says, 'I never knew, and never shall know, a worse man than myself.' What does this say about Thoreau's opinion of himself? Is he saying he's lazy and worthless, floating around Walden Pond all day in his boat?"

Several hands went up. Rick called on Alan Garry, an earnest young man with a pitted complexion and pale, thinning hair. "It doesn't mean Thoreau thought badly of himself. He sees himself for who he is. No better or worse than anyone."

Rick liked the comment, and a good discussion followed; the class went along well. With ten minutes left, he raised a question on the last line in the book, "The sun is but a morning star." "How is it significant as the summing up of *Walden*?" he asked his students.

Several hands went up. That same moment a man in the blue uniform of the campus police entered the room. "Professor Forrester?" he inquired.

"Yes."

"Please dismiss your class and come with me."

"What's going on?"

"Just dismiss your class, sir."

Rick told his students to go ahead with their reading in Thoreau, specifically "Civil Disobedience." He'd see them next week. He picked up his briefcase and walked over to the policeman. "What's this all about?"

"I'll be driving you to your house," the officer said.

"Why?"

"I'm following orders, sir."

They walked into the corridor—with classes in session it was oddly quiet—then down three flights of stairs to the lobby of Humanities. Parked directly outside was a white cruiser with blue trim and the seal of the State University of New York on the door. Rick slid into the passenger's seat and the car began moving slowly along a campus walkway. Soon the driver turned onto a college thoroughfare, picked up speed, merged onto Main Street in Appleton. At the minipark he braked for a traffic light, made a right onto N. Elm, then a left on Hazel. Rick felt chilled even as sweat was building up on his chest, under his arms. Hazel hit Elting Street, and in minutes the campus policeman was pulling into Rick's driveway.

Three squad cars were parked in it; official vehicles were also on the street, including the Appleton Rescue Squad ambulance. Rick got out, ran past the garage/shed to the deck stairs. Waldo was barking in his pen. Rick pushed open the back door to the house. His son was sitting with a female officer in the living room.

A young man, also in the brown and tan of the Appleton Police, was standing by the kitchen range. "Professor Forrester?"

"Yes."

"It is my duty to—tell you—that—"

"Yes—?"

"—your wife—"

"What? Say it!"

"—is dead."

Rick reached out, took hold of the counter to steady himself. "What happened?"

"That's all I can tell you. Detective Sergeant Skeen is upstairs investigating."

Rick dropped his briefcase beneath the pendulum clock, walked into the living room, and sat with his son, holding him, trying to comfort him and to gain control of himself. Andrew had an empty, faraway look on his face; he said nothing, never moved. Rick pressed his son's upper arms, his shoulders, then left him with the woman and went into the front hall, turning at the stairs. An officer in eyeglasses stood just outside the master bedroom, but to Rick he appeared at the top of a steep hill. When he got to the landing, Rick said who he was. The officer gave a somber nod. Rick thought he might say, "You can look," but he said nothing and Rick, preparing himself, looked on his own.

In jeans and a blue shirt, Chloe lay face down on the floor, head twisted to the side. One of her arms was tucked under her chest; the other, stretched out, extended off the carpet, her fingers almost touching a small, jagged hole in the floor. Close by lay Rick's shotgun. Through the shredded material in the center of his wife's back, raw flesh protruded. The slanted part of the ceiling was dotted with pellet holes and splattered with blood, bits of flesh, cloth fibers, in an area the size of a bicycle wheel. A copy of *Golf Magazine* lay near the gun.

Several people were in the room; some wore uniforms, others civilian clothes. Rick broke away, stumbled the length of the landing to the bathroom. He lowered his head at the sink, cupped cold water in his hands and splashed his face, rubbed it vigorously with a towel, then caught his reflection in the mirror. Rick struggled to take a full breath. He gasped, half-choking, feeling ill. Somehow he managed to gain control of his emotions and left the bathroom. He saw two men in the bedroom doorway: one corpulent, dressed in a blue sharkskin suit; the other tall, wiry, with an almost skeletal face, in tan gabardine.

"Professor Forrester?" said the heavy man as Rick walked up.

"Yes."

"I'm Dr. Russo, Ulmer County Medical Examiner. First, let me say I'm deeply grieved. Please accept my sincere feelings of sorrow." Dr. Russo gestured to the man on his left. "This is Detective Sergeant Skeen, Appleton Police Department."

The officer mumbled something by way of expressing sympathy; or perhaps it wasn't sympathy. Rick didn't like him and he didn't like Rick.

"When did it happen?" Rick asked Dr. Russo.

"One and a half to two hours ago. Your son came home from school and found her. He had the presence of mind to call Emergency Central."

Rick closed his eyes, fingers pressing into his forehead.

"If I might ask you a few questions, Professor Forrester," Dr. Russo said. "How would you describe your wife's mental state over the past weeks or months?"

"Sometimes she was afraid, other times perfectly normal. It—it fluctuated," Rick said.

"Had she ever mentioned suicide, talked about it?"

"Not to me."

"Was she menopausal?"

"No. At thirty-nine? No."

Dr. Russo glanced at Skeen. "Darryl, I have to run. A farmhand in Crawfordville, burning brush, tripped and fell into the fire." He gestured to the bedroom, telling Skeen he could release the body.

"OK, Dr. Russo."

"Good day, Professor," the county official said, "and again, my condolences." He started down; a heavy man, he still moved quickly.

Detective Sergeant Skeen slipped a small spiral notebook and a mechanical pencil from his inner jacket pocket. He had a fishhook-shaped scar on his chin; a tattoo on the back of his right hand depicted a coiled rattlesnake. He asked Rick how he'd spent his day.

"At the college."

"Did you come home for lunch, or for any other reason?"

"No."

"Can you identify the weapon?"

"It's my shotgun."

"Was it available to your wife?"

"Yes."

"Where was it kept?"

"In her closet."

The detective's front teeth, top and bottom, angled inward in a kind of reverse buck. "Any reason it was stored there?"

"She asked for it, so that was where I put it."

"Why did she ask for it?"

"She wanted protection."

"From?"

"She never said."

"Was the gun loaded?"

"No."

"Were shells available?"

"Yes, on a shelf in her closet."

"How many?"

"Two."

Skeen tucked away the notebook. "Do you have any questions?"

"That jagged hole in the floor," Rick said, pointing. "What is it?"

"Your wife apparently test-fired the shotgun before turning it on herself," Skeen said.

"*Test-fired it?*"

"Yes, it's not uncommon with suicides."

"How so?" Rick said.

"Suicidal individuals are besieged by insecurity, fear, doubt," Skeen said. "They want to make sure the gun works."

"My wife was familiar with the gun," Rick said. "She'd fired it many times."

"You're trying to say something, Professor," Skeen said.

Resenting the detective's patronizing tone, Rick said it might look like a suicide but he wasn't sure it was.

"You have a right to your opinion. It's a suicide," Skeen said.

"I think you're wrong."

"No husband likes admitting that his wife killed herself," Skeen said.

There came a clacking of the front-door knocker. The door opened and Sara and Stan Silverman came in with the chairman of the English Department, Albert Dollar. Sara was Chloe's closest friend in the community and Stan, an Appleton attorney, had done the closing on the house five years ago.

"Anything else, Professor?" Skeen said.

"I'd like my wife's rings," Rick said. "Also the magazine—"

"You'll have the rings. The gun and magazine go to the state lab in Albany," the detective said. "I'll get them back to you in two to three weeks."

The men exchanged penetrating last looks. Halfway down the stairs, Rick heard a commotion at the back door. His daughter Lisa was rushing in, sobbing uncontrollably.

■ ■ ■

Twenty minutes later Albert Dollar was asking Rick if he and the kids would be staying someplace else that night. Martha and he had plenty of room—

"We'll be driving to my mother's in Woodbridge," Rick said.

"Good, nothing like family. Rick, there's no rush, take all the time you want. We'll cover your classes."

"Thanks, Albert."

In the living room, Sara Silverman was holding Lisa, who was still crying. Andrew sat on Sara's other side, his eyes dry, staring at the wood-burning stove. Upstairs, two men in dark clothes were carrying Chloe's body, in a maroon bag strapped to a chrome stretcher, down the stairs. Rick walked into the hall. A police officer opened the door and the men went through, then wheeled the stretcher to a black station wagon parked on Elting Street. They slid the body in and the car pulled away. Rick stood in the doorway staring at the vacated spot.

PART II

CHAPTER
28

Too many people were at Lash's Funeral Home in Woodbridge to fit inside the main parlor, so upwards of one hundred stood outside. Lawrence Davidson, Rick's brother-in-law, gave the eulogy. The forty-nine-year-old banker recalled the time when he and Holly had visited the Forresters shortly after they had moved to Appleton. On a fine October afternoon they all drove into the Shagg Range and walked on a wooded trail. At one point he and Rick were thirty or forty steps ahead, and looking back he saw Chloe, with Lisa, Andrew, and Holly, and in Chloe's hand was a bough of red and yellow leaves, and she was laughing. It was the brightest, happiest laugh Larry had ever seen or heard, and it was the way he would always remember Chloe Forrester, as a totally alive and vivacious woman.

After the service, many extended their sympathy to Rick and his children, introducing themselves as Chloe's clients, professional associates, old friends from Queens.

■ ■ ■

Later, a smaller group gathered at the home of Rick's mother in Woodbridge. Margaret Forrester had prepared a smoked Virginia ham with scalloped potatoes and string beans and a huge salad, and there was plenty to drink. Rick spent a good deal of time with Chloe's mother, her three brothers, and two sisters, all of whom were in profound emotional agony. How could it have happened? That was all they wanted to know. Efet Cika, a little woman whose dark hair hadn't a strand of gray, said she had read ominous signs in her coffee grounds a few weeks ago. A dark presence, a man with evil intentions, had invaded her daughter's life. One thing she knew, Chloe had not killed herself. She loved her children too much to take so final a step.

The eldest daughter, Harmonia, said she had checked Chloe's stars on the day of her death. The heavens on that afternoon were brutally aligned for those born under the sign of Aries. Such individuals were in huge emotional turmoil between one and three p.m. Added to those troubling signs, Harmonia went on, were Chloe's personal struggles—her dashed hopes, her remorse—and the poor dear girl had nowhere to turn. At the end all she wanted was to escape her pain.

The family looked at Rick. What did he think? If anyone should know, shouldn't he?

It was nothing he could prove, he said, but he believed that someone had come into the house. Terrified, Chloe took the shotgun from her closet. They struggled—she and the intruder—and the gun went off. "There's a hole in the floorboards testifying to it," Rick said. "The man positioned her over the barrels and pulled the trigger."

"If it was a handgun, I could see your scenario played out," Zino Cika, the middle brother, said. He was a wiry man with a middle-European nose and narrow, intense eyes; he had often visited Rick and Chloe when they lived in Woodbridge. "But to position a frantic woman over the barrels of a shotgun—"

"—would take a strong man," Rick said.

"Did the cops see anything suspicious when they came to the house?"

"No."

"What about the hole in the floor?"

"Suicides often 'test fire' a gun, the detective told me."

"Rick, shouldn't you be talking to the police?"

"When and if I have something tangible to offer them. Right now all I have is conjecture," Rick said. "Suicide in a family spreads around a lot of guilt. I could be making a murder out of a suicide. Why? Because murder is easier to live with. But that morning, my last morning with Chloe, it was as if we were starting over. We'd come full circle and now we were picking up pieces of our lives."

Efet Cika began to weep. Harmonia took her mother in her arms, caressing her, speaking to her softly. And the brothers Cika came over to Rick.

■ ■ ■

In the early afternoon of the third day at Margi's, Rick drove to Appleton and parked in his Elting Street driveway. He had a job to do, a job he dreaded but felt compelled to perform. Wanting to give himself a little time before starting in, he walked along the top of the embankment. The water had subsided; about eighty percent of the land, once covered, was land again. All along the downslope, the high-water level had left a brown, horizontal line, reminding him of the murky stain on ships' hulls in dry dock. The oxbow, subsumed by last week's cloudy sea, was beginning to regain its shape as a crescent moon.

Enough procrastination. On the kitchen counter, when he went in, lay a note-sized piece of paper. He read the words written on it: "Dear Rick, Lisa, and Andrew—We sang and prayed and felt a sweet Life Force returning to the house. Welcome home! Sara, Stan, and Albert."

As Sara was leaving that day, Rick recalled, she had asked for a spare key. She and Stan would like to come in while he and the kids were away. Why, he didn't know, and didn't ask. Rick set the note down, continued through to the front hall, and climbed the stairs. When he reached the second-floor landing, he stopped at the master-bedroom doorway, prepared himself, and looked in. The first thing he saw, on Chloe's bureau, was an Easter lily. His eyes rose to the ceiling: spackled smooth, painted. On the floor, in place of the stained oat carpet, lay a new shag rug, a calming blue-gray.

Rick stood on the threshold, deeply moved by the kindness

of his friends. But another emotion began to sweep in, crushingly. All along he had thought of the task as a way to purge his excruciating guilt. He felt cheated. The obligation to clean his wife's blood had been taken from him. His last and only immediate connection to her death was gone. In front of the Cika family he had spoken of an intruder; someone had come in and killed Chloe. But it wasn't so; he was only trying to deny the horrid reality.

Rick walked about the house hoping to sense a sweet Life Force in the air; he didn't sense it. In the fireplace room, on the small table with sweetheart roses hand-painted around the edge, he spotted Chloe's appointment book. He picked it up, glanced at a few names, set it back down—and had to leave, or break entirely down. Soon he was parking in front of 97 N. Elm. On the way in he checked his mailbox: empty. Knocked on the landlady's door. Mrs. Delvecchio appeared in a pale, washed-out housedress, her musty hair carelessly pinned.

"What-a you want?"

"I'm leaving."

"When?"

"By the end of the month."

"You owe me the extra."

"Why?"

"Destruction of property."

"Mrs. Delvecchio, I improved your property," Rick said. "When I moved in, it was a garbage dump."

"You put nails in the wall."

"I'll pull them out."

Rick climbed the stairs, went by the light blue door without looking at it, unlocked his attic door. Scattered inside lay a dozen pieces of mail. He picked them up, depositing them on the coffee table. Three or four envelopes were hand-scripted; one had no stamp on it and only his first name. He sat on the sofa, opened the envelope, and took out a card depicting a mountain lake in early summer. Inside: "Dear Rick, I was very upset, shocked beyond belief, to learn about Chloe. May God bless you and your children and guide you through this tragedy. Love, Noreen."

He read the other notes, then stood and looked about his garret. Once his home. Giving himself a push, he began the dismantling. Unloading shelves in the kitchen, putting canned goods and cereals on the table, saving what he could in the refrigerator, emptying his closet and laying his clothes on the bed, clearing personal effects from the bathroom. Next to his well-used toothbrush was a green one, like new. He held it for a second, then tossed it in the trash with a tired bar of soap.

∎ ∎ ∎

Two days later he and his kids and Waldo moved back into the Elting Street house, and the following day, unseasonably cold, Rick resumed his job at the college. His colleagues were generous in their offers of support and he particularly thanked his chairman, Albert Dollar, for granting him time...and for coming by with the Silvermans and taking an oppressive task off his hands. He was deeply appreciative....

CHAPTER
29

Coming home from the college one afternoon in mid-April, Rick saw his daughter on the stairway going up to her room. He called out to her. Stopping, one hand on the banister, "Hi, Daddy. An Appleton policeman was just here asking for you," she said. "He had the shotgun and wanted me to take it. Like he almost shoved it at me!"

"What did he look like?"

"He was tall, he had a weird scar on his chin. I told him to put the gun on your workbench."

"I'm sorry about that, Lisa."

"Daddy, get rid of it, will you? Having it around gives me the creeps!"

"I will. Promise."

Angered by the incident, Rick went down the deck steps and slid open the shed door. There, on his bench, lay his Beretta and a plastic evidence bag containing Andrew's golf magazine and a couple of 20-gauge casings. Gun gave him the creeps as well. He stowed it, closed the door. As he was leaving the shed he decided to bring the magazine inside for Andrew, but as he pulled it from the bag he began having second thoughts. Maybe it wasn't a good idea. And when he saw that the lower corner was stained a dark reddish brown, he was convinced of it.

But questions—questions Andrew refused to answer— lingered, troubling Rick. If Andrew had called to his mother, something he usually did when coming home from school, and she hadn't responded, what would he think? He would think she was sleeping, or maybe out taking a little walk. With that line of reasoning, Andrew wouldn't have "found" her at all, at least not so quickly. But he *had* found her, and Rick could only assume that Andrew had had a special reason for going upstairs to see her beyond merely saying, "Hi, Mom." And, seeing his mother lying on the floor, he froze, and the magazine fell from his hands....

In a quandary, Rick flipped idly through the pages, seeing the various articles—how to get ten extra yards on your drives, the tried and true way to get out of a bunker—but gave them no heed, lost as he was in the mystery of that afternoon. About to toss the magazine into a trash basket, Rick glimpsed a section called CHAMPS' CLINIC—queries by amateur golfers to well-known pros and the pros' answers. It seemed like an interesting feature, and out of curiosity Rick read the first query.

Dear Johnny,

I'm twelve, playing in the low-80s, and I had one 77 this year and a couple of 78s, and a hole in one too! My dream is to play on the PGA Tour. What advise can you give me to help make my dream come true?

Sincerely,
Andrew Forrester

His eyes blurring, clouding, Rick struggled through the pro's reply:

Dear Andrew,

When I was your age I had the same dream. Don't lose it—always keep it before you. As to what you can do to prepare for a Tour career: practice hard, play by the rules, lead a healthy life, and above all make it fun! Hoping to see your name on the Leader Board soon.

Johnny Miller

■ ■ ■

A village employee was working on the planters, cleaning them and putting in flowers, as Lisa, with two Appleton High classmates, approached the minipark. One of the girls, Monica Salem of the cerise hair and snug-fitting jeans, had shocked Lisa last fall when she said she'd first had sex when she was fourteen. She and Milo Balducci, a mechanic at King's Mobil, had done it on a blanket in the back of his pickup. Since then she'd slept with eleven different guys. She kept a list, a kind of scorecard, with their names on it—descriptions of their bodies and commentary on their techniques; plus she rated them, 1 to 10, as to how good they were. The best was Jeremy Hackman, a teaching assistant in the English Department at Appleton State, who scored a 9½. Lisa didn't believe everything that Monica said but she never questioned her, though eleven did seem a lot.

Muriel Lewis was altogether different. She played varsity soccer and was involved in student politics and the drama club. She wasn't hot-looking like Monica but was easier to be with, in Lisa's opinion, because she didn't have sex on the brain. Lisa put herself somewhere between the two. They all walked into Hobo Deli to get a soda and right away she thought she saw Greg at the counter buying a sandwich. But it wasn't. It was somebody who looked like Greg, with dark, heavy eyes and a beard, but not nearly so handsome.

Greg really didn't interest her anymore and she didn't want to start with him again. She almost wanted to run into him as a test—to listen to herself say no if he asked her to go hiking in the Shaggs.

Monica was broke and Muriel said she'd loan her a dollar. The man with the beard shuffled by, unwrapping his ham and cheese on a roll. Chuck, the chain smoker with the herky-jerky movements, was behind the counter, adding up the order of a woman with frantic eyes who, when she went to pay, couldn't locate her wallet inside her purse. Monica was muttering under her breath and the woman gave her a dirty look, and Lisa walked to the soda machine and dropped in two quarters, pushing the button for an Orange Crush. Opposite the machine was a cream and sugar bar and a display of coffee beans, all different blends. Three small tables, empty at the moment, occupied the floor near the bar. A man was filling a bag with beans; he sealed it and looked up. Her eyes met his. For a second he kind of stared; then his face broke into a big smile.

"Lisa!"

She was confused: knowing she should hate him for all that had happened, yet feeling a certain excitement. Controlling her emotions, "Hi, Evan."

He set down his purchase and came over, gave her a little-more-than-friendly hug. "It's wonderful seeing you. You're just getting prettier and prettier and prettier! How are you?"

Her thoughts, emotions, were totally jumbled. "I—I'm all right."

"I've been wanting to write you about your mom," he said, "and I still will. I'm just now getting over the shock. She was an extraordinary woman, very beautiful and very talented. It was a terrible loss."

Lisa didn't know what to say.

"What have you been up to?" Kendrix asked.

"Just, you know, going to school. Not too much."

"That was such a great comment you made about poetry, I'll never forget it," Evan said. "Andrew was talking about science and you said a poem could also get you to the moon."

The commotion in her chest was making her uneasy. "I remember."

"How is Andrew?"

"He—he's different. I hardly know him."

"An emotional blow like that, you don't get over it right away. It takes time. Tell him—" Evan's hand cradled her elbow,

"—tell him if he ever wants to talk, I'm a phone call away. Will you do that?"

"Sure."

He was smiling, but it was more than a smile; more than just friendliness. "Well, see you again, Lisa." Evan kissed the side of her face; his lip, just touching her ear, sent a tingle down her spine. Then he walked to the counter, paid for his coffee, and left the deli.

"Who was *that*?" Monica asked, coming over with Muriel.

"A friend."

"Some friend. How is he?"

"I wouldn't know."

"Right."

"Monica, chill, OK?" said Muriel.

The girls took their sodas outside. A minute later Evan glided through the intersection in his Porsche, giving Lisa a wave and a smile.

"He has to be a ten," Monica Salem said.

■ ■ ■

As he was correcting student essays in his living room one evening in early May, the phone rang. Rick went into the alcove and picked up. "Hello."

"Mr. Forrester?"

"Yes."

"This is Dick Flanders, director of our Junior Golf League. I'm calling because Andrew missed practice last Tuesday and Thursday and then again today."

"I didn't know that," Rick said.

"I know how much he loves golf, and frankly I'm confused," the director said. "I have him in the number-one spot in our opening match this Saturday against Ellentown. He's a great boy and a fine young player, Mr. Forrester. Is he all right? I know he lost his mother and I'm concerned and I just hope—"

"Thank you, Mr. Flanders," Rick said, breaking in. "Why he hasn't been at practice, I can't say. I'll have him call you."

Rick took down the man's number, thanked him again for his concern, and climbed the stairs to the second floor. Andrew's door was closed and he knocked and went in. The boy was at his desk, drawing a graph on lined paper.

"Mr. Flanders just called," Rick said. "Evidently you missed a couple of practices and he wanted to know why."

"I quit the team."

Rick took the loose clothes from a second chair, placed them on Andrew's bed, and sat down. "How come?"

"I don't want to play anymore."

"Did you tell Mr. Flanders?"

"No."

"Don't you think you should?"

"He's going to get the idea, isn't he?"

Rick was surprised at the comment, the derisiveness of it. "That's beside the point. The right thing to do is to call him."

"Dad, what difference does it make?"

"It makes a difference. Not to tell the coach you've quit is wrong. He's counting on you, Andrew."

The boy stared at the graph paper, unmoved.

"Quitting golf is your decision," Rick said. "I have no problem with that. What worries me is you."

"Well, don't worry. I'm OK."

"You might think so but you're not yourself."

The boy continued with his assignment.

"I'm talking to you, Andrew."

"I hear you."

"I saw your letter to Johnny Miller. That didn't seem like a kid who wanted to quit."

Andrew's pencil lay on his desk; his eyes stayed on the graph.

"What is it? Tell me, Andrew."

"It's nothing."

"Well, I've been in touch with a therapist. I've met with him," Rick said. "He's a kind, understanding man. His name is Desmond Street, and he'd like to sit down with you and have a good, easy-going talk."

"I'm not going, I'm not doing it!"

Rick was stunned by the outburst. "Then talk to me."

The boy turned in his chair, facing his father. With great feeling, he blurted out, "None of this had to happen!"

Rick spoke calmly without feeling calm. "But it happened, Andrew. It's terrible for all of us."

"Why didn't you do something?"

"I left my apartment, I was here for you and Lisa, I did everything I could for Chloe."

"You walked out on us!"

"Your mother wanted to be with Evan. What could I do, Andrew? Ground her like Lisa?"

"You could've gotten in his Porsche, driven to his house, and rammed it through his door!"

I could have, Rick thought. I didn't.

Andrew reached out and yanked his father's Navy Cross from the wall, slapping it down on his desk. "I don't want this anymore. I don't believe you even won it!"

The comment stung, and Rick had an impulse to respond in anger. He kept his emotions in check. "I'm sorry that's how you feel," he said. "Good night, Andrew."

Leaving the medal where it lay, he walked out.

CHAPTER
30

The geraniums were in full bloom in the minipark as Rick turned at the corner and looked for a parking spot on Main Street close to Ulmer County Savings. Nothing. But across Main he spotted one. He made a u-turn, pulling to the curb in front of the large Victorian house, one of the truly handsome houses in Appleton but run down, badly in need of repair. He'd heard talk that the bank had acquired it, not to restore but to raze, needing space for employee parking.

Rick got out of his station wagon and waited for a break in the traffic, college paycheck in his pocket. Fridays the bank stayed open until six, and by the time and temperature display above the entrance, it was 5:33p/68°.

Just as he was about to cross, someone was calling his name. He turned, looking in the direction of the shout. Coming toward him, on the sidewalk sloping up from the Walloon River, was Greg Horboychuk. Rick hadn't seen him since their mano a mano in the mountains.

The veteran extended his hand. Cautiously, Rick put out his: he could find himself flat on his back, a knife at his throat. "My heart goes out to you, man. I heard about it," Greg said.

"Thank you."

"Society's fucked—it makes people do crazy things," Greg said. "I've been sitting by the river, trying to fathom what it all means. God damn war! It killed so many of us. One morning the Good Shepherd disappears. Like vanishes. Then Jean-Jean the Artist splits for Haight-Ashbury. Now they have him in the slammer on willful indifference to human life."

"What happened?"

"They're saying he laid some heavy shit on his girlfriend and she o.d.'d."

"That's not good," Rick said.

"Dynamite chick, went to Appleton."

Something clicked in Rick's head. "Do you know her name?"

"Christine."

Rick felt a painful wrench in his stomach. "How did you find out?"

"Word travels."

"Greg, I have to run."

"Can you give me something, man?"

"Haven't got it today."

Rick hurried back to the corner, then walked quickly on N. Elm to his old rooming house, thinking the police had nailed the wrong man in Christine's death; and so it went on. One woman at a time. He knocked on the light blue door. It opened; standing inside, looking out at him, was Crusher, in black trousers and an orange rayon shirt. A glum Crusher.

"Hey, Rick."

"I just got word."

"Come on in. The girls left for White Plains about an hour ago."

"How are they?"

"Wiped, totally out of it. Lemme getcha a beer."

"No, thanks."

"I've been on the road," Crusher said. "When I come in around four, they was both beside theirselfs. What in hell's going on? So they tell me. Christine had a bad trip on the Coast. Her friend, that pothead who says he's an artist? He rushed her to the hospital. Too late."

Crusher had a swig from the bottle of St. Pauli Girl in his hand. "Christine's old lady called Nory's mom. Thing is, I had good news. Remember I was telling yuh about Dover? Every piece fell into place—it's a done deal. Four hundred thousand big ones comin' my way. And I din't even have a chance to tell Maria! Anyways, all Christine's old friends and classmates are gettin' together. I'm leavin' in twenty minutes. Come on down wit me."

"I don't think so, Crusher."

"Why not?"

"I wouldn't fit in."

"What are yuh talkin' about?"

"I'm not one of Christine's old friends or classmates."

"So? You're Nory's friend, right? Maria's friend, my friend."

"I haven't seen Noreen for a while, it might be awkward," Rick said.

"Fuck awkward! How do yuh think I nailed Dover? Yuh gotta go after what yuh want. In case yuh din't know, some towhead lawyer's makin' moves on her. Two minutes after I meet him, right here in the apartment, he tells me he's a Rhodes Scholar. Hello, my name is Cliff Bremmer, I'm a Rhodes Scholar. I mean what kind of asshole is that? Nory Russell is one in a million, Rick. I heard your wife was a beautiful woman and Kendrix come by and snaked her away, no sweat. If I was goin' wit Nory and the likes of Cliff Bremmer was sniffin' aroun'? He'd be one sorry son-of-a-bitch he was ever fuckin' born!"

"I'm not going with Noreen," Rick said.

"Not now, but you was. You think the spark is dead?"

"Crusher, I have to run. Extend my condolences."

Rick went out, hurried along. When he arrived at Ulmer County Savings, the assistant manager, a woman with skinny legs in a chocolate-brown suit, was walking away from the glass doors, keys dangling in her hand. Rick rapped on the glass but she didn't even turn, just gave her keys a shake.

Enraged, he wanted to break down the door, chase after her. Give her a piece of his mind. It took him a few moments to collect himself. He was late; the woman was doing her job.

CHAPTER
31

Rick began the job of restoring Chloe's old office by tearing down the warped, water-damaged sheetrock, then extracting the ruined insulation and shoving all the debris into a couple of trash barrels and several lawn-and-leaf bags, and carrying everything out to his station wagon. He drove three miles to the Appleton Land Fill, a stretch of barren, smoking land. A great battle might've just taken place; a thick, disagreeable odor hung in the air.

Rick followed a badly rutted road to an area designated "BURNABLES." A huge man on a bulldozer was leveling trash nearby, all the while keeping an eye on his territory, in case anyone was dumping in the wrong place. Rick, evidently, was, because the man, a latter-day Genghis Kahn astride a snorting steed, bellowed, "That shit don't go there, Mac! Over there! 'DISPOSABLES!'"

Rick did as commanded, left the war zone with a minor grazing only, then stopped by True Value in the village and bought the material he needed. Back home, he carried everything into the basement, positioned his stepladder....

■ ■ ■

Spring came to Appleton. On the oxbow, turtles at the end of their long cold sleep found tufts of matted grass to sun themselves on, their shells shining like mirrors. Ducklings, smaller than tennis balls, followed tightly behind their mother. Muskrats plied back and forth between shores, as if paying visits to in-laws or neighbors. Canada geese were coming in for evening landings, splashing down, a raucous group. A big snapper was prowling. It moved ponderously along; every so often its head, shaped like an anvil, would appear, a foot ahead of its hulking shell.

Rick thought it would be nice having dinner with his kids on the glass-topped table on the deck—hamburgers on the grill, a big salad. But his kids weren't enthused. He had no proof that Lisa was seeing Greg again but he knew his daughter; something was going on. Andrew—he didn't know what to think about Andrew. A second attempt to have him see a therapist had failed. Whatever was working inside the boy, he was keeping a lid on it.

■ ■ ■

Last day of the semester at Appleton State—warm, hardly a cloud in the sky, a perfect May afternoon. Rick got into his car behind Grove Hall and rolled past the fire house and police department to Main Street. The sidewalks were crowded with young people, in shorts and tops, enjoying the weather, talking, carrying on. Rick braked as two eighteen-year-old girls, holding hands, dashed across the street, then again as a kid in cut-off jeans and flowing hair sliced in front of him on a skateboard.

The crowd was especially heavy as Rick approached the minipark. Benches were taken and people, young and old, were standing about in the sun. Planters in full bloom: geraniums, petunias, marigolds. The traffic light at the intersection turned red. Roughly tenth in a line of vehicles from the light, Rick came to a full stop directly in front of The Roaring Twenties, and just coming out, a double-chocolate cone in one hand, a double strawberry in the other, was Evan Kendrix.

He lifted the chocolate cone, took a big lick, walked to the corner smiling. It was the smile of insouciance itself, of someone loving life and all the treats it offered. Rick had a flash urge to swerve out of line and run him down—screams, chaos, sirens. The light changed and he moved slowly along to the corner.

Turning onto N. Elm, Rick glanced through his passenger's

window at the gathering of people—and spotted Evan once again. He was talking with great ardor to a girl in jeans and a blue halter top—the recipient of the strawberry cone—his hand, that moment, touching her dark brown hair, brushing it intimately to the side. Rick had a peek of her young, smiling face, then had a second, closer look—blaring of horns, squealing of tires. He cut back into his own lane just in time to avoid a Budweiser truck. Next thing he knew he was in his driveway staring through his windshield at the hoof-cloven top of Chloe's convertible.

He made himself a vodka and tonic, sat on the deck, finished it and made another, remembering the day he'd waited for Chloe to come home after her first interview with a well-known, highly regarded Appleton psychiatrist, who she hoped would help her get started in her chosen career. She'd left the house a little before two and it was just five when she returned, telling Rick that she and Dr. Kendrix had hit it off really well.

"You must have."

"He offered to train me," Chloe said. "In time, if it goes well, he hopes to send me referrals."

"You were gone long enough."

"He has a private pond and a canoe. He took me for a paddle."

"How charming."

She bridled at the irony "What's your problem, Rick? I try to tell you good news and—"

"You were with him for three hours!"

Rick heard Lisa crossing the driveway, walking rapidly. She came up the deck steps, her bluejeans torn at one knee, a lot of skin showing at her stomach. Wrapped around her hand was the drawstring to her canvas book bag.

"Oh. Hi, Daddy," she said, brightly.

"Where've you been?"

"I stopped at the Appleton library and got a couple of books for my science report," Lisa said. "Then me and Monica walked down to the minipark and met some friends. How about you? Did you have a nice day?"

"What friends?"

"Kids from high school."

"Just kids from high school?"

"People came and went. There was a big crowd."

"Was Evan Kendrix there?"

Her complexion deepened. "I saw him."

"You had an ice-cream cone with him, Lisa."

"All right."

"So you lied to me."

"That's better than having you get all bent out of shape, isn't it?"

"I don't think so."

"He bought me a cone. Big deal."

"I saw how he touched your hair!"

"Next time I'll slap him across the face. OK?"

"There won't be a next time, Lisa."

He saw the look of defiance on her face. "Well, I have homework," she said, and made for the door.

"Whatever you're doing after school, wherever you're going, I want a note from you!" he shouted after her. "Do you understand?"

She didn't answer and he followed her in; she was halfway up the stairs. "Lisa, do you understand?"

"You want a note from me."

"I want the truth from you!"

He went back out, sat on the deck with his drink, thinking to grab his Beretta, drive to Kendrix's and end this outrage. Shout to Evan from his driveway and when he came out, let him have it, both barrels, shoot the predacious son-of-a-bitch down—Boom! Boom! There, god damn it, miserable bastard! Never again!

Rick was breathing heavily, his index fingers locked in the shape of a hook. Inside, he made a new drink.

■ ■ ■

At Commencement Exercises in late May the main speaker was U.S. Representative Martin Hoteling, who had graduated from Appleton State twelve years earlier. Always the environmentalist, he spoke about the need to balance economic growth with sound conservation measures. He urged everyone, regardless of career goals or political beliefs, to protect the nation's natural resources. Rick, sitting among his colleagues in the third row of folding chairs, thought the speech honest, pertinent, and, best of all, brief.

After the Rev. Harvey Sargent of the Reformed Church of Appleton bestowed a final blessing, guests and graduates began strolling about the college grounds, hugging and kissing one another, laughing; here and there students, in the arms of classmates they would likely never see again, cried openly. In the center of the great lawn, fifty tables were set up; staff personnel were in the process of distributing box lunches tied with red ribbon.

His obligation met, Rick walked toward Grove Hall, doctorally attired, greeting those students he knew, had taught through the years, now college graduates, all eager to have him meet their parents, grandparents, siblings. Which, patiently, he did. As he was nearing Grove, he saw Noreen in her cap and gown standing in the shade of a campus maple with Maria and Crusher, two older couples, Rick's colleague Terry Randolph, and a tall, good-looking man with blond hair, in white trousers and a Masters-green blazer who was holding Noreen's hand. The Rhodes Scholar.

Arrogant creep.

In his office on the second floor, Rick stowed his academic garb in the closet, then began giving the various circulars, letters, and announcements scattered about his desk an end-of-semester once-over; after a few minutes he swept everything into his wastebasket and walked out.

Ten minutes later he was parking at his house. A note on the kitchen counter caught his attention. He snatched it up. "Daddy, at Galaxy Shopping Center with Monica and her boyfriend. Home by four. Lisa."

He made himself a drink, took it outside, stood at the deck railing looking across the floodplain. *Galaxy Shopping Center, a.k.a. Evan Kendrix's pond.*

CHAPTER
32

Rick was driving north on Rt. 23 en route to see his old friend, the gunsmith Dave Ballard, who some years ago had sold him the Beretta. Dave would offer him something; it didn't matter to Rick how much. He just wanted the gun out of his life.

Once through Kingsley-on-Hudson, he picked up Rt. 26 and five miles outside of Woodbridge came to a small frame building, painted red, its roofline resembling a swayback horse. He pulled into the parking area, got out, and opened the back door of his station wagon. Lying on the seat was his Beretta, loosely wrapped in a blanket; on the floor were several boxes of shells. He grabbed the gun by its stock and walked to the door. A sign—**David Ballard, Gunsmith**—was artfully burned into a piece of oak. Tacked to the siding was a scrawled note: "Friday 3 p.m., had to close early. Open tomorrow at 10. Dave."

Rick uttered a mild oath. Next visit he'd use his brain and call ahead. He peered through the barred window at the interior of the shop: guns, some new but most from an earlier time, in racks, lying on the counter, standing in corners. As he was going back to his wagon, a dark gray pickup pulled in and a man with thin reddish hair and puffy, chipmunk cheeks stepped out.

"Dave left for the day," Rick said, pointing to the note.

"Oh. OK." His eyes flicked to Rick's gun. "Beretta, beautiful! What's the chokes onto it?"

"Modified and improved cylinder."

"Barrel length twenty-six inches, am I right?" He had a high, scratchy voice.

"You are."

"Would you mind?" He held out a hand with sausage-like

fingers.

Rick passed him the shotgun and the man weighed it, lifted it to his shoulder, swung it left and right. "You wouldn't be sellin' this," he said.

"Actually it's why I'm here."

"Whatcha want for it?"

"I don't have a figure," Rick said.

"Dave will offer you two hundred, I'll give you five. Cash on the barrelhead."

"I'd like to see Dave first."

He passed the Beretta to Rick, took a card from his wallet. "Do yourself a favor, gimme me a call. Within the week, six hundred." The man went to his pickup and drove off.

Rick glanced at the card. **Clarence Gunn, Firearms**. Then, below, "*Gunn's the Name, Guns Are My Business.*" He slid the card into his wallet, tucked the Beretta behind the driver's seat—realizing, right then, that he'd just had an opportunity to part with the Beretta, and for a good price; and had let it go by.

What's my problem? Rick thought, covering over the shotgun.

■ ■ ■

They were having a drumstick cookout on the deck, a light westerly breeze coming in, ducks swimming about on the oxbow, the maples on the lower property shading them from the dropping sun. As was their custom, Andrew cleared the table when they finished and Lisa helped with the dishes, telling her father that Muriel Lewis was having a party and she wanted to go to it.

"Is she the one with the purple hair?" Rick asked.

"No, that's Monica Salem."

"When's the party?"

"She said about eight."

"Whenever you're ready, I'll give you a lift."

"Dad, it's nothing. I'll walk."

"Are you sure?"

"It's not a problem."

He looked at his daughter, so wanting to believe her; the doubt, the worry, was killing him. "How will you be getting home?"

"Muriel has an older sister. She'll give me a lift."

■ ■ ■

Later that evening, when his preoccupation with Lisa didn't subside—when in fact it got unbearable—Rick decided to go out for an hour, hoping a change in environment would alter his mindset. He checked on Andrew, then drove into town, parked on lower Main, and walked up the street to P&B's. "A Cornerstone of Appleton" it said on the awning over the door. Rick went in, his first time in the establishment since early spring.

Two patrons were in Townies' Corner, the smaller part of the L-shaped bar, and several students and five or six working men stood at the longer section. Nolan Schrade, among the men, greeted him with a handshake.

"Rick, good seeing you. What a terrible thing for you and your kids."

"Good seeing you, Nolan."

"I always think of that day in the Medical Center. Your daughter was ready to scratch my eyes out. Feisty little bobcat! How's she doing?"

"About the same."

From Townies' Corner, The Walker gave him a smile barely discernable in the smoke surrounding her like a diaphanous shawl. Nolan said, "Let me buy you one, Rick."

But Tom Kellerhouse, the bartender and Rick's former student, was already setting down a rocks glass, amply filled with Wild Turkey 101. "On the house, Rick. Glad to see you up and about."

"Thanks, Tom."

"Next one's on me," Nolan said to the bartender. To Rick, "How's it going?"

"Not so great."

"Give it time. Time heals. One fine morning you'll be your old self again."

"Let's hope. What've you been doing, Nolan?"

"The old Garner Homestead on Route 207? Bricks was in sad shape. So that was what I done all day, pointed bricks. I had a good day."

Of all the times he'd had a drink with Nolan Schrade here in P&B's, Rick had never known the journeyman to have had anything *but* a good day. His life was a good day. Someone was tapping Rick's shoulder. "I'd like to give yeh my condolesons."

It was The Walker. "Thank you, Edna," he said.

"Life is full of heartache. If yeh ever want to talk or anythin', I've a place in the Walloon Trailer Park, 15A. Come by, we'll have a cup of coffee, whatever yeh'd like."

"That's kind of you."

"Well, good seeing yeh again, Rick."

She had a tug on her cigarette and drifted off. Once, here in P&B's, they'd talked. He'd stopped in for a drink after a night class, and she was standing at the bar having a Southern Comfort and smoking cigarette after cigarette. She wasn't thirty-five but was already haggard—bad teeth, rough skin, coarse brown hair. Whenever Rick saw her in town she was always walking, stepping along as if she had an important engagement and couldn't be late. Her name was Edna but he always thought of her as The Walker.

Tom came by and placed a second jigger in front of Rick, flipped it over. "On Edna."

Rick made a gesture of appreciation toward the smoke-clouded woman.

He continued talking with Nolan, working on his Wild Turkey—fearful Lisa wasn't where she said she'd be. Rick tried to suppress his thoughts, block them out. He had another taste of Wild Turkey; and the idea came to him. He only wondered why he hadn't thought of it before. He reached in his pocket for a dime and walked over to the pay phone near the door, found the Salems' number in the local phonebook dangling on a chain. A girl picked up. Loud background noise—music, laughter, talking.

"Monica?" Rick asked.

"No."

"Lisa Forrester, please."

"There's about a million kids here." The girl was giggling.

"Will you look for her?"

Giggle. "There's no way—stop it, Randy. Is there a message?"

"I'll call back."

He re-hooked the receiver, went back to his place beside Nolan and started on his second drink, Nolan's. They talked about the blight attacking area elms. Right now all elms in Ulmer County were stressed real bad, Nolan said. The beautiful elm in the minipark, right here in the village, was losing its leaves. He gave it another year.

"Like the chestnuts of an earlier day," Rick said.

Nolan gave his head a sad shake. "That was a great tree. All of 'em just died, like overnight."

The journeyman began a long story dealing with his father, the best damn worker he'd ever seen. Nolan thought *he* could put in a good day's work, his father put him to shame. One time when he was seventeen, working with his old man in town putting a new roof on the bank, what was then First Federal Bank of Appleton, he slipped and a bucket of mortar went tumbling and he almost went with it and his father fired him on the spot, and Nolan walked away and never worked with his old man again. But that man could work. He put his son to shame.

Rick finished Nolan's drink and started on The Walker's, becoming increasingly convinced that Lisa was at Evan's. He called the Salem house again, fumbling twice with the dial before getting it right. A boy answered and the party seemed quieter. Rick asked him if he'd seen Lisa.

"Who?"

"Lisa Forrester."

"She ain't here."

"Are you sure?"

"I'm sure."

"Was she ever there?"

"I didn't see her."

"Put on Monica."

"Right." The kid hung up.

Back at the bar Rick finished The Walker's drink, shoved some singles beneath his glass, and told Nolan he was leaving.

"Next time don't make yourself such a stranger."

"I won't. See you, Nolan."

"Don't forget your pipe."

"Oh. Thanks." He shoved it into his pocket.

"Safe trip home, Rick," the bartender said.

In his car he drove through the back streets of Appleton, upstairs at his house checked Lisa's bed, empty, behind the wheel again, drove down Elting Street. The great trees bordering the street resembled huge dinosaurs waiting to pounce. Rick crossed the bridge, following Rt. 289 toward the mountains at 30 m.p.h. He was drunk but he wasn't crazy. To get pulled over on a mission to save your daughter? No way. He would bring her home. Above him, on the great open road of the sky, boxy clouds tumbled along like tractor-trailers destined to crash and burn.

■ ■ ■

Evan had spent the evening with her, and now, at Karen Clendenin's car in his driveway, they kissed good night. She started the engine, waved, and drove away, her dimming tail lights reminding him of their relationship. He had asked her to come to Corfu with him, and she'd made the necessary arrangements, though she'd only be staying for two weeks; and he was thinking, now, even that was too long. She was really a very conventional, ordinary woman. That aside, Karen reveled in the sexual trip she was finally allowing herself. Like tonight was the first time she'd ever ridden the pony. Starting at a nice rhythmic canter slowly building to a gallop, the while watching herself in the plate window. Into it big time. Woman could fuck. But it was becoming abundantly clear to Evan that they really weren't getting anywhere, anywhere meaningful. On her days off, she could spend the whole day in the mall. As he envisioned their relationship, he'd see Karen for another couple of weeks, then break up with her before going to Corfu…by himself.

Evan walked into the center of the turnaround. Ultimately, he saw himself with Sue. She was a changed woman, no longer daddy's little girl. Her business was doing exceptionally well. Two coffee houses in San Francisco, one in Sausalito, and soon a "Kendrix's" would be opening in Gualala, just up the coast; and talk was in the air about a national franchise. In *Sex and Marriage,* he'd done an important chapter on marrying the same person twice. If it hadn't worked the first time, odds were—and statistics said—it wouldn't the second. But with certain couples it did work, and extremely well. Why? Because in the interim both parties had grown emotionally and psychically; in short, they had given up their roles and had accepted themselves for who they were. Not secondarily was a strong, pre-existing chemistry. Evan liked believing that he and Sue fit that profile perfectly. In a year or two he could see himself giving up psychotherapy as a career and reuniting with his family in California, devoting himself to sculpting and writing and traveling.

Evan lifted his arms to Mt. Chodokee, drinking deeply of the cool, refreshing air.

■ ■ ■

Hands tight on the wheel, Rick steered off Rt. 289 onto Chodokee Road, turning at a mailbox with an imposing "1" on it; his rear wheel bumped heavily, as if in and out of a ditch. Two moons, one chasing another, ducked behind a cloud. Lo-beams illuminated Kendrix's studio. Halfway to the turnaround, Rick spotted lights in the psychiatrist's house; he drove closer, stopping well shy of the split-rail fence, braked, turned off the engine. Sat behind the wheel, gave himself a moment to psyche himself…and noticed what appeared to be—he strained to see through the windshield—a person, a human form, crawling to Evan's house. Wild Turkey at it again! Or was he really seeing a man scraping along on the ground? A voice told Rick to make dust. Then he remembered why he was here. To get Lisa. Now more than ever—with, who knew, a madman on the property—he had no choice; and he stepped out.

As he was closing the car door, the moons reappeared— something was shining on the backseat. It was the walnut stock of his Beretta poking out of the cover. Grateful to have it, he opened the door, fumbled in one of the boxes for a couple of shells, loaded the gun, and started toward the path. In all his years of hunting, he had never listened or looked about so keenly. He reached the path; the man was still dragging himself along. Rick went closer, approaching at an angle, and the man suddenly twisted about, lifting his torso, and Rick almost blanked out at the horror of it. The man was Evan, or a gruesome replica of Evan, his face dotted with ghastly pockmarks, each dripping blood, one eye swollen shut, shirt perforated and soaked dark red. But it was the wound lower down that so shocked, so horrified Rick. The psychiatrist's entire pelvis was blown away, obliterated.

Rick went even closer, leaned over, wanting to ask Evan the uppermost question on his mind. Was Lisa here, was she OK? Guttural sounds in Evan's throat, red trickles from his mouth. Suddenly the psychiatrist reached up and grabbed the barrels of the gun, near the muzzle, yanking Rick off balance. He fell forward, just catching himself, their faces almost touching. Drowning in his own blood, his single eye glowing in the moonlight, Evan tried to say something; it was impossible for Rick to know what it was. He pulled the gun away. Evan's hand slipped from the smooth steel and he tumbled back, convulsing, near death.

Rick ran to the house, kicked open the door, moved from room to room, shouting his daughter's name over and over. Nothing, no one. Back outside, he stood there, looking down at Evan. The psychiatrist's face twitched grotesquely, blood and bile spilled from his mouth. Then he lay still, motionless as one of his stones, his good eye fixed on Rick.

■ ■ ■

Somehow he had driven himself home. In his driveway, he sat behind the wheel, sweating; got out and threw up. Wiped his mouth with the back of his smeared hand tasting Evan's blood, gagged on it, grabbed his gun and started toward the shed— just as a car, coming along Elting Street, slowed and turned in. Bootlegging the Beretta, Rick stumbled to the shed, laid the gun on his bench, stood there in the dark waiting for the car to drive off. He heard the quick patter of a familiar footstep.

"Daddy?"

"Yes, I'm here."

"What are you doing?"

He stayed in the shadows. "Nothing. Where were you?"

"At Muriel's."

"Muriel's?"

"Yes. What's the matter?"

"You said Monica's."

"I never said Monica's! I said Muriel's."

"I thought you said Monica's."

"Daddy, what is it? Why are you hiding?"

"I'm all right. Go inside, Lisa—I'm glad you're home."

She gave him a slow, distressed look and went up the steps. Rick flipped on the fluorescent lights, opened the box of cotton patches, unscrewed the top to the Hoppe's. The pungent aroma of the solvent, as he doused a patch, caused his stomach to tighten spasmodically. He ran the patch down the outside of the barrels; it came away a deep dark red. He retched violently. In his pen, Waldo was barking. Unable to continue, Rick capped the bottle and went out, locked the shed door. Upstairs in the house he took a long, hot shower, rinsed away the lather, crawled into bed, cocooning himself in sheet and blanket.

A car was coming down Elting Street, its headlights gliding along the wall. He waited for it to slow, turn in, stop in his driveway; car continued on. Rick closed his eyes—dinosaurs ready to pounce, trucks destined to crash and burn....

CHAPTER
33

When Rick awoke the next morning, he lay in bed having a sick, terrible feeling that something horrendous had happened; but his mind was a blank, nothing was coming through. Then, by degrees, fragments of the evening began emerging. P&B's—upside down jiggers, trying to reach Lisa, talk of elm trees with Nolan. Rick dragged on jeans and sweatshirt, held the banister on his way downstairs. In the kitchen he poured himself a glass of orange juice, drank it while looking across the floodplain, trying to recall what he'd done after leaving the bar—

In brutal suddenness, an image jumped before his eyes: Kendrix on the ground, horribly wounded, reaching up and grabbing the barrels of his shotgun. Or was he having hallucinatory meanderings, the whole evening a 101-induced nightmare?

There was a way to find out.

He set his glass on the kitchen counter and went out to his wagon, pulled open the rear door. Boxes of shells, yes. Shotgun, no. Beginning to hyperventilate, he rushed to the shed—to find the door locked. 17-33-6. Was that the combo? He gave it a try; miraculously the lock separated and he went in. On his workbench lay the Beretta, a bottle of Hoppe's next to it, also several patches, one already stained. He worked feverishly wiping down the Beretta from stock to muzzle. About to break the gun and examine the inside of the barrels, Rick heard the familiar sound of crunching stones. He waited for the car to back out; what he heard was the clunk of a shutting door.

He laid the Beretta on his bench and crossed to the doorway. Stepping from a light brown sedan was a tall, bony, angular-faced man who spotted Rick and began walking toward the shed. Peeking out from his drab, waist-length jacket was the rottweiler-like snout of a holster.

"Good morning, Professor. Detective Sergeant Skeen, Appleton Police."

"Good morning."

"We had an incident in the township last night. With your permission, I've a few questions."

"Go ahead."

"Do you know someone named Evan Kendrix?"

Rick wasn't seeing well; he sensed his eyes weren't focusing. "I know him, not well."

"When was the last time you saw him?"

"Saw him?"

"What is it about 'saw him' you don't understand, Professor?"

The J-shaped scar on the detective's jaw was more pronounced, more welt-like, than Rick remembered. "It was on Main Street sometime in April."

"How about last night?"

"I told you, I haven't seen him since April."

Skeen sniffed the air, glanced inside the shed. "Dr. Kendrix was found outside his house at seven fifty-five this morning, shot dead by shotgun blasts."

Rick said nothing; his face felt like the skin side of a stretched muskrat pelt.

"Where were you last night between nine thirty and eleven?"

"P&B's."

"Then what did you do?"

"I came home and went to bed."

Skeen had a second look inside the shed, another sniff. "Thank you, Professor. Your cooperation is helpful." He strode to his car and backed out, tires spitting stones.

Rick returned to his bench, broke the gun, made to look

down the barrels; he hadn't fired last night but he wanted to make sure they were clean. Just then his daughter's voice startled him.

"Dad, I thought you were sleeping. I left a message for you." She was standing just outside the sliding door. "I'm meeting a couple kids and we're hiking to Spoon Pond."

"OK."

"Last night you really scared me."

"Last night?"

"When I came home."

"I'm sorry."

"Are you all right, Daddy?"

"I'm OK. Lisa, there's something I have to tell you."

"What is it?"

Rick went to the door of the shed. In the better light, she looked at him with alarm. "The Appleton police were just here," he said, and paused.

"And?"

"Evan Kendrix was—he was found outside his house this morning. Dead."

"*What?*"

"Someone shot him."

"Oh my God!"

"I knew you'd hear. I wanted you to know."

"That's awful! *Who*—?"

"They—they don't know yet," Rick said.

"Daddy, you look really sick," she said. "Do you want me to stay home?"

"No, you go ahead. Just be careful." He pressed her upper arm. "I love you, Lisa."

■ ■ ■

When Skeen had left the investigation to pay Professor Forrester a surprise visit, only one vehicle was on Kendrix's property, that of his assistant, Sergeant J.C. Berchtold. Now, as he spun down Kendrix's long driveway, he saw, in addition to J.C.'s car, Chief Eldrid's car, a state trooper's cruiser, a sheriff's sedan, the medical examiner's car, a reporter's car, and a shiny black station wagon. Prominent psychiatrist shotgunned to death outside his home, it didn't take long for word to spread. And it hadn't taken *him* long to finger the killer.

Skeen parked and got out. There was only one thing that bothered him as he walked toward the chief. The trooper had Eldrid's ear. Once a trooper himself, Eldrid had quit three years ago to head the APD, wanting the "slower pace of a village cop." But lingering in Eldrid's mind—everyone in the department knew it—was the belief that troopers were king.

Skeen greeted his boss. "'Morning, Chief."

"Darryl," the chief said. "You know Vic Maldonado out of the Ellentown barracks."

"Sure do. How's it going, Vic?"

Maldonado was a big man, beefy, with a flat, steam-rollered nose. "Not too badly," he said. "How's it with you, Darryl?"

"Working on a solid lead."

"Well, I'm letting Vic have the case," Eldrid said. Fifty, the chief had a paunch and a prissy little mustache, red like his hair. What hair he had.

The scar on Skeen's chin started to pulse. "Chief, I was here this morning with J.C., first on the scene," he said. "Plus, I have a suspect. What does Vic have?"

"An agency backing him called the State Police."

"It don't take an agency to bring someone in."

"Darryl," Maldonado said, "I understand how you feel." He spoke as if he had pebbles in his mouth. "I'll keep you on the case as a consultant."

Skeen didn't say, "Go fuck yourself," but it was on his tongue. To Eldrid, "We're capable of handling this, Chief."

The paramedics were wheeling Kendrix's body to the station

wagon. Dr. Russo, in his customary sharkskin, was in his customary rush; he didn't stay and chat with the three law enforcement officers for more than a minute. Soon the black wagon was rolling down Kendrix's driveway.

"Darryl," said Chief Eldrid, coming back to the topic, "murder cases are time-consuming. They burn up a budget. Why burden ourselves when—?"

Just then Sergeant Berchtold walked up holding a small, police-department baggie, knees of his bluejeans soiled. He had flat-lying brown hair and a clean, smooth-shaven face, early thirties. "Got an even ten," he said, giving the pellets in the baggie a shake, along with a smattering of dirt.

"Good work," said Skeen. In his opinion, J.C. was a fine detective, a loyal sidekick for the past seven years in the investigative wing of the APD. A born-again nut, but who cared?

Berchtold was about to hand Skeen the baggie when the chief said, "Let me see that, J.C."

Eldrid held it up to eye level. Skeen had the notion that the chief was buying time, couldn't decide. Also eyeing the pellets was Maldonado. "Look like 7½'s, possibly 8's," the trooper said.

Skeen had to admit Maldonado had a good eye but it was typical trooper bullshit tossed out to impress Eldrid. Just then, from one of the Appleton policemen searching the bushes and woods just off the parking area: "Detective Sergeant, got something!"

Skeen, Chief Eldrid, Maldonado, and Sergeant Berchtold crossed the shale to where Frank Buford, early twenties and the only black officer on the force, was standing. "Take a look," Buford said, pointing to the leaves and tufts of grass at his feet.

Lying there, half hidden, was a matchbook. "Turn it over," Skeen said.

Using a stick, Buford flipped it. On the cover: "P&B's. Cornerstone of Appleton, N.Y."

"That's where my suspect was last night," Skeen put in quickly, "by his own admission."

"When did you learn this?" asked Eldrid.

"Where do you think I just come from? I have a suspect, chief. You won't believe what he was doing when I stopped by."

"Tell me anyway."

Skeen didn't say and after a couple of seconds Chief Eldrid said, "Vic, it looks like Darryl's got something going. We're going to keep it."

"No problem," Maldonado said, pushing around the pebbles in his mouth. "I'll help out any way I can." Then to Skeen, "Good luck, Darryl," and he plodded to his cruiser.

J.C. Berchtold held open a new plastic bag, and Frank Buford, pinching the matchbook between two twigs, dropped it in.

"Who's your suspect?" Chief Eldrid asked Skeen as they walked away.

"A professor at Appleton State. His wife and Dr. Kendrix were keeping company. Remember the woman who killed herself, lived on Elting Street?"

"Mrs. Forrester."

"Her husband, Rick Forrester. When I stopped by just now, he was cleaning his shotgun."

The chief gave a small guffaw. "You're kidding me."

"Gun lying right there on his bench," Skeen said, "box of patches, Hoppe's in the air. The whiskey on his breath 'most knocked me over."

Eldrid nodded toward Berchtold. "Good work, J.C. You too, Frank." He gave the plastic bag containing the loose shot to Skeen and they continued walking. "Forrester looks like a prime suspect," the chief said. "But don't shut yourself off from normal investigative procedure. Make your interviews, turn over all stones."

"Got it," Skeen said.

"If only to cover our ass."

"Right."

"Bring it home, Darryl," the chief said getting in his car.

CHAPTER
34

Rick stepped out of his Ford wagon with an overnight bag and began walking on a down-sloping path toward Michael Bostwick's large, rambling house. The land immediately surrounding it gave the appearance of a huge rock garden—scattered stone outcroppings, trees, flowering bushes. No grass. Behind the house, fields and forest stretched away, and in the not too distant distance rose the Adirondack Mountains. The house stood alone, reminding Rick (as it had on visits past) of a fort, a stronghold in the wilds.

A side door to the house opened and an Irish setter barked once and came loping across the property. Rick patted the setter's head. "Casey, you old bird dog, remember me?"

A familiar voice: "I remember you."

Michael Bostwick was coming out of the house—tall, his great shock of gray hair silver in the afternoon sun. They met on the path, embraced. Michael said Jane had stayed in New York. Their daughter, Beth, had just had her first child, so he was here by himself. Yesterday, on the Dunbar, a hatch had come on so thick he'd thought a storm cloud was moving in. He'd kept two browns, both fourteen inches, returned seven others, all nice fish.

"Did you bring your gear?"

"I didn't," Rick said.

"Not a problem. I've a new Payne I want you to try."

They entered the house via the side door to a room, more like a hall, with a stone floor, a big cast-iron stove, and a massive ice box—and it was just that, an ice box. In the middle of the floor stood a solid twelve-foot wood table.

"Your room's on the second floor," Michael said. "First door on the left."

"OK."

Michael put his hand on his friend's shoulder, came in a half step. "How're you doing, Rick? We've got a lot to talk about, but that's uppermost on my mind."

"I'm not sure it's sunk in yet," Rick said, "what with everything happening. Maybe one day I'll break down and grieve, possibly in jail."

"We'll keep you out of jail," Michael Bostwick said.

Rick went into the living room, rustic furniture cushioned in green, and climbed a broad stairway. On his last visit to Farlow, three years ago, he and Chloe had had a room looking east to the Adirondack peaks; his room now was smaller and had a less dramatic but still marvelous view of the forest. When he returned to the kitchen, Michael had a platter of sliced ham, cheese, lettuce, and tomatoes waiting; a cutting board with a loaf of rye bread lay on the table, along with a jar of mustard and a thermos of coffee.

They put together sandwiches, talked, continued catching up. Kids, careers, their twenty-fifth reunion at Andover. Rick hadn't attended, Michael had. He said the school had a new gym and an indoor hockey rink. No more shoveling the snow off Rabbit Pond. "I walked out to it for old time's sake," he said. "What did I see? A muskrat chewing happily on a shoot. I can report that the Bostwick-Forrester reign of terror is long forgotten."

They both laughed, but then Michael's voice took on a more serious tone. "OK, to the business at hand," he said. "Yesterday when you called you gave me a snapshot of your brush with the law. A man in Appleton was killed Friday night, and Saturday morning a detective stops by your house to ask a few questions. Now you can fill me in. Why did he stop by?"

Rick sifted through the details in his head, wanting to bring them out in some semblance of order. The simple fact of sitting with his old friend had eased his worry, the pounding preoccupation. "The man killed—murdered—was the man Chloe was having an affair with, a local psychiatrist named Evan Kendrix. Skeen, Detective Sergeant Skeen, thought visiting her husband would be a good place to start."

"How did it go?"

"For him, great. He has me down as a suspect."

"How do you know?"

"He saw me cleaning my shotgun."

"Maybe you'd just come in from a morning hunt."

"Unlikely. I was frantic, and hung-over."

"Rick, start from the beginning. You're losing me," Michael said.

Rick talked about Lisa and Kendrix, his fear that the psychiatrist was trying to seduce her, and how he went looking for her Friday night. When he got there, he found the psychiatrist near death, brutally shot in the face and chest, and in the groin. "I was horrified, terrified. Was a lunatic on the property, was Lisa all right? Then, without any warning, Kendrix reaches up and grabs the barrels of my gun, almost pulling me over."

"You went looking for your daughter with a shotgun?" Michael sat back a little, alarmed.

"When I arrived at his place, I saw a body, the body of a man, dragging himself along. I had the gun in my car—"

"Is that standard for you, Rick? Riding around town with your shotgun?"

"That afternoon I'd tried to sell it."

Michael scraped at the two-day stubble on his chin. "Go ahead."

"I yanked the gun away from Kendrix, ran into his house looking for Lisa, shouting her name—no sign of her. I came back out, stopping to look at Kendrix; and right then he died."

"Did you call the police, your local rescue team?"

"I thought of it. But with blood all over me, all over my gun—I panicked. When I got home I started to clean the gun, got sick—combination of Kendrix's blood and Hoppe's turned my guts—plus the booze. I was a fucking mess. I went inside, took a long shower, and in the morning went back to wiping away the evidence, and that was when Detective Sergeant Skeen pulled in."

"So he has his man, he thinks."

"Not 'thinks.' He's one hundred percent certain I murdered Dr. Kendrix."

Michael nodded, his eyes level on his old prep school friend. "Are you a hundred percent certain you didn't?"

"I didn't go there to kill him, I know that. I went there to get Lisa and bring her home."

"Answer the question, Rick."

"Everything points to me," Rick said. "Motive, building like a storm over two years. And the evidence! After Skeen left that morning, the morning he surprised me with a visit, I broke the gun and looked down the barrels. Michael, I have never stowed a gun after firing it without cleaning the bores. What I saw sent the chill of death through me—bits of wadding and specks of powder—small amounts, what you'd get from a single discharge in each barrel."

Michael's eyes closed, much longer than an ordinary blink. "What you're telling me—"

"Yes. My rage, the alcohol, my desperation to save Lisa, all conspired—I'd killed Evan Kendrix. That was what I believed Saturday morning when Skeen left. And the dirty barrels were proof! I doused a patch and just before pushing it through a voice was saying 'Don't do it.' A voice I knew but couldn't place. 'Don't do it, Rick!' I didn't think, didn't listen. I ran the patch through both barrels, not once but twice."

"You didn't hurt your case," Michael said.

"But I did," Rick said, "badly, irreparably. Looking at the

deposits, forensic experts would have seen they were old. Fresh deposits in a barrel are dark, crisp, they sit up. The deposits I saw Saturday morning were gray, they lay flat."

"Rick, you were hung over, your vision was impaired."

"They were old deposits, Michael."

"It's academic," the lawyer came back. "They're gone, wiped away. How can old residue *that no longer exists* help us?"

"It can't," Rick said, "but it could have. If I'd listened, we wouldn't be having a trial."

"You're putting too much on conjecture," Michael said.

"I'm not, I'm talking fact."

"Then how did those 'old' deposits get there, if you always clean your shotgun after using it?"

"I wasn't the last person to use it," Rick said.

"Who was?"

"The person who spoke to me, saying 'Don't do it, Rick,' fired it on a rainy day last March."

Michael nodded quietly. Then he got up from the table and looked out the kitchen window at the sky. "I feel a great hatch coming on. Let's hit the stream," he said.

■ ■ ■

In his police department office early in the morning, a few days after the Kendrix murder, Detective Sergeant Darryl Skeen was scrutinizing the shotgun pellets in the clear plastic baggie he'd just removed from the evidence locker. Trooper Maldonado's gravelly voice—"Look like 7½'s, possibly 8's"—had awakened him at five thirty. Wanting to take measurements himself before the ballistic expert from the capital district would arrive at nine to establish their official size, Darryl had gotten quickly out of bed.

Now, in his office, he took a slurp of the coffee he'd made when he'd first come in. Also on his desk were five boxes of shotgun shells—two open, three sealed—that he and J.C.

Berchtold had taken from Professor Forrester's tool shed on a search warrant. On the side of each box was a picture of a ruffed grouse, then the manufacturer's name and the specs of the enclosed shells: Winchester. Gauge 20. Shot Size 7½. Field Grade.

To have ballistic expert Ken Ventriglia classify the pellets as 8's, when Professor Forrester didn't have 8's—that would be embarrassing; in short, it would throw the case against Forrester out. But there was something besides the damage to his reputation that motivated Darryl Skeen now....

It had been seven years since the incident at Onderdonk State College near the Canadian border. When his kid brother Cal, who was majoring in veterinarian medicine, found out that his chemistry professor was carrying on with his girlfriend, a nursing major, Cal slugged the son-of-a-bitch right there in the classroom, broke his jaw. He was expelled, charged with assault and battery, got two years, and later that spring Professor Roth was given tenure. For fucking a co-ed and reckless indifference to the well-being of one of his students. Something happened to Cal in prison, he never said what—it was like he gave up on life. Seeing him today wasn't a pretty picture. The best, the smartest of the five Skeen brothers, all of them in law enforcement except Cal who wanted to be a vet. You could find him in Pat O'Hare's in upstate Jaspertown any day of the week. Looked like an old man, slouched there at the bar.

Skeen reached into his desk drawer and pulled out a small box of polished wood. Opening it, he took out a micrometer. On his desk lay *Jim Whitney's Cartridge Catalog* in its 18th edition, the recognized bible for all rifle, handgun, and shotgun ammo. Skeen picked up the baggie with the ten pieces of shot—*7½'s, possibly 8's*.

This one's for you, Cal, he thought.

CHAPTER
35

Driving down Hazel Street Rick saw his daughter walking toward him, several books in one hand and a stuffed gym bag in the other. He braked to a stop. Through his open window he said he was on his way to visit Margi. Did she want to come along?

Lisa put her books and canvas bag on the back seat, then sat in front. Her hair looked mussed, and Rick noticed a rip in the upper sleeve of her shirt. Where Hazel met N. Elm, he headed north toward Woodbridge. "What happened? You OK?"

"Just now on the bus a girl in my class, Dawn Gravino, shook a copy of the *Appleton News* in my face," Lisa said. "Then she goes: 'What's it like having a murderer for a father?' I grabbed it away from her and we started fighting."

Rick gave her hand a squeeze. "Lisa, to have you involved like this really hurts me," he said. "Sad part is, you'll probably hear stuff like that again. Try to ignore it."

They passed Westgate Industries, then, farther along, the entrance to the town landfill. Rick asked Lisa why she had so much stuff with her.

"Last day of school."

He should have known that, he thought. "That's usually a happy day, isn't it?"

"Usually."

"Lisa," he said after a while, "so you know what's going on—right now a grand jury is hearing evidence. I'll likely be indicted and one of these days arrested. It's why I'm seeing Margi, to make plans if bail is denied."

"Why would they deny it?"

"It's a capital case. They might consider me a threat to run."

"Run where?"

"Anywhere, instead of facing the music."

"But you didn't kill Evan!"

"Your friend on the bus thinks otherwise, as do others. As does the district attorney of Ulmer County."

Out of Appleton township, N. Elm became Rt. 23. Trailers: shades pulled, blinds closed. Roadside businesses. One dealt in religious lawn ornaments, another sold firewood, mountains of unstacked logs. Bert & Sons offered 24 Hour Towing plus a big selection of used cars. Billboards by the score, telling you what to look for in Kingsley-on-Hudson or Appleton, depending on the direction you were driving. On a gloomy stretch of road a tavern appeared; maybe its name, Happy Days, enticed an occasional traveler. Whoever might stop in, it was the most desolate-looking place Rick had ever seen. Ahead, a steel bridge, similar to the one in Appleton, spanned the Walloon River meandering its way north.

A VW van on the side of the road, painted orange and blue and green, had a flat front tire; to Rick it appeared to be genuflecting. *Make Love, Not War.* On the approach to Kingsley-on-Hudson a sign with a left-pointing arrow directed a motorist to the Ulmer County Jail. Rick went by, pretending he hadn't noticed, and turned onto Jefferson Avenue, a thoroughfare lined with trees and two-story frame houses. Chloe had once told him it was the kind of street she dreamed of living on when she was a little girl in the projects. An old man in a baggy brown suit shuffled along on the sidewalk in front of the Jefferson Avenue Sanitarium.

Once through the city, Rick picked up Rt. 26, years ago the old "plank road," now a four-lane highway. The first roadside tavern he'd ever entered on his own, the night after his eighteenth birthday, was just ahead. As a boy, he'd heard intriguing tales about the Avalon Inn. Things "went on" inside the Avalon. Women were waiting to meet you. Not that night. Now the building was a place that sold doll houses and miniature furniture. The road crested, and coming into view were the Catskills, a deep purple. No one could call them awe-inspiring but there was something grand about them still. On a steady rise Rick gave his station wagon a little pedal. Two pickups and a van were parked in the lot at Dave Ballard's gun shop.

"Dad," Lisa said, "before we visit Margi can we go to the cemetery?"

"Sure. Good idea."

In the hamlet of West Harleyville, a few miles from Woodbridge, they passed a well-known area restaurant, Scileppi's. Rick's closest friends growing up were the Scileppi brothers. In Woodbridge, at the village green, Rick made a right and soon parked at a thin line of hemlocks atop a grassy hill. He and his daughter walked through the trees. The land sloped downward, graves marked with headstones; there were no standing memorials in the Woodbridge Artists Cemetery. It ended at a crumbling stone wall and then a great field stretched away, and in the near distance Mount Lookout rose. At the summit stood the never-finished Mountain House, a casualty of the Depression, savaged equally by vandals and by time.

Rick and Lisa began walking through the cemetery, deeply still; many stones bore the names of people he'd known through the years. They stood at his father's grave. The Woodbridge sculptor who had engraved the great slab of bluestone did not lie far away.

RODERICK HENLEY FORRESTER
Sept. 3, 1898–Jan. 5, 1961
He was a man, take him for all in all,
I shall not look upon his like again.

Rick stayed for a moment, shaking his head slowly, then

joined his daughter at a smaller stone in the family plot, newly placed.

CHLOE CIKA FORRESTER
March 30, 1936–March 23, 1976

The great rush of fresh sorrow was too much. Enough of this haunted graveyard, of memories of his dead. He pressed Lisa's hand and went to the top of the cemetery where he sat on a stone bench beneath the hemlocks watching his daughter. What must she be thinking, feeling? She dropped to her knees, then leaned all the way forward in an attitude of prayer. Or was it? Her hands clenched and she struck the stone, her face crunching up, cries of pain, of anger, rending the quiet. Rick got to his feet, thinking to go to her, but a wiser part of him prevailed. This was between daughter and mother, between them alone. Lisa rested her forehead lowered on the stone, and she wept.

In time she came up the rise in the cemetery, wiping her cheeks, breathing deeply, and sat beside her father. He asked no questions, said nothing at all. Lisa leaned her head against his chest and after a while she was calmer.

"Daddy?"

"Yes, Lisa."

"There's something I want to tell you."

"Now is a good time."

"It's about Evan."

What isn't? Rick thought.

"The day he bought me the cone? When we finished, he asked me to go for a drive with him. I said I couldn't, I had to get home. But it wasn't what I was thinking. I liked Greg, we were really good friends, maybe for a while there I was in love with him; but it started with Greg because I wanted to get back at Mom. After she died, it was even stronger—the need to *really* get back at her. For leaving us. Leaving us that way! After promising me, holding me and promising me, she would never—she would never kill herself."

"She promised you that?"

"Yes." Tears were flowing down Lisa's face. Rick pressed a handkerchief into her hand.

"It was a dagger in my heart, Daddy. She betrayed me," Lisa said. "I said no to Evan but I knew he'd ask me again, and I wasn't sure I'd say no. I thought I'd probably say yes. And in my mind…in my mind we'd be in bed, and I could hear myself saying to her, 'How do you like this, Mom? Huh? How do you like it?'"

Rick remembered—it was just yesterday, wasn't it?—taking nature walks with Lisa in her little sun dresses when they lived in Woodbridge, identifying birds, looking for wild flowers….

Lisa used the handkerchief, wiping her eyes, her cheeks. "It was all so confusing to me, how she took up with Evan. That was the end of everything, even her. I loved Mom, I loved her so much! I want to love her the way I used to, when we danced and painted and laughed in the rain."

"You will," he said. "One day you will, Lisa."

"And one other thing," she said.

He waited awhile for her to go on. A solitary woman, in a long skirt with her gray hair in a bun, walked into the cemetery and stood at a grave.

"You came looking for me, to take me home," Lisa said. "And now you're in trouble. I'm sorry, Daddy. I'm really, really sorry."

"It's OK. It's all right, Lisa."

They sat together on the stone bench overlooking the flat-lying stones. Responding to a tug on his eyes, Rick looked upward. Clouds, like wandering sheep, were grazing in the sky.

CHAPTER
36

He had just finished the repair on the water damage in the basement, had showered and changed; now, as he was coming downstairs from his bedroom, Rick heard the clack of the front-door knocker. When he opened the door, Detective Sergeant Skeen and Sergeant J.C. Berchtold, in uniform, were standing there. "Professor Forrester, I have a warrant for your arrest in the murder of Evan Kendrix of Appleton," Skeen said, showing him the document.

Almost as a courtesy, Rick glanced at it. Berchtold took a half-step forward informing him that he had the right to remain silent. In the officer's hands were a set of handcuffs.

■ ■ ■

"That way, Forrester," the prison guard said. "Start walking."

"That way" was down a long cinderblock corridor. In orange pants and top—everything was jailhouse issue except the shoes—Rick slowed his pace, thinking to let the guard lead the way.

"No. Keep ahead of me, two steps. Always walk ahead of a corrections officer."

The man, impersonal but not unfriendly, wore a dark blue uniform with a nametag fastened to the jacket above his badge. "S. Prentiss." He'd seen Rick through the entire processing—fingerprints, mug shot, interview, physical—and now they were headed for Tier 33. Maximum security. In Rick's hand, as they walked along, was a mesh bag containing extra shorts, socks, a towel, a few toilet articles—

The corrections officer pressed a button above a steel door; it opened to a steep flight of concrete stairs. "From up here you get a great view of the Hudson," he said.

Rick started up. At the top of the stairs, Prentiss unlocked and swung open another door, and Rick looked down a long passageway. On his left ran a cinderblock wall; immediately on his right prison bars marked off one side of a large open area. Inmates were moving about, talking, reading newspapers or paperback books, playing cards at small tables. Some thirty-five or forty cells were tucked against the far wall, all doors uniformly open.

After twenty steps along the passageway, Prentiss stopped. "You're in 27," he said, pointing. "Cell doors open each morning at seven and stay open all day, close at ten sharp. If you so much as stumble into someone else's cell you'll be looking at two weeks in solitary for the first offense. Any questions?"

"No."

Prentiss unlocked the door to the common area and Rick went in. The inmates stopped whatever they were doing to size up the new arrival. Rick angled across the common area toward 27. Then someone shouted, "Hey, Penny Loafers, welcome to Crowbar Hotel."

Raucous laughter.

"Let me know when you're taking your first shower, Penny."

More laughter.

"Know somethin', that's the college professor who shot the shrink."

"Yeah, shot him in the balls."

"Shrink was fucking his wife."

"That so, Professor? Shrink fuckin' your wife?"

Rick entered his cell. It had, in it, a narrow concrete bed, a wash basin, steel toilet, and a plastic storage box. The only light came from the common area. Rick opened the box and pulled out a thin olive-drab blanket. He wanted to lie down but with his cell door open he felt vulnerable, despite the regulation. He continued sitting. From time to time someone sauntered by, stopped, faint shadow sliding in. Rick didn't glance up, kept staring at the concrete floor. But then a shadow lingered so long he felt compelled to look.

The man, standing some three or four feet away, toes of his scuffed street shoes touching the steel door track, had pasty skin, cropped red hair, and muscular, tattooed arms. Instead of a full orange suit, pants only, plus T-shirt. He ran his hand across his midriff, just below the drawstring of his pants, smiled a small, depraved smile, and moved on.

Rick walked over to his basin. Trickle of tepid water. He wet his hand, ran it behind his neck, returned to his slab; tired but unable to relax, afraid to close his eyes.

"Klein, Acker, Youngman—visitors!"

It was Officer Prentiss shouting the length of the tier. Three inmates converged at the common-area door. The guard opened it and they stepped out.

Rick stayed in his cell for the rest of the afternoon, alternately lying down, sitting up, and pacing back and forth between washbasin and open door. He ventured out for the evening meal. Picked up his tray and sat with two inmates at the table across from his cell. No one spoke. The meal consisted of canned corn, canned string beans, and meat—difficult to say what kind. Rick looked around for utensils. All he saw was a plastic spoon. Then he realized that the inmates were all eating with spoons, a bendable variety. Rick had a bite of the corn, the beans, somehow worked loose a piece of meat. Chewed and chewed and finally, with difficulty, swallowed.

Three tables away, staring at him, was the man with the red buzz-cut hair in the t-shirt.

Rick lowered his eyes, didn't look around or say anything; thought to get up and go back to his cell. Then one of the men at his table, across from him, was saying, "Professor Forrester?" He was about thirty, bald, with dark, lively eyes and a compact, wiry build.

"Yes," Rick said.

"I'm a friend of Greg Horboychuk's."

"I know Greg," Rick said.

"One day the cops raided Bums' Landing there in Appleton by the river," the man said. "OK, I had weed on me but I wasn't movin' it. Lawyer I have says I'm lookin' at five years. For a second offense, five years?"

"It seems like a lot."

"My name's Floyd, Floyd Zero."

"Rick."

"You play handball?"

"I used to."

"We could play tomorrow during rec. I love sports, I was first-string running back at DeWitt Clinton High. All Metro. And wrestling. A hundred and forty-five pound class. Made it to the state regionals one year. Lost my last match by one point or I would've went to the nationals in Dez Moines."

"That's impressive," Rick said. Man in t-shirt with red hair still staring at him. "What time do you want to play?"

"Two o'clock," Floyd said. "It's the only time they let you out—by law they got to, one hour."

"This is barf city," the man on Rick's left said, and got up with his tray.

"Floyd," Rick said, "who's the guy with the red hair? In a t-shirt. He keeps looking at me."

"Merlin Litwack. Stay away from him."

I'd like to, Rick thought.

"He raped and strangled a nine-year-old girl in Sawyerton," Floyd said. "When the mother come in he raped her too—then cut her throat."

■ ■ ■

Overhead lights glowed dimly in the common area outside

his cell. Rick lay on his concrete slab; his cot at home, that he had come to hate, was a featherbed by comparison. Whenever an inmate on the tier yelled out a curse, a name, an incomprehensible epithet, he jumped. The night wore on, hot, stifling. He had no idea what time it was, maybe two thirty, glad for one reason only—that his door was shut and locked.

His thoughts wandered. Lines, a whole passage he'd memorized years ago in Thoreau's "Civil Disobedience," came to mind:

> *I was put into a jail once...for one night...and as I considered the walls of solid stone and the door of wood and iron, I could not help being struck with the foolishness of that institution which treated me as if I were mere flesh and blood. I saw that, if there was a wall of stone between me and my townsmen, there was a still more difficult one to climb or break through, before they could get to be as free as I was.... It was like travelling into a far country, such as I had never expected to behold. It seemed to me that I had never heard the town-clock strike before, nor the evening sounds of the village—*

"Penny Loafers, how many times that shrink fuck your old lady?" echoed through Tier 33.

Rick covered his ears.

"Did he do her up the ass?"

"Shut up, Litwack!" an inmate shouted.

"I ain't talking to you, asshole! Penny, answer me! Was he fucking her up the ass?"

■ ■ ■

Shortly after the cell doors opened that morning, Prentiss shouted: "Forrester, visitor!"

Rick took the steep steps down (ahead of Prentiss). Michael

was waiting for him in the main reception area. "Sorry for the delay," Michael said. "The court has accepted your house on Elting Street as bond. You're free on your own recognizance, restricted to Ulmer County. I asked him how much cash it would take on top of your house. He said fifty thousand. We shook hands on it, and I left. There's no rush, just let me know the money's there and I'll take care of it."

"Thanks, Michael."

"How was your day in jail?"

"Don't ask. Just get me out of here."

Rick signed a few papers, changed into his clothes, and walked out with his lawyer.

"Let's have a good breakfast for ourselves," Michael Bostwick said, driving away from the jail grounds. "This is your neck of the woods, name a place."

In the town of Bloomdale, just north of Appleton, Rick said to slow down as they approached a shopping area with cracked, pot-holed blacktop and ringed with rural, nondescript places of business. "Over to your right," Rick said. "Rt. 23 Eatery."

Michael avoided breaks in the blacktop, parked near the restaurant. Inside, all places were taken at the counter; two of the seven booths were unoccupied. Ulmer County breakfast: working men in rough pants and shirts loading up for the day. In time a heavy-set blondish woman came over and took their order. Two coffees, two specials. All business, she didn't crack a smile.

The coffees arrived first, and when Rick picked up his mug his hand was shaking. Michael looked him over, then glanced around. "I'm having a déjà vu experience," the lawyer said.

"How so?"

"The setting. You and me together, with plumbers and roofers just like now, your mood about the same. Only difference, that was a bar; and it was night, and we were young."

It took Rick a moment to retrieve the occasion. Seniors, one day before graduation, all 125 in the class and all in their new, charcoal-gray suits and silk ties, had just had the traditional graduation-eve banquet at Andover. Speeches by class leaders, a sneak reading of the class poll before it came out in the yearbook. When the banquet ended, Michael had caught up with Rick outside the Commons and suggested they walk into downtown Andover.

"Guys bought us a couple of beers," Rick said, sipping coffee.

"They did. You weren't a happy camper."

"True."

"Do you remember what I told you?"

"What did you tell me?"

"You had to go up to your father, when parents arrived the next day, and tell him."

"Well, I didn't," Rick said.

Their breakfasts came, two eggs over easy, sausages, home fries, toast; refills on the coffee.

"I was hoping you'd go up to him and say, 'Dad, guess what my classmates voted me in the senior poll?'"

"I couldn't do it," Rick said.

"Do you wish you had?"

"Yes. But it wasn't going to happen."

They continued with their meal. After a while, picking up the thread, Michael said, "Pretend I'm your father, Rick. Tell him now what you didn't tell him then."

"Michael, drop it."

"Then tell me, your old friend."

"Why? You've forgotten?"

"I have."

"Like you've forgotten you were voted Most Likely to Succeed, I suppose."

"Jurors have a way of knowing when a defendant is hiding something." Michael said. "Just say it, get it off your chest."

"Michael, you're my lawyer, not my therapist." Rick had a last sip of coffee and signaled for the check.

■ ■ ■

When the phone rang later in the week, Lisa picked up, talked for a while with the caller, then came out and told her father it was for him; her eyes were smiling. In a semi-whisper, "It's Noreen."

Rick walked in from the living room, pulled out the little white chair in the alcove, hesitated for a second to recalibrate his thinking, then picked up and said, "Well, this is a surprise."

"Rick. I—I've been thinking about you," she said. "I can't stop thinking about you. When the story broke that you were charged with murdering Evan, I was bowled over. Still am. It's like I had a bad dream and now I'm living the dream."

"That sounds like me," he said.

"How are you holding up?"

"I'm not, really," he said. "I spent a night in jail and never want to see it again. It's like an evil tease—they give you a hint of the horrors of it, then hit you with twenty-five years."

"You're not sounding overly positive," Noreen said.

"I'm not. We don't have a scintilla of exculpatory evidence."

"Something will turn up, Rick. Have faith."

"I'm trying. How are you?"

"I'm getting ready for law school, looking for a place in New York. I have a part-time job in Scribner's. It keeps me pretty busy."

"Still going with that Gatsby lookalike?"

"He was insufferable. I ended it a week after graduation."

"Your mother must be heart-broken. He was a perfect 4.0."

She laughed. The sound of her laugh warmed him, gave him hope.

"The other day in White Plains I ran into Vincent Ciccarelli," Noreen said, "Christine's old boyfriend. The Appleton police had interviewed him, he said, as a 'person of interest.' Evidently they'd gone through Evan's journals and his name had popped up. They talked for twenty minutes and that was it."

"He didn't know Kendrix," Rick said.

"That was what he said, and it's the truth. But he seemed different," Noreen said. "Then I thought of course Vincent seems different, he's still in mourning for Christine. Rick, I don't want to get in Michael Bostwick's way but—you need help. *Someone killed Kendrix.* If it's OK with you, I'd like to serve as your attorney without portfolio."

"Noreen," he said, reaching out to her across space and time, "how can I say no to that?"

■ ■ ■

That summer, Lisa worked as a lifeguard at the village pool and joined the swim team, sometimes getting to the pool by seven in the morning for practice. Andrew was the pro's assistant at Locust Tree, polishing and regripping golf clubs and taking care of the practice range, with playing privileges. Rick took walks in the Shagg Range, on one occasion stopping on a rocky ledge. On his left were trees, a mountain upslope; on his other side was a sheer, thirty-foot drop, a narrow chasm with a fast-flowing stream at the bottom of it. He sat down and listened to the sound of the falls at the head of the stream, the sun warm on his shoulders, then lay on his back and looked up at the cloudless sky. His mind spun lazily. He wondered how Noreen was doing; he missed her tremendously. He walked down the rocky ledge to where the stream emerged from the chasm. He took off his clothes and walked into the pool. The water was icy cold but finally he took a plunge and began swimming against the current. He got halfway to the waterfall, then let the rushing water sweep him back to the pool, imagining they were together, laughing, frolicking—

But pressing on Rick's mind most was the trial. He had met

with Michael in August and September, always leaving with the feeling that they weren't getting anywhere, weren't developing a strong case, and on their last meeting in October, Michael said he had come to the conclusion, after conferring with a senior partner in his firm, that it would be a mistake for Rick to take the stand. Nothing was to be gained by it; they could lose the trial by letting Rick testify. Instead, they would fall back on an established courtroom tactic of making the prosecution prove its case. Rick said nothing for a long while. They were sitting on his deck watching colored leaves fall to the ground. Finally he said he hadn't killed Kendrix and not taking the stand would sow doubt in the jurors' minds. What was the defendant hiding? they would ask themselves. Michael said it wasn't a concern; it was the bedrock of law against self-incrimination. But he couldn't shake Rick's mind. Close to stepping aside, Michael decided, ultimately, to continue with the case on his friend's terms.

The days wore on. The first deep frost hit Ulmer County and the yap of Canada geese V-ing south filled the air. Increasingly, Rick was haunted by a conviction that something was waiting for him on Evan Kendrix's property.

He knew how it would look if he were caught but he had to revisit the scene, for all the risk. At the first glimmer of light on a cold morning in late November, ten days before the trial, Rick got out of bed, pulled on clothes, and went downstairs. He let Waldo out, made coffee, stood at the back door looking across the floodplain to the Shagg Range. After a third taste from his mug, Rick put on a warm jacket and grabbed his keys. His breath vaporized as he crossed the deck and walked out to his car. Waldo came running up. At first Rick thought to put him in his pen, then changed his mind. He gave Waldo a boost and soon they were passing the old stone houses on Elting Street and crossing the bridge over the Walloon River.

Once past the Lufkin & Jenkins orchard, the road started

to curve and rise; where Chodokee Road came in, Rick cut off Rt. 289 and made a right at a rural box, rolled past Evan's sculptures, parked shy of the turnaround and turned off his headlights. Ringing the entire area was a yellow police ribbon, in places sagging to the ground. He remained seated for a couple of minutes, staring ahead in the dim light; the place was dark, lonely, frightening. He began having second thoughts but pushed them away and opened his door—

"Rrrufff!"

He had forgotten that the dog was with him in the car. "Waldo, *chill*. We shouldn't be here."

He issued a couple of "OK"s and the dog ran off, disappearing in the shadows. Rick started walking toward the path, crossing the shale to the drooping ribbon. A gust swirled off Mt. Chodokee, scattering leaves. Rick stepped over the ribbon. A night bird cut sharply over the red, barn-like building. He stopped, looked about, having vivid images of his last visit, then moved closer to the house. A sign on the front door in large letters jumped out: POLICE. Right about here was where Evan had reached up and grabbed the Beretta. Rick cast a glance down the length of the driveway. They catch me here, I'm dead, he thought. He crossed in front of the darkened windows, turned at the north corner and walked to the back of the house, then angled to the down-sloping path leading to the pond. Heavy mist hung over the water, partially concealing the dock. When he got there, the canoe was gone. Rick stood on the edge of the dock, looking out, water slowly becoming visible as the mist rose. Silence…broken by a splash near the opposite shore.

Rick's heart started thumping. He turned, thinking he'd better leave. In one of the windows in Kendrix's house he saw—thought he saw—a woman peering out; next instant she backed away, vanished. What's going on here? Rick thought. From the turnaround came the sound of loud barking. Rick retraced his steps, half-running. An Appleton cop was probably trying to subdue Waldo, and the big springer spaniel wasn't cooperating. But as Rick circled the house and stepped onto the shale, he didn't see any squad cars. His dog, just visible in the dim light, was scratching at the ground in a frenzied manner.

Rick went closer. "What in hell are you doing, Waldo?"

Whatever it was, the dog didn't stop. Giving in to panic, Rick caught hold of his collar, gave Waldo a boost into the car, and sped away. So much for something waiting for me on Kendrix's property, he thought.

CHAPTER
37

He had started reading a *Times* article in the living room about an Olympic athlete when the phone rang. Rick laid down the paper and went into the alcove. "Hello."

"Rick, Michael here. Jury selection is next Tuesday. I'll pick you up at eight thirty in the morning."

"OK."

"You'll get to see R. Lincoln Centerwall in action," Michael said.

"I can't wait."

"I'm taking on a second lawyer. A colleague in the firm, Leonard Cashman. See you Tuesday."

Rick put down the phone and went back to his chair. It was mid-morning on a cold, cloudy day; he had a fire going in the stove and his kids were in school. He picked up the sports section of the paper and his eyes went to the small headline below the fold. It wasn't a big story but it had caught his eye, and he started again from the top.

Olympic Athlete Dies in Crash

Vincent Ciccarelli, 27, of Yonkers, a gold-medal winner at the Olympic Games in Montreal, was killed in the early morning hours of November 25 when the car he was driving failed to negotiate a curve and hit a tree on a rural stretch of road west of Armonk, New York. State Trooper Damon Stinemyer, who investigated the accident, estimated Ciccarelli's speed at the moment of impact at 95 mph. The Olympic athlete was alone in his late-model BMW sports sedan when the accident occurred, the trooper said.

Ciccarelli, who worked for his father's construction company, Ciccarelli & Sons, based in Yonkers, won his gold medal in skeet shooting, defeating world champion Helmut Windschuh of East Germany by one point.

Jesse Delafield, the principal of White Plains High School, spoke of Ciccarelli as a man of intense desire. "Vincent's dedication, not only to his sport but to all aspects of life, was exemplary to the highest degree," Delafield said. "He was a young man who never wavered in his commitment to honesty and integrity."

Ciccarelli is survived by his mother and father, Frank and Louise Ciccarelli, of Yonkers, his brother William, also of Yonkers, and a sister, Ruth Bellinkamp of Baltimore, Maryland.

Rick set aside the paper. What the hell is this all about? he thought.

CHAPTER
38

Assistant District Attorney R. Lincoln Centerwall was a big man, heavy of shoulder with a battering-ram forehead, who clearly saw himself as a force to be reckoned with. For the better part of the day, the two lawyers (Leonard Cashman, the new defense lawyer, observed and occasionally spoke to Michael) engaged in a mano a mano to seat jurors each perceived would help his case. Challenges, both for cause and, on occasion, no cause at all, flew about the high-ceilinged, tall-windowed, turn-of-the-century courtroom. The judge, Wilbur Cruikshank, watched the proceedings with quiet interest. He had a rough, weathered face and narrow eyes, as if he had driven cattle for the better part of his life. His dark blue, soft-textured robe didn't seem in keeping with his persona. Rough denim would be more the ticket.

Finally the twelve seats were filled and two alternatives chosen, and Rick and his two lawyers headed back to Appleton. Michael and Cashman, a loose-limbed man with a quick smile and an easy-going manner, were generally satisfied with the selection. The jurors seemed to them a fair-minded group of local men and women. As for R. Lincoln Centerwall, Cashman termed him a hard-nosed county lawyer who would dearly love to bury a couple of Ivy-educated attorneys from the New York firm of Pooley, Manning, & Maxwell. Less kindly, Michael called Centerwall a pig-headed son-of-a-bitch. There was no disagreement. Rick said the judge reminded him of a marshal in the western states of the 1880s, tough but even-handed. Cashman came back and said it wouldn't surprise him if Cruikshank kept a Colt "Peacekeeper" on the bench.

■ ■ ■

Exactly one week later, they were back in court, stepping off
the elevator on the second floor. The wide corridor was busy
with attorneys and witnesses and courtroom personnel walking
hurriedly about. Rick and his lawyers went directly to the
defense table, with Michael sitting between him and Cashman.
And then, quite suddenly, a jowly bailiff was announcing: "All
rise! The Honorable Wilbur Cruikshank of Ulmer County
Court!"

He climbed three steps to his bench. Nothing sentimental
or mild-mannered about Wilbur Cruikshank. Rick could see
him pointing to the limb of a nearby oak and ordering, "Hang
the bastard!"

Minutes later the jurors filed in, took their places, and
Cruikshank gestured to a thin-lipped clerk who read the
indictment in the case now before the court. Not one to dither—
had to get his 250 longhorns into Dodge by sundown—the
judge hammered down his gavel. "The trial of New York v.
Roderick John Forrester is now in progress. Assistant District
Attorney of Ulmer County, R. Lincoln Centerwall, will make
his opening statement." He gave a nod. "Mr. Centerwall."

Attired in a sharp blue suit with twin vents and a red-and-
blue paisley tie, Centerwall walked to the center of the floor.
He had superb posture, a large Roman nose, and his protruding
brow that gave the effect of a bumping apparatus. He moved
toward the seven men and five women seated in the jury box.

"Good morning, and a crisp December morning it is," he
said, rubbing his hands together, as if to warm them up. But to
Rick it seemed more a gesture of glee: in anticipation of tearing
apart his opponent's case. "What we are participating in, here
in this grand, historic courtroom in Kingsley-on-Hudson, is
as American as Old Glory itself," Centerwall went on. "It is
our democratic way of administrating justice—to have citizens
from all walks of life determine a defendant's fate. Let me thank
you in advance for your patience, attentiveness, and your sense

of civic duty."

Rick remembered how peremptory challenges had flown back and forth between Centerwall and Michael during jury selection. "Juror seven, you may go." "Juror ten, you may go." Now, among those selected to decide his fate, he recognized the woman who groomed dogs, the man who drove an oil-delivery truck, the man who sold refrigerators at Montgomery Ward, the woman who owned an art gallery in Woodbridge. The foreman, Adam Straiger, slouching in the first seat in the front row, worked for a carpet-cleaning concern in Sawyerton. He had narrow shoulders and a sallow complexion and appeared (then as now) sorely lacking in essential vitamins.

R. Lincoln Centerwall launched into his opening remarks. "Ladies and gentlemen, the case before us today is one of violent, premeditated murder. Dr. Kendrix of Appleton, a renowned psychiatrist and author, was killed by two successive shotgun blasts. The evidence showing that Roderick J. Forrester, also of Appleton, committed the crime, is staggering, both in its abundance and strength of conviction. An eyewitness, who will be testifying before us, saw Professor Forrester step out of his station wagon on the night of June 11th, the night Dr. Kendrix was killed, carrying a gun with a long barrel or barrels. Lab tests performed on this gun, a Beretta 20-gauge shotgun, found traces of blood on it that matched Doctor Kendrix's blood type, AB—the rarest of all types, I might add."

The assistant D.A. took a step closer to the jurors. "Dr. Kendrix had an affair with Professor Forrester's wife, starting in late summer of last year. Chloe Forrester was a lay psychotherapist—that is, she practiced therapy without license or professional degrees, under the supervision of Dr. Kendrix. Mrs. Forrester was a beautiful woman, thirty-nine years old, mother of two. Why do I use the past tense to describe her? Because Mrs. Forrester committed suicide in March of this year. Three months later Evan Kendrix was murdered, shot down in a parking area outside his home on the night of June 11th. Detective Sergeant Skeen of the Appleton Police Department, who investigated the suicide, also investigated the murder. He knew of Kendrix's affair with Mrs. Forrester. After setting up his investigative team at the murder site, at eight thirty in the morning on June 12th, he played a hunch, as the police like to say, and drove to the Forrester house. What do you suppose he found when he pulled into the Forrester driveway?"

Centerwall paused, as if to give someone on the jury a chance to speak up. "He found, as he will testify to, Professor Forrester in his workshop, a small building detached from the main house, bleary eyed, whiskey on his breath. And what was the defendant doing?" The smile on the A.D.A.'s face was one of feigned incredulity. "He was cleaning his shotgun!"

Centerwall continued with his case against Professor Forrester, each statement more incriminating than the one preceding it. Thirty minutes later he summed up. "Emboldened by alcohol consumed at a local tavern, Professor Forrester drove to Kendrix's house on the night of June 11th. He claims he was looking for his teenage daughter. But Lisa Forrester was not at Kendrix's that night. Evidence will show that Professor Forrester lay in wait for Kendrix in the bushes bordering the western side of his turnaround, and when Dr. Kendrix stepped out of his house for a breath of air at approximately ten forty-five, Rick Forrester shot him with both barrels of his gold-triggered Beretta shotgun. Roderick Forrester, a professor of literature and gentleman hunter of game birds, became at that moment a brutal, cold-blooded murderer! And the prosecution will prove this to you irrefutably, beyond a reasonable doubt, in the trial now before this court."

Centerwall strode to his table. Judge Cruikshank scribbled a few notes on a lined pad, then looking up, "The defense will now make its opening statement. Mr. Bostwick."

"Thank you, Your Honor."

Michael Bostwick, in a gray flannel suit and blue-and-gray silk tie, took three steps toward the jury box. "Good morning, ladies and gentlemen. I agree with the prosecution that the case before us today is one of violent murder. Perhaps it was premeditated but we can't say, because the man or woman who killed Dr. Kendrix is at large and we do not know the details or facts of the crime. There were no witnesses to it. The prosecution would like you to believe that Professor Forrester's shotgun is the murder weapon, the 'smoking gun.' Let Mr. Centerwall prove it. The prosecution's case is based solely on circumstantial evidence."

Michael then spelled out his case in Rick's defense. "Professor Forrester," he said, "is a concerned and involved parent, a thoughtful and rational man. Some three months before June 11th, his wife died tragically, and since then he's been raising their two children, Lisa and Andrew, now sixteen and thirteen respectively. Rick Forrester did not *like* Dr. Kendrix, but murder him? And spend years and years in prison leaving his children motherless *and* fatherless?"

Michael detailed what had occurred on the afternoon and evening of June 11th. "The assistant district attorney appears to have witnesses and evidence supporting guilt," Michael said, "but contrary to what he says or believes, the man or woman who shot and killed Evan Kendrix is not in this courtroom. The prosecution has built its case not on fact but on assumption. It will not stand, ladies and gentlemen. And when the time comes for you to begin your deliberations, I'm confident you'll see this to be true and return a verdict of not guilty."

■ ■ ■

Centerwall, opening his case for the prosecution, called as his first witness the medical examiner of Ulmer County.

With the same quick step Rick remembered from last March, Dr. Russo walked to the witness chair, a well-fed man in sharkskin. Oath taken, he said who he was and what his duties, as medical examiner, were. For any unattended or mysterious death, he was summoned to determine how, and under what circumstances, the individual had died. Only on his word was a body removed. Following a death, not always but when deemed necessary, he performed autopsies.

After several preliminary questions, Centerwall asked Dr. Russo to state the cause, or causes, of Dr. Kendrix's death.

"Severe trauma and bleeding caused by shotgun blasts."

"Blasts, plural?"

"Yes, one from a distance of about ninety feet that caused him to fall—wounds to his chest, upper arms, and face; the other at point-blank range. It was the second blast, aimed at Dr. Kendrix's genitalia, that caused death."

"Where, in relation to Dr. Kendrix's body, was his assailant standing when he fired the second shot?"

"He was standing between Dr. Kendrix's legs." Dr. Russo spread two fingers on his left hand, inserting his right index finger between them at a 45-degree angle.

"Did you perform an autopsy on Dr. Kendrix?"

"I did."

"What was the condition of his genitalia?"

"There was nothing left to examine."

The assistant district attorney gave Dr. Russo's comment time to sink in. Then he asked the medical examiner to explain why a blast to a man's genitalia would cause death. "A man's penis and testicles are non-vital organs," Dr. Russo replied. "However, the bleeding would be extremely heavy and the individual would succumb, in time, to trauma and loss of blood."

Centerwall clasped his hands before the middle button of his jacket. "Dr. Russo, if someone had it in his mind to commit murder—to shoot a man lying on his back with a shotgun—where is it likely, in your opinion, he would direct a blast?"

"Objection," Michael said. "Dr. Russo is a medical examiner, not a psychologist. Furthermore, it's a question that has no right or definitive answer."

"Mr. Bostwick," the judge said, "I see the professions of medicine and psychology as having a close relationship. I'm interested in Dr. Russo's opinion. Overruled."

Centerwall repeated the question, and Dr. Russo answered, "As stated by Mr. Bostwick, there is no definitive answer. Probably the thorax. Perhaps the cranium or throat."

"Then why would an assailant aim and fire at a man's genitalia?"

"I'll tell you my thoughts as I was examining Dr. Kendrix's body," Dr. Russo said. "I could only think whoever shot this man didn't care if he killed him, so long as he destroyed him as a sexually functional individual."

Michael objected again, this time on his feet. "This is blatant speculation, Your Honor. In my mind it smacks of prompting, for the sole purpose of inciting the jury."

"Sustained. Strike the statement from the record," he said to the stenographer. "You may continue, Mr. Centerwall."

"No further questions," he said.

Judge Cruikshank looked at the defense table. "Mr. Bostwick, you may cross-examine."

Michael approached the witness. "Dr. Russo," he said, "the first shotgun blast to Doctor Kendrix was to his chest, face, and arms, is that correct?"

"Yes."

"Would that blast, by itself, have been fatal?"

"I saw no puncture wounds, no penetrations, that seriously endangered vital organs."

"In your opinion, was Dr. Kendrix incapacitated by the first blast?"

"Definitely."

"Would he have been able to stand?"

"With difficulty and for a very short time."

"How about sit up?"

"Having taken pellets to his chest and face? Again, with great difficulty."

"What were the conditions of the psychiatrist's hands when you were first called to the scene?"

"They were caked with blood."

"Dr. Russo," Michael said, "how and at what point was Kendrix's blood—I'm not disputing it's his blood—transferred to Professor Forrester's Beretta?"

"Most likely the proximity of the gun barrels to the wounded man—eighteen inches at most. Perhaps the weapon brushed Dr. Kendrix's clothing."

"Do the blood traces on Professor Forrester's shotgun make it, by definition, the murder weapon?"

"By definition, no. But given the circumstances—"

"Thank you, Doctor."

Centerwall's next witness was Sergeant Ken Ventriglia, a muscular man with bushy eyebrows that met over a large, beaked nose. Stationed at district headquarters in Albany, he was the chief firearms and ballistics expert for the New York State Police. Yes, he had measured the shot Patrolman Berchtold had recovered from the murder site and also the autopsy shot. Using a micrometer in Detective Skeen's Appleton office five days after the murder, with Skeen and Berchtold present, he determined the pellets to be .095 of an inch in diameter—in common terminology, 7½ shot.

In cross-examination, Michael asked the sergeant if he had measured every pellet in Detective Skeen's possession. Ventriglia said he had selected three pellets, at random, from both the murder site and the autopsy.

"Is that standard practice, to select a few pellets and say *all* are the same?" Michael asked.

"If a medical doctor gives you ten piece of shot from a victim's body," the trooper said, "one is going to be a clone of the other."

"Then why not measure a single pellet and be done with it?"

"You could. But it gives a better appearance if you measure three or four."

"And better appearance is what we're after, isn't it, Sergeant?"

Patty Lewis took the stand. She had a pear-shaped body, very little on top, a lot below. Moon face. At Centerwall's request, she stated that she lived in Appleton, was a sophomore at Appleton State, and was Muriel Lewis's sister. Muriel and Lisa Forrester were best friends.

"What happened on the night of June 11th, Patty?"

"I drove Lisa home from a party at our house around eleven o'clock and saw Lisa's father leaving his car in his driveway carrying a gun with a long barrel, or maybe two long barrels."

"Were there any other distinguishing characteristics about the gun that you noticed?"

"A portion of the gun, the middle part, reflected the headlights almost like a mirror," Patty Lewis said.

"How did you know it was Lisa Forrester's father?" Centerwall asked.

"I recognized him. He was my English professor last year."

"Did he do anything with the gun, other than carry it?"

"When he saw my car, he tried to hide it."

"How does one hide a gun with long barrels?"

"He kind of tucked it in against his side."

Michael, in cross, asked the witness what grade Professor Forrester had given her last year.

"C minus."

"Was that a fair grade, in your opinion."

"It was terribly *un*fair. It blew my cume for the semester."

"Thank you, Patty."

Susan Kendrix took the stand in a finely tailored light gray suit. She spoke about her ex-husband. They had divorced three years ago but were planning to remarry. His horrific murder had shattered their dream of reuniting their family. After the funeral service, she and their son Jared returned his ashes to nature.

"Can you describe that occasion?" Centerwall asked.

Susan's hands rested on the top knee of her modestly crossed legs. "On Dr. Kendrix's property is a pond, which he dearly loved," she said. "It brought him great peace and comfort to sit by it, to canoe on it. Jared and I paddled out in his canoe, said prayers; then Jared emptied the urn. His father's ashes mingled in the water—" tears were spilling from her eyes, "—and we said goodbye."

Centerwall thanked the witness and Judge Cruikshank said the defense could cross-examine.

"How do you do, Mrs. Kendrix?" Michael said.

She gave a small nod.

"Your husband—excuse me, ex-husband—is the author of a well-known book called *Sex and Marriage*," Michael said. He paused momentarily, as if pondering the issues it covered. "Dr. Kendrix counseled individuals, and couples, struggling in their relationships. Does that express the type of work he did?"

"One aspect of it. It's not the only reason one sees a therapist."

"Of course. I read Chapter 9, 'All Manner of Transference,' with special interest," Michael said. "In it Dr. Kendrix says the profession of psychotherapy is not the safest in the wide range of human employment. Would you agree?"

"He said there are safer ways to make a living. I agree with his statement, not yours."

"Dr. Kendrix speaks of the phenomenon of 'negative transference,' where instead of love for the therapist the patient feels anger and even hate. There's an example he gives of a young man who acts out his anger—anger at his father—and attacks his therapist with a knife. Do you recall that section or passage?"

"It's familiar to me."

Michael took a step closer to the witness. He saw her as confident and self-assured, certainly attractive. Liked fucking, didn't like men. "Did Dr. Kendrix ever say anything to you about such matters, namely concerns for his safety as a practicing psychotherapist?"

"Evan had a wonderful way with those who saw him professionally, instilling in them confidence and trust."

"No exceptions?" Michael said.

"In his entire career, he may have had concerns about two or three patients at the very most," Susan Kendrix said.

"Concerns?"

"That they might want to do him harm."

"That will be all, Mrs. Kendrix. Thank you."

CHAPTER
39

R. Lincoln Centerwall led Sgt. J.C. Berchtold, Skeen's assistant in the investigative wing of the APD, through several queries regarding his career in law enforcement, then went straight to the heart of Dr. Kendrix's murder, asking Berchtold to relate where and how he had obtained shotgun pellets pertaining to the murder of Dr. Kendrix.

"I uncovered ten pellets at the murder site on the morning of July 12th, and Dr. Russo provided me with pellets at the autopsy. Any number were available, and I chose five."

Centerwall went to the evidence table and picked up a pair of plastic envelopes. He brought them over to the witness; on each was a notation in indelible marker.

"Are these the pellets you uncovered at the murder site and were handed at the autopsy?"

"Yes."

"Where specifically on the murder site did you search for pellets?"

"Dr. Kendrix left a trail dragging himself toward his house," Berchtold replied. "At the start of that trail was where he took the blast to the groin. That was where I looked."

"Did you find every pellet that went through Dr. Kendrix's body?"

"I found every pellet that was there to find."

"Your Honor, I would like to enter these shotgun pellets as prosecution Exhibits A and B," Centerwall said. "Exhibit A, the murder-site shot. Exhibit B, the autopsy shot."

Cruikshank gave a grouchy nod. "So entered."

Centerwall returned the envelopes to the evidence table. "Detective Berchtold," he said, "do you consider Exhibits A and B important evidence in this case?"

"Yes."

"Please explain."

"Every shotgun shell has pellets, or shot, of a specific size," Berchtold said. "The pellets in Exhibits A and B are 7½'s. After the murder, on a warrant, Detective Sergeant Skeen and I found five boxes of 7½ shells in Professor Forrester's shed. That gave us a match."

At the evidence table, pointing, "Are these the boxes of shells you found in Professor Forrester's shed?" Centerwall asked.

"They are."

"Your Honor, please recognize these shotgun shells as prosecution Exhibit C. Five boxes with 7½ shot."

The judge nodded.

"One final question, Sergeant. In shotgun terminology, what does '7½' mean?"

"It's a term meaning the size of a shot, how big it is. It's like saying a size 9 shoe. Unlike shoes, the larger the shot, the lower the number. Not counting buckshot, a 2 is the largest pellet, a 9 the smallest."

"Thank you, Officer Berchtold," said Centerwall.

Michael pushed back his chair and walked around the end of the table. Approaching the witness, "Sergeant Berchtold, you said you had a 'match' when you found five boxes of 7½ shells in Professor Forrester's shed. A match as to what?"

"With the shot in people's Exhibit A and B."

"In your opinion, is 7½ a common size of shot?'"

"Yes."

"The term 'rifling.' Can you explain it for us?"

"It refers to the spiral grooves inside the barrel of a rifle or handgun. It imparts spin to a bullet, making for accuracy."

"It also leaves a unique 'fingerprint' on an expended round, so investigators can trace it to a specific gun. Is that correct?"

"Yes."

"Now then, Sergeant, what distinctive markings are on expended shotgun pellets?"

"There aren't any."

"Why is that?"

"Shotguns have smooth bores."

"So the pellets in prosecution Exhibit A and B match the pellets in Exhibit C—those five boxes of 7½ shells you seized—in size only. That's really all you can say, isn't it?"

"Yes."

■ ■ ■

"Darryl Skeen. Detective Sergeant in the Appleton Police Department."

"How long have you been with the Appleton police, Detective Sergeant?" Centerwall asked.

"Nine years." He had on a brown suit, tan shirt, and a black string tie; a silver pin, in the shape of a Colt .44, held the ends of the string together.

Centerwall spoke to the witness in conversational tones. "How would you describe your duties as a Detective Sergeant?"

"I investigate crimes within the village and township of Appleton."

"Did you investigate any crime, within this jurisdiction, on the morning of June 12th?"

"I did," said Skeen.

"Can you tell us about it?"

The detective stated that he had received a call from Emergency Central at seven twenty-five a.m. A local man, Bert Meade, who worked for Dr. Kendrix tending his grounds, had found the psychiatrist's body lying on the path to his house. Skeen and his assistant, J.C. Berchtold, drove to Kendrix's residence at 1 Chodokee Road. After an hour on the scene, Skeen drove back to Appleton.

"For what purpose?"

"To pay Professor Forrester a visit at his house on Elting Street."

"Continue."

"When I got there, I saw Professor Forrester standing in the doorway to his shed. I got out of my vehicle and walked up to him."

"How did he appear to you?"

"His eyes were bloodshot, he didn't seem that steady on his feet, he looked pale; and I could smell whiskey on his breath."

"What did you say to Professor Forrester?"

"I told him we'd had an incident in Appleton and I wanted to ask him a few questions. He didn't object so I asked him what he'd done last night between nine thirty and eleven."

"His answer?"

"He said he was at P&B's. Then he came home and went to bed."

The assistant D.A. nodded. "Was Professor Forrester busy when you approached him in his shed?"

"At that exact minute, no. He was standing in the doorway."

"Prior to that, had he been doing anything—as you judged it?"

"He'd been cleaning his shotgun."

"How did you determine that?"

"It was on his worktable. I saw a wooden dowel leaning against the table and some stained, used patches lying around; and Hoppe's was in the air."

"Hoppe's?"

"It's a solvent used for cleaning guns."

"The shotgun you saw on Professor Forrester's worktable, had you ever seen it before?"

"I had."

"On what occasion?"

"Earlier in the year I'd investigated a suicide on Elting Street in Appleton," Skeen said. "The gun was on the floor next to Mrs. Forrester's body."

"Did you make positive identification between the suicide weapon and the gun on Professor Forrester's worktable?"

"Yes. There were characteristics I remembered."

The A.D.A. looked at Judge Cruikshank. "With the court's permission, I would like Detective Sergeant Skeen to point out these characteristics."

The judge waved a gnarled finger to proceed.

Skeen ambled over to the evidence table and picked up the shotgun. "First off," he said, "the pistol-grip stock. Second—" flipping the gun casually, "the—"

"That's bad protocol," Rick said to Michael. "Call him on it."

Michael spoke up. "Your Honor, for safety's sake, Detective Skeen should break the gun before going on."

"For what purpose?" countered Centerwall, looking sharply over.

"To determine if it's loaded."

"Mr. Bostwick, do you have reason to believe the gun is loaded?" asked the judge.

"Every gun is loaded until proven otherwise, Your Honor."

"Something your client should know," Centerwall said, glaring at Michael.

"Enough of that," Cruikshank said pointedly to the A.D.A., then banged his gavel to quiet the courtroom. "Open the gun, detective."

Skeen thumbed the breaking lever and the barrels dropped forward. Two shells zipped past his hip and landed, bouncing and rolling on the parquet floor and stopping in front of the jury box. Gasps came from the gallery and members of the jury.

The assistant D.A. gave Michael a withering look. "Is this some kind of joke?"

"I don't see it as one," Michael said.

Skeen set the Beretta down and walked over to pick up the shells. Examining them, "These aren't live rounds."

"What are they?" Centerwall demanded to know.

"They're called dummies," Michael replied.

From the gallery came more than a few chortles.

Skeen handed the dummies to Centerwall, who set them on the evidence table, and Skeen continued talking about the gun's characteristics. The over-under barrels; the polished, engraved receiver; the gold-plated trigger. The assistant D.A. entered the Beretta as prosecution Exhibit D and Skeen returned to the witness chair.

"Now then, Detective," Centerwall said, still ruffled, aggravated, "what did you do after interviewing Professor Forrester?"

"I went back to the murder site and continued with the investigation."

"Were there any developments?"

"Patrolman Berchtold had uncovered pellets from the shale—Exhibit A. And Patrolman Darnell found a P&B's matchbook in the woods bordering Dr. Kendrix's turnaround."

Centerwall entered the matchbook as prosecution Exhibit E and told the judge he had no further questions. He stepped away and the judge told the defense attorney he could cross-examine.

Michael stopped ten feet from the witness. "Detective Sergeant Skeen, do you recall coming to Professor Forrester's house on the day of his wife's death?"

"I do."

"When you left, did you take any items with you?"

"The suicide weapon and a golf magazine."

"For what purpose?"

"It's standard procedure to take items from a crime scene or the scene of an unattended death for analysis."

"You said the gun and magazine would be going to the state lab in Albany, isn't that so?"

"Objection," Centerwall said. "We're talking about the murder of Dr. Kendrix, not the death of the defendant's wife!"

"The witness has testified that the weapon, in both instances, is one and the same," said the judge. "That makes the testimony worth listening to. Overruled."

Michael to Skeen, "Did you or didn't you tell Professor Forrester that his Beretta, currently prosecution Exhibit D, and the golf magazine, purportedly belonging to his son, would be going to the state lab for analysis?"

"I don't recall."

"Then tell us, if you would, where this analysis was done?"

"At the police station in Appleton."

"By?"

"Myself."

"Do you have any records of that, Sergeant?"

"No."

"Don't police keep careful and accurate records on such matters?"

"It was a suicide, analysis was a formality."

"You're calling it a suicide," Michael said.

"I'm calling it what it was," said Skeen.

Michael retreated to his table, picked up a single sheet of paper. "Your Honor, I have here a document, stamped with an official Ulmer County seal. With your permission, I would like to approach the witness and ask him to read from it."

The judge examined the document, handed it back. "Go ahead."

Michael passed it to Skeen. "Please read the heading," he said, adding, "out loud."

"'New York State Department of Health, Certificate of Death'."

"Now Line 1."

"'Name: Chloe Cika Forrester'."

"Now," said Michael, "skip to item 23."

Skeen read, "'To be completed by Medical Examiner only'."

"Continue," said Michael.

"'Signed: Edward Russo, M.D. Ulmer County Medical Examiner.'"

"Now go to line 27A."

"'Specify if accident, homicide, suicide, undetermined, or pending investigation'."

"And what is the entry?" asked Michael.

Skeen hesitated.

"Well, Detective Sergeant?"

"It says 'Apparent Suicide'."

"An *apparent* suicide," Michael said. "Signed by the Medical Examiner of Ulmer County. But to you it was a suicide, no questions asked. Just like when you saw Professor Forrester cleaning his shotgun, you told yourself here's the man who killed Evan Kendrix. You had Roderick Forrester tried and convicted on the morning of June 12th, isn't that so?"

"No. I had cause for suspicion."

Michael had no further questions, and R. Lincoln Centerwall announced that the prosecution was resting its case.

CHAPTER
40

Michael Bostwick called three character witnesses—the chairman of the English Department, Albert Dollar; the dean of Liberal Arts and Sciences, Jeffrey Bernard; and Rick's colleague, Terry Randolph—all saying in various ways that Rick Forrester was a responsible and dedicated professor at Appleton State, who had just finished a biography on the life and times of the 19th Century American writer and naturalist, Henry David Thoreau.

Centerwall saw no reason to cross-examine. Why should he breathe life into testimony that was clearly putting the jury to sleep?

Michael called on a firearms dealer, Clarence Gunn, who told him, after taking the oath, that he'd met the defendant at Dave Ballard's gun shop in Woodbridge on the afternoon of June 11th.

"Did he introduce himself?"

"No. But I remember him." Gunn pointed a fat finger at the defense table. "He had a shotgun in his hand, an over-under Beretta. Wanted to sell it to Ballard."

"Was Ballard interested?"

"No, he was out. He'd went somewhere."

Michael stood at the evidence table. "Is this the gun?"

"It's the one he had, or one just like it." Squeaky voice: vocal cords needed oil.

"Did Professor Forrester tell you why he wanted to sell the gun?"

"No, but I told him I'd buy it from him. Still would. Single trigger, engraved receiver—"

"Thank you, Mr. Gunn."

Centerwall queried the firearms dealer on his business. Perfunctory questions. Then he asked him if he was in trouble with the IRS.

"You mean them bloodsuckers in our government?"

"I meant the Internal Revenue Service," Centerwall said.

"That's what *you* call it. I say bloodsuckers!"

■ ■ ■

Here we go, thought Michael, as Rick took the witness stand. After a string of questions as to name, profession, and a rundown of his early years in Ulmer County—caddying at the Woodbridge Golf Course, hunting and fishing—Michael fast-forwarded to the present, asking his old friend to describe his reasons for choosing Thoreau as a subject of scholarship.

"He had always appealed to me," Rick said. "His knowledge of nature, his stance in the anti-slavery movement at the time, his philosophy of passive resistance."

"What is passive resistance, Professor Forrester?"

"It's the accomplishment of goals without bloodshed. Its basic tenet is nonviolence."

"Did passive resistance, as you describe it, make a mark on history?"

"It influenced many people, most notably Mahatma Gandhi of India. It brought democracy to his country."

Michael Bostwick nodded; he and Rick had had several rehearsals, and Rick knew the next part of his testimony was closer to the moment; was, in fact, the main show. Michael had given him fair warning. He would be walking on a mine field. It was his call to take the stand, fine, but Michael was calling the shots from here on. Everything Rick would say on the stand could be used against him in cross-examination. The focus would be on Rick's peaceful nature and his fatherly concern about his daughter.

Now, looking at Rick as he sat in the witness chair, Michael asked him if he had driven to Dr. Kendrix's house on the evening of June 11th.

"Yes."

"For what purpose?"

"I believed my daughter might be visiting Dr. Kendrix."

"Did you have reason to believe this?"

"Yes."

"Please explain."

"I saw Dr. Kendrix and Lisa together in a mini-park in Appleton. He touched her hair affectionately."

"Did your daughter and Dr. Kendrix know each other prior to this incident in the mini-park?"

"Yes. When he and my wife were going together, they had met and talked in the house."

"How old is your daughter, Professor Forrester?"

"She just turned sixteen."

The direct examination went on for twenty more minutes, with questions designed to create reasonable doubt that the defendant was capable of so brutal a crime as the one now before the court. Summing up, Michael asked Rick if he had killed Dr. Kendrix on the night of June 11th?

"No. I did not. I stumbled on the scene. Someone else had shot him."

"Thank you, Professor Forrester."

■ ■ ■

R. Lincoln Centerwall approached the stand, his head lowered aggressively, as if he were eschewing the verbal for a more direct tactic in his cross-examination. But he stopped well short of the witness and said, "Professor Forrester, will you confirm that Dr. Kendrix had an affair with your wife?"

"Yes."

"You testified that Dr. Kendrix knew your daughter through his relationship with your wife. Is that correct?"

"Yes."

"You were terrified that Dr. Kendrix might take this friendship with Lisa a step further, or a couple of steps further, is that not true?"

"I wasn't terrified. I was concerned."

Centerwall came closer to the witness; it was more of a stalk. "You called your daughter's friend from P&B's, a bar in Appleton, you said, to see if she was at her house. Is that a fair statement?"

"Yes."

"Is that why you'd gone into the bar, to make the call?"

"No."

"Were you drinking that night?"

"Yes."

"What were you drinking?"

"Wild Turkey."

"Professor Forrester," Centerwall went on, "Wild Turkey comes in differing alcoholic content, as do most spirits. Commonly called 'proof.' What proof was the Wild Turkey you were drinking on the night of June 11th?"

"Objection, Your Honor," Michael said. "This is extraneous. Mr. Centerwall is fishing."

"He may be," the judge said, "but I find it interesting. Let's see what he catches. Overruled." To the defendant, he said, "Answer the question."

"A hundred and one."

"How many drinks did you have that night? Do you recall?"

"Three."

"Do the bartenders at P&B's use measuring devices inserted in the bottle, or do they simply uncap a bottle and pour?"

"They uncap and pour."

"That night, did you know the bartender?"

"Yes."

"In what capacity?"

"He was a former student of mine," Rick said.

"Approximately how many ounces of bourbon were in the drinks you had that night? In each glass."

"Two."

Centerwall pushed on. "That means you had six ounces of 101-proof whiskey in your system on the night of June 11th. Over how long a period?"

"An hour and a half to two hours."

"Were you feeling the effects of the alcohol?"

"Yes."

"Is it fair to say," Centerwall continued, "that between the Wild Turkey and your own deep-seated anxieties concerning your daughter and Dr. Kendrix, that you were in a disturbed, agitated, and intoxicated state when you left P&B's that evening?"

"I left the bar. I was feeling all right."

"Feeling 'all right,' you drove to Dr. Kendrix's to rescue your daughter, is that correct?"

"Yes."

"And you saw the man who had wrecked your family, pushed your wife to the brink of suicide, and was currently, you feared, making a play for your teenage daughter, lying on the ground, brutally shot. Is that what you saw, Professor Forrester?"

"I saw what appeared to be a human body lying on the ground."

"Did you go up to this 'human body?'"

"Yes."

"Carrying your shotgun, is that correct?"

"Yes."

"Which you just happened to have in your car," Centerwall said.

"That same day I had tried to sell it." Rick said. "It was in my car for a reason."

"A convenient reason, to be sure," the assistant district attorney said.

Michael jumped to his feet. "Objection! Mr. Centerwall is twisting testimony to serve—"

"Sustained. Mr. Centerwall, need I remind you—?"

"Understood, Your Honor." He refocused on the defendant. "It must have pleased you no end, Mr. Forrester, seeing the individual who had stolen your wife and was looking to seduce your daughter, lying there, his sexual organs obliterated!"

"It didn't please me at all."

"Words are cheap, Professor Forrester. It's easy to fabricate a story of innocence, but deep down, helped along by six ounces of high-octane whiskey, you proved the old saw: *in vino veritas.* You went to Dr. Kendrix's on a mission, accomplished the mission, and left Kendrix lying on the path to his house like so much roadkill! By all the evidence, all the testimony we've heard, it comes out loud and clear: on the night of June 11th—acting on an alcohol-liberated rage—you shot and killed Evan Kendrix!"

"I didn't kill Evan Kendrix," said Rick.

"You couldn't stand it for another minute," Centerwall went on. "Dr. Kendrix had spat in your face, kicked you where it hurts once too often. Aided by a substance known to embolden the weak, you lay in wait for him in the bushes fringing his turnaround, where a P&B's matchbook dropped from your pocket, and expended a round from your $3000 artfully engraved gold-triggered Beretta into Dr. Kendrix's face and chest, then, at close range, fired another round into his testicles!"

"That isn't true," Rick said.

"Tell us about the truth, Professor Forrester," Centerwall said. "Like you told it to Detective Sergeant Skeen on the morning of June 12th. 'I came home from P&B's and went to bed.' You went to bed all right, but not from P&B's. From

Evan Kendrix's, where you concealed yourself in the bushes and shot him down as he inhaled the cool evening air off Mount Chodokee. Vengeance is mine, sayeth the Lord. Not on the night of June 11th it wasn't. It was Rick Forrester's!"

"Someone else shot Evan Kendrix."

"Some fictitious character, I suppose," said Centerwall in full frontal attack. "You're a man of letters but this isn't a classroom, we're not interpreting poetry—we're getting to the truth of a bloody and heinous murder!"

"I didn't kill Dr. Kendrix."

"What evidence do you have to support that, Professor Forrester?"

"My intentions to sell the gun, given in testimony."

"Yes, you had good intentions. And we know what road they pave, don't we? Any other 'proof?'"

"My testimony given to Mr. Bostwick."

"How long have you known Mr. Bostwick?"

"Thirty years."

"Well, you *are* old friends," said Centerwall. "Where did you meet?"

"In high school."

"High school? Phillips Andover Academy, the leading private school in the nation, where privileged boys 'prep' for Yale, Harvard, and Columbia, a *high school?* When *do* you tell the truth, Professor? Or have you read so many books in your career as a scholar that you no longer distinguish fact from fiction? Your 'high school' pal and you made up your whole defense, and you know it!"

"That isn't true. Every word—"

"—is a lie," countered Centerwall. "You sit before us a killer, Professor Forrester. You planned and then executed the murder of—"

"Objection!" Michael was on his feet, furious. "The prosecution's statements are beyond the pale. Their only purpose is to—"

"Sustained." Cruikshank glanced at the stenographer. "Remove Mr. Centerwall's last comment."

"Starting with—?"

"'You sit before us a killer.'"

The assistant district attorney, trying to hide a self-satisfied smirk, said he had no further questions. Rick went to his table, clasping his hands together to keep them still.

"Mr. Bostwick, you may continue," said Cruikshank.

"The defense rests, Your Honor."

At the comment, Centerwall gave Michael a supercilious turn of the head. *What defense?*

■ ■ ■

Later that evening, Michael and Len Cashman were sitting in their suite at the Governor Whelan, throwing around ideas, jotting down points for Michael's closing argument tomorrow; but uppermost in their minds was Centerwall's cross-examination of the defendant, Rick Forrester.

His coffee long since finished, Michael picked up the cup anyway, hoping for a last drop. The room—his room in their two-room suite—had fleur-de-lis wallpaper, dark blue drapes, and a maroon wall-to-wall carpet. It was an old hotel in an old, historic city, and the room had a certain colonial, if somewhat tired, look about it. "I had my doubts about taking the case," Michael said. "Rick's like a brother. Does a doctor operate on his brother? Now I know firsthand why the answer is no."

He stood, walked about the room, pulling aside a drape and looking out at a small park. Standing tall in the center of it, well-illuminated, was a statue of the old governor himself. Michael turned around and spoke to his colleague at the firm. "I should have stuck by my experience as a trial lawyer," he said. "What I knew would happen, if Rick took the stand, happened. I believe we've lost this one, Len. Or I have."

"It's not over yet," Cashman said.

"Right. I'm going to save it tomorrow with a brilliant closing argument."

Cashman gave his head a bewildered shake. "You've known Rick since you were kids. What gives with him anyway? Why would he insist on testifying?"

"I can give you a thought," Michael said. "I'm not Catholic but I know what confession is. You go into the booth and tell your sins to the priest. It's not so different from taking the witness stand. Instead of a priest, you have a judge. And a jury. Rick has a lot he carries with him, a lot of guilt, misgivings. What better place, *what better place*, to redeem yourself than on a witness stand? No way was he going to sit this one out. If it killed him, he would testify."

Michael sat down on the edge of his bed, head heavy in his hands. "I can give you another thought," he said, looking up at his colleague. "This trial is like no other in vast annals of jurisprudence. The defense and the prosecution are one and the same. Rick Forrester v. Rick Forrester. That may be why we're not doing so well."

They spent the next half-hour discussing, jotting down talking points for Michael's closing argument, when the telephone rang. Michael reached for it. "Yes."

"Mr. Bostwick?"

"Speaking."

"This is Sergeant Berchtold of the Appleton P.D. I'm in the lobby."

A pause. He looked at Leonard. "What can I do for you, Sergeant Berchtold?"

"I'd like to talk to you, sir. I'm not in uniform. I'm not carrying a gun."

CHAPTER
41

"Judge Wilbur Cruikshank. All rise!"

Cruikshank stepped up to his chair; the second-floor courtroom, standing room only, quieted. Through the high windows a gray, early winter light drifted in. R. Lincoln Centerwall sat with his hands before him, right hand covering his left. Michael, at the defense table with Cashman and Rick, stole a glance over his shoulder at the journalists and court officials standing against the rear wall. The door near the jury box opened and seven men and five women filed in and took their assigned places.

"How did Berchtold leave it?" Rick asked.

"He said he'd be here at the opening gavel," Michael said.

When the jurors were settled, the judge tapped the wooden block on his bench, then spoke to the defense lawyer. "Mr. Bostwick, are you ready for your closing argument in New York v. Forrester?"

"I am, Your Honor."

Michael looked at Cashman, giving a small, disappointed shrug. Before leaving his table he gave a second look at the gallery. Sergeant Berchtold, in uniform, and a bald, portly man in a three-quarter coat, had just walked in. Michael turned to the judge and asked if he might approach.

Cruikshank nodded.

"What is this?" Centerwall asked in a firm, annoyed voice.

The judge indicated that both lawyers should step forward. Michael hadn't spoken for more than fifteen seconds when Centerwall started in. Cruikshank told the A.D.A. to simmer down. He allowed each lawyer five minutes to state his position, then declared a twenty-minute recess. The jury went back out and Cruikshank left the bench.

Michael, sitting with Rick and Leonard Cashman, said he had no idea how Cruikshank would rule. The judge didn't like when a tree fell across his trail; used up valuable time; still, Michael seemed to think his request had a chance. Centerwall sat at his table, jaw set, hands tightly interlocked. In twenty-five minutes Cruikshank reappeared, the jury came back in, and the judge said he would allow Sergeant Berchtold to testify for the defense, with full privilege of cross-examination to the prosecution.

"Mr. Bostwick."

"Thank you, Your Honor."

Michael called the Appleton police officer to the stand and began the questioning. "I'd like to review your testimony when you testified for the prosecution, Sergeant Berchtold."

The detective gave a small, tight nod, his forehead deeply lined; he looked uncomfortable, suddenly testifying for the other side.

Michael ran him through a series of questions on the pellets he had uncovered on the morning of June 12th. Then Michael said, "When Sergeant Ventriglia of the state police came to take an official measurement of these pellets, you were present with Detective Sergeant Skeen—is that correct?"

"Yes."

"What were Sergeant Ventriglia's findings?"

"He mic'd them out as 7½'s."

"Was that a problem for you?"

"No."

"Had you, or anyone you know, expressed an opinion as to the size of these pellets prior to Sergeant Ventriglia's finding?"

"Only casually."

"Could you elaborate on that, Sergeant Berchtold?"

Drops of sweat beaded the sergeant's hairline. "On the morning of the initial investigation, March 12th, I put the pellets I'd found in a plastic evidence bag and handed it to Chief Eldrid of the Appleton P.D. He held it up and had a look. Detective Sergeant Skeen was standing right there and so was a state trooper out of Ellentown. The chief was examining the pellets, like I said, and the trooper pipes up: '7½'s, maybe 8's.'"

"He could tell at a glance?"

"It's not difficult if you're familiar with shot," Berchtold said.

"What was your opinion?" Michael said.

"Yes. 7½'s, possibly 8's.'"

"Of the two sizes of shot, 7½ and 8," Michael said, "which is more common, more prevalent among hunters? I'm asking for your opinion."

"I'd say 7½'s," Berchtold said. "A 7½ strikes a balance between hitting power and spread. It's a favorite of bird hunters in the northeast."

"Who, as a group, uses 8's?"

"Also bird hunters. Like anything else, it's personal preference. Skeet shooters use 9's in competition but often practice with 8's."

"Can you tell the court why a skeet shooter might use 8's in practice?"

"On average, there are 250 fewer pellets in an 8 cartridge than a 9," Berchtold said. "That makes hitting a clay pigeon more difficult with an 8. It keeps the shooter honest."

Michael paused momentarily. "Sergeant Berchtold, tell us what happened last summer, when you were working alone in your police department office. Give us the approximate date."

"I was doing a report on a minor crime, sometime in late July. I made a typing error. As I was erasing it—"

"Could you speak up, Sergeant?"

Berchtold raised his voice, not by much. "As I was erasing it, the eraser twisted from my hand, landing on the floor. It was under my desk, and when I reached for it, the brush end of the eraser knocked something away—something round and very small. It rolled out of sight and was gone in an eye blink."

"Did that strike you as odd?"

"It got me thinking," Berchtold said. "We have shotguns in the department and shotgun ammunition, two dozen boxes of riot-type ammo, mostly buckshot and 2's—but this pellet was bird shot. I asked myself, What is a piece of bird shot doing under my desk?"

"Did you come up with an answer?"

"No," Berchtold said, "but it wouldn't leave me alone. Then the day I testified, here in court, I remembered what the Ellentown trooper had said, '7½'s, maybe 8's.'" Berchtold stopped; his jaw seemed to lock.

"Please continue, Sergeant," Michael urged.

After a while he said, "Yesterday afternoon I went to the murder site on Dr. Kendrix's property hoping to find another pellet. I called up my neighbor, Joe Brink, and he came with me; he's here in court right now. When we got to the spot where Kendrix took the blast to his groin, the shale was all tore up, like a coyote had smelled blood and started scratching, digging, nothing like how I'd left it on the morning of June 12th. Anyways, I hadn't looked for thirty seconds when I saw a piece of shot. I dropped it in an APD baggie, then looked and dug around for another hour, hoping to find a second pellet. But that was it."

At the defense table, Rick stared at Berchtold in disbelief, his mouth falling open; quickly he caught himself, closing it.

"Then what happened?" asked Michael.

"At home I measured the pellet using a micrometer," Berchtold said. "Joe Brink was sitting right next to me. It measured .09 of an inch; he confirmed the finding. Under 'Shotgun Ammo' in Jim Whitney's *Cartridge Catalog*, that's an 8."

"Do you have the pellet with you?"

Berchtold pulled out a file card from his jacket pocket; holding the single shot in place was a strip of transparent tape. Written on the card were the size, where found, and the date found. Michael showed the pellet to the judge and jury, then presented it as defense Exhibit A.

Cruikshank nodded.

Michael asked Berchtold, "What does this pellet say to you, Sergeant?"

"It tells me someone tampered with the evidence in the Kendrix murder case."

Michael felt the seriousness, the heft of Berchtold's words. "Tampered with it how?"

"By discarding the pellets I found on June 12th, and the autopsy pellets, and replacing them with 7½'s."

"Where were the original pellets kept?"

"In our evidence locker at the station."

"Who has the key to this locker?"

"Chief Eldrid and Detective Sergeant Skeen."

"Sergeant Berchtold," Michael said, "are individual shotgun pellets easy to come by?"

"If you have ammo handy, yes."

"Were any boxes of shotgun ammo handy during the early part of your investigation?"

"The boxes on the evidence table, people's Exhibits C, sat on the Detective Sergeant's desk."

"Not in the evidence locker?"

"Later on they were but not for the first few weeks."

Michael looked at the judge. "Your Honor, I would like to remove a single shotgun shell from a box in prosecution Exhibit C."

"Go ahead."

He went to the table, lifted the flap on one of the boxes, and picked out a shell, then came back to the witness, holding the bright red cartridge for all to see. Speaking to Berchtold,

"What is printed on the side of the shell?"

"The number 7½."

"The pellets hardly seem accessible. They're solidly encased," Michael said.

"You have to cut through the hull."

"Would you be willing to demonstrate for the court?"

The witness chair had flat, sturdy arms. Berchtold reached into his pocket for a small, compact knife, opened the blade. The shell was 2½ inches long, and he selected a spot about an inch above the brass, slicing clean through. The police officer held the slightly longer section in his fingers; it was brimming with shot.

Michael showed it to the judge and jury; in the process two or three pellets spilled out, skittering across the floor. Then he set the two sections on the evidence table, naming them with Cruikshank's approval defense Exhibit B. Coming back to the witness, "Sergeant Berchtold, can you now explain the existence of the pellet that rolled across the office floor last summer?"

"Whoever tampered with the evidence, a shot got away. Transferring fifteen pellets all told, maybe more than one."

After several long seconds Michael asked the detective why he had come forward.

"First off, I didn't know if I could—" Berchtold looked down in an effort to regain his composure, "—or even if I should. Last night I talked it over with my wife, and she said if I didn't stand up for what was right, I might just as well turn in my badge. How could I let Professor Forrester, or anyone, go to jail for twenty-five years for a murder they didn't commit? I couldn't. That's why I'm here."

Michael paused respectfully. "Thank you, Sergeant Berchtold."

Cruikshank gestured to Centerwall. "You may cross-examine."

The assistant D.A. walked up to the witness, his forehead

swollen with indignation. "Yesterday you took it upon yourself to revisit the murder scene, is that correct?"

"Yes."

"You hoped to find a pellet in the spot where Dr. Kendrix took the fatal blast."

"Yes."

"And some animal, we're led to believe a phantom coyote, had scratched at this spot earlier on, and lo! a pellet was there waiting for you."

"For anyone who went looking," Berchtold said.

"That boils down to you, Sergeant. Who else but you would've even *noticed* the pellet? This testimony of yours, and the evidence you 'found'—with all due respect to this court— is inadmissible. You're a police officer. Does that make it OK to skirt the rules of evidence? You have a pellet in your possession that you found, you say. You go home and measure it. The shot measures .09 of an inch, an 8. As if your good friend and neighbor was going to disagree!"

"Joe Brink is an honest man! He'll testify under oath."

"It's your testimony that's crucial here, detective. Let's talk about micrometers," Centerwall said. "Correct me if I'm wrong. To get a reading, you turn the threaded screw on the device until you pinch the object you're measuring. Let's say you're measuring the thickness of a piece of cardboard. You turn the threaded screw until you 'catch' the cardboard between the—" Centerwall pressed his thumb and index finger together.

"Anvil and spindle," said Berchtold.

"Thank you. We'll say the cardboard measures .12 of an inch on the dial. Are you with me, Detective?"

Berchtold didn't answer.

"Wouldn't it be possible, at that point, to give the threaded screw another little turn, considering that cardboard is relatively soft?"

"You could."

"So your reading would then be .10 of an inch, or thereabouts," Centerwall said. "In other words, a smaller reading."

Berchtold didn't comment, and Centerwall went on. "Unless the object we're measuring is rock hard, like a piece of glass or steel, its measurement really depends on how hard you turn the screw. Is that correct?"

"If you bear down, yes. But—"

"What is the difference in size between a 7½ and an 8 pellet, would you know offhand?"

"Five thousandths of an inch."

"A tiny, tiny amount," said Centerwall. "Sergeant, what are shotgun pellets made of?"

"Lead."

"Not an especially hard metal." Centerwall made to turn a knob or dial. "You could flatten a lead pellet .005 of an inch in a micrometer, wouldn't you say? And by doing so, effectively reduce a 7½ to a smaller 8?"

"It would still be a 7½," Berchtold said. "It would only mean whoever was mic-ing the pellet was doing a bad job of it!"

"Perhaps intentionally."

"Check out defense Exhibit A. See if it's flattened or compressed!"

Centerwall was amused; he smiled in a patronizing manner. "You're married, as you stated. Twin girls, a child on the way. Is that correct?"

"Yes."

"Car payments, mortgage. Taxes. Appleton is known for high taxes. It's hard to make ends meet, isn't it?"

"We manage," J.C. Berchtold said.

"'Manage.' I take that as a synonym for 'scrape by.' If Detective Sergeant Skeen were to lose his job for evidence tampering, you'd become the top detective in the Appleton P.D., isn't that so?"

"I resent that comment."

"At a handsome salary increase."

"And that one!"

"'Detective Sergeant Berchtold'—what a great ring that has! Just sully the good name of Darryl Skeen, it's yours."

"Your Honor," Michael said, breaking in, "this is not a cross-examination, it's the ruthless attack on a man's character!"

Centerwall didn't wait for a ruling. "You didn't find a pellet at the murder site, Detective Berchtold. You planted one and *then* found it! You stabbed a fellow officer in the back so you could get his job in the department!"

Michael stood, his voice cracking with anger. "The assistant district attorney is out of line, Your Honor! His blatant *ad hominem* comments should be stricken from the record."

The judge glowered at Michael. "At your request, counselor, a prosecution witness has testified for the defense. Overruled. You will have the opportunity to re-direct." To Centerwall, "You may continue."

"I have no further questions."

Once Centerwall had sat down, Michael approached the witness. "Sergeant Berchtold, suppose Detective Sergeant Skeen—on his own, in good standing—were to leave the Appleton Police Force and take a job elsewhere, would you be in line to take over the job he now has?"

"Yes, but that doesn't mean—"

"What are your qualifications, as you see them, to take over Skeen's job?"

"My length of service, going on eight years, as a detective. I'm a respected member of the community. I'd have the backing of my fellow officers."

"You're confident of that," Michael said.

"I am, yes."

Michael nodded. He liked Berchtold; he was a man with a solid core. "If Skeen were to lose his job as a result of your testimony today, Sergeant Berchtold, would you have their backing then?"

"No."

"Without it, would you likely take over as top detective?"

"No. I'll likely be asked to leave the force."

"Why? You've done a tremendous job. Through your persistence and hard work, you uncovered key evidence—"

"There's a code among cops," Berchtold said. "I didn't live up to it." His eyes clouded.

"Then what did testifying against your boss bring you?"

"Bring me?"

"Yes. Why did you do it?"

"Because I had to. The code among cops isn't the primary code in my life."

"Thank you, Detective Berchtold," Michael said.

CHAPTER
42

After closing arguments and a thirty-minute recess, Judge Cruikshank instructed the jurors on the fine points of the law in New York v. Forrester, adding at the last moment that the clock of justice was in their hands, not his. If they chose to discuss the case into the wee hours of the morning, that was their right and privilege. "We await *you*." Thus charged, the jury filed out.

Michael said it was unlikely that their first go at it would last an hour. For one, the afternoon was pressing on. A message would come in saying the jury had taken a vote, had established a procedure, and wanted to start actual deliberation in the morning. Words to that effect. But no message came in. One hour stretched into two; darkness settled over Kingsley-on-Hudson. Two and a half hours along, the bailiff finally handed Judge Cruikshank a note.

Both tables were very still. Was this it? Cruikshank studied the note, folded it, and spoke to the lawyers. "The jury is suspending its deliberations for the day. Court is in recess until nine a.m. tomorrow." He gave his block a rap.

"OK," Michael said, "good."

■ ■ ■

Rick was relieved that the jury hadn't ended the trial then and there, considering the strength of Centerwall's closing argument, especially the summing up. It was going through Rick's mind now as he drove south on Rt. 23. *"Perhaps you are aware, ladies and gentlemen, of the Supreme court ruling rendered last month, October 4, lifting the ban on the death penalty in the United States. Gary Gilmore killed two Brigham University students earlier in the year, and now, with the lifting of the ban, he faces execution. In Utah it's by firing squad. However monstrous that crime, Professor Forrester's murder of Dr. Kendrix is no less monstrous. Here in New York we have the electric chair. I am asking you to convict Professor Forrester of the premeditated murder of Evan Kendrix so that he, like Gilmore, will pay the ultimate penalty for his crime."*

Rick wanted to get home and see his kids but felt too emotionally shaken to be with them now; he needed time to settle down. And then he saw on his right the neon windows of the dark and gloomy Happy Days tavern. Any port in a storm. Rick swerved off the road and pulled into the parking area.

As he walked to the entrance, he noticed an 8-point buck lying in the bed of a pickup, the deer's hide matted and bloody near its shoulder. The door to the establishment demanded a hard pull, as if to turn away anyone without the strength, or will, to enter. He managed and went in. The place was shadowy, minimal lighting. A solitary patron in checked wool pants sat at the far end of the bar, slouching over a draft. The bartender, a big, beefy individual with thick hair low on his forehead, saw the new customer and came over; his small eyes, shiny as anthracite coal, seemed to penetrate the gloom.

"What ken I getcha, pal?"

"A beer."

"Bud or Schlitz?"

"Schlitz."

But the bartender didn't move; staring, leaning across the bar, he said, "Rick! Son-of-a-gun!"

It was his oldest boyhood pal, Dom Scileppi. "Dom. What a surprise!"

"Jeeze, I been reading about yeh, seeing yeh on TV—and out of the blue yeh stop in!" He put out meaty arms and grabbed Rick by the shoulders. "I don't hardly believe it! Jeeze, it's been a while." He searched Rick's face. "Bad stuff you're goin' through.

How you doin'?"

"Hanging in, I think. This your place?"

Dom pulled away but stayed close. "Three years now."

"I've passed it a hundred times. How's business?"

"People drop in. Hunters, fishermen, guys going home from work." Dom grinned, the smell of a meatball sandwich, plenty of garlic, heavy on his breath. "What I was thinking of, just recent," he said, "was the day your dad took us to Ebbets Field. We must of been eleven. We seen Dolf Camilli park one—remember?"

"It was a great day."

"Afterwards we went to Nedick's. I had two dogs and an Orange Crush. I been thinking about all that, seeing your name in the papers. Like that time we was still-hunting for grays—me, you, and Frank. You had his old .410 with the double hammers. We was spread out, maybe a hundred yards between us, like in a triangle. 'Boom!' comes through the woods. The .410. Then I remember, Jeeze, we didn't tell Rick it had hair triggers, is he OK? I go running over the ridge and you're sittin' on a downed pine, a big gray layin' at your feet."

"It was my first squirrel."

"That goes back. I don't think the war had started yet."

"It hadn't."

"Boy, them was happy days," Dom said, "trappin', huntin', fishin' on the reservoy. Borrowin' boats layin' on the shore—OK, we busted a few chains—then rowin' to all the good spots. Stringer would have eight or ten bass on it when we quit. Yellow perch. Bullheads. Remember that big wall-eye I caught? Went thirty-five inches!'"

"I sure do."

Dom's voice lowered. "Tell me, am I gettin' it right, Rick, all this I'm hearin'? But lemme me get yeh a brew."

He set a draft before Rick just as two hunters ambled in, looked like a father and son. Dom served the new customers, stayed with them jawin' for a while, laughing. Rick had a swallow of beer. He would sometimes sleep over at Dom's in the Scileppis' three-story roadhouse. In the bar was a television with a screen no bigger than a book and if you looked real hard you saw men running around in a snowstorm—looked like baseball.

Now, drinking a beer, Rick saw his old friend leaning across the bar speaking with the father and son. Dom had an older brother, Frank, who—when they were all kids—had a girlfriend, a waitress in the roadhouse, and one time when Rick was spending the night, Dom told him that Frank was upstairs fucking Roberta. Rick didn't know what that meant but didn't say anything, and Dom asked him if he wanted to go look. Well, sure. He followed Dom up to the third floor and they went into one of the five or six bedrooms and Frank and Roberta were in bed. To Rick it looked like they were sleeping. Her hip was outside the covers, and Dom slid his hand between the cheeks of her ass, high up between, and kept it there kind of smiling, then pulled it away. "Go ahead, Rick, feel her snatch." Rick didn't know why he should but at the same time wanted to, only just then Roberta yanked the covers over her legs and Frank woke up and yelled and Dom and Rick ran out. Dom was laughing and they went down to the bar and watched shadowy men circling bases in a blizzard. Men and women at the bar talking, drinking. Something was different. Rick couldn't explain what it was, just that something was different. Mr. Scileppi brought over short beers to his son and the Forrester boy....

Dom broke away and shuffled over; leaning in close, he said, "I was wondrin' if I could do anything for yeh, Rick."

"Like what?"

"I know a lot of people."

"Thanks, Dom. I don't think so," Rick said.

"I'd hate to see you get sent up."

"I wouldn't like it either."

"If yeh change your mind, jus' let me know. Favors are owed." Dom shifted to a new topic. "Seeing your name and all, just the other day somethin' else come to me—going to church on Sundays. Jeeze, how yeh rung them bells! Yeh rung them like a saint, my mother used to say. 'Dominick,' she'd say, 'why don't you become an altar boy like Rick?' What, and learn all them lines? What language is that?"

"Latin."

"Who speaks that anyway?"

"Not too many people."

A new customer came in, a man with grimy hands wearing a greasy cap and a thin blue jacket. Dom set down a beer before him, took his money, returned to Rick. "This morning, over to Crawfordville, I dropped me a 12-pointer," Dom told Rick. "Beautiful buck, third this season."

"Aren't you only allowed one?"

"So they tell me. Let me getcha another."

"I have to be running, Dom."

"A short one." He held Rick's glass under the tap, stopping when it was two-thirds full. Smiling, "Like the old days, remember?"

■ ■ ■

A fire was going in the iron stove when Rick got home. He and his family sat in front of it and he gave them the latest developments. A member of the Appleton police force had taken the stand for the defense, of and by itself a bonus. Sergeant Berchtold had uncovered a pellet in Evan's driveway smaller than the pellets the prosecution was claiming had killed Evan; and he testified to that effect.

Waldo was sitting next to Rick, who was patting the dog's head. "Berchtold said the pellet was probably scratched up by a coyote," Rick went on; then, directly to the dog, "A wily old coyote, Waldo, smelling Evan's blood, starting digging, and there it was. A crucial piece of evidence. How about that?"

"Rrrufff!"

Margi and the kids had a rare laugh.

Rick saw no reason to speak of Centerwall's powerful closing argument, invoking the death penalty; nor did he mention the fear that had gripped his heart when word had come in from the jurors after the first two hours of deliberations. He said that he had stopped by a roadside tavern on his way home and had bumped into his oldest boyhood friend, Dom Scileppi.

■ ■ ■

"They were hard days for everyone," his mother was saying, seated with Rick at the kitchen table after Lisa and Andrew had gone to bed. The topic of Dom Scileppi had led Margi into recalling how Dom's father, before opening his tavern, had driven through the Bluestone Art Colony in an old Ford truck with baskets strapped to its running board and fenders filled with vegetables that local restaurants and grocery stores could no longer sell. Luigi would blow his screechy horn and artists would come out and buy tired lettuce and beans and eggplants. "The Depression had come roaring back in the late thirties," Margi said. "No one had a dime, but your father kept sending out his work. He opened the mail one day and there was a check for a hundred dollars from Century. They had bought one of his stories. It was the first time I'd ever seen him cry. Rod was a difficult man, he had his failings; but he was a great provider."

Rick had another bite of the pot roast, a taste of wine. For some reason, he felt a surge of anger and grief. "I never felt close to him as a kid," he said. "He took me places but he never let me in. In all those years when I was growing up, he never hugged me, sat with me in a chair. Didn't recognize me."

"He was set in his ways," Margi said.

"I remember one winter's day when I was about eight, Rachel and Holly were playing with paper dolls, decking them out in dresses for different occasions. They had a friend over, another girl. I went in and sat down with them and my job was dressing 'Skip,' putting on a cowboy outfit; then he became a fireman. We were having a wonderful time, laughing, talking, making up stories. My father walked in, saw what I was doing, and called me over. Girls play with dolls, not boys, he said. Boys chop wood. No more dolls for me."

"Rick, your father meant no harm."

"Couldn't he see we were having fun? What was he afraid of? That his son would develop… tendencies?"

"He loved you. In his heart your father loved you very much," Margi said.

"Why don't you agree with me, say it was wrong? What he did that day was wrong."

"Your father only wanted what was best for you, and in his mind—"

"I remember as a kid wondering why you always took his side," Rick said. "And you're still doing it."

"That isn't true."

"It is true," Rick said. "When the chips were down, when it counted, it was your husband you backed. One time he was explaining a game to my sisters and me. I forget the details of it but I wasn't interested; it was way too complicated and my mind drifted and when it became apparent I wasn't listening, he blew up. Ranted, carried on, sent me to my room in tears, and ten minutes later you came in and do you know what you said? Do you remember what you told me? My father was very upset and I should go down and hug him and say I was sorry for not paying attention. And I went downstairs and hugged him and apologized, and I hated it, hated myself for doing it!"

Rick took the jug of wine and half-filled his glass. "How many times did he spank me because I'd done something bad? I would cower in my room waiting for him to come up. Did you say anything, Mom? Stand in his way at the foot of the stairs? Then, worst of all, when you came up for commencement exercises at Andover, and driving home afterward he started telling me how disappointed he was that I hadn't won any prizes. Other kids had won prizes, why hadn't *his* son? And you sat there in the front seat and let him go on and on. I'd gone to the school for him, stayed there four years for him, and that was what I got for it, to be called a failure by my father? It was the last thing I needed. In a senior poll that came out the night before graduation, I was so humiliated, so crushed by it—I was voted Class Phony—that I thought of killing myself. We came to a traffic light in a village outside of Boston, and I had my hand on the door handle ready to jump out and disappear down the side streets of the town. Forever."

Rick lowered his head, shook it solemnly. "I died that day in the back of the car driving home with you and Dad," he said. "Do you know why I jumped from my ship to save that poor pilot's life? It wasn't bravery 'above and beyond,' as the Navy called it. He was looking up at me, his plane was going under, and I said to myself, what do I have to lose? And I jumped."

From the pocket of her gray cardigan Margi reached for a handkerchief, touched her eyes with it. "Rick," she said, "I want you to know something."

The handkerchief stayed in her hand, rolled, reminding him of the hanky she always had when he was a boy and they were going into a store, perhaps into someone's house. She would fish it out of her purse, wet it with spit, and use it to clean his face.

"I didn't know a word of English when I stepped off the boat. With a letter of introduction, I went to see a Mrs. Jacob Forrester who had eleven children and a big house in Green Harbor, Massachusetts. Proud Irish lady, Ellen Flynn, ambitious for her children."

Margi was telling the story he and his sisters had heard many times "Her kids would drift in and out, and I got to know them," she went on. "The oldest was your father, a star at Columbia, on the faculty, a poet. And one day, maybe I'd been with the family two years, he asked me to walk with him on the beach, and we sat on a dune and talked about the sand and the ocean and my family in Germany, and his plan to strike out on his own as a writer; and then he asked me to marry him. We'd never even held hands, nothing! I was engaged to a boy in Germany who worked in a coal mine. I wrote him to say I wasn't coming back. Rick, I never woke up, never snapped out of that moment on the dunes. Why is Roderick Forrester Junior asking me to marry him? Today I know why. I was the only woman in the world who wouldn't complain, who'd live with him in the art colony where we went—two little rooms and a screened-in porch, no running water, making do with what we had—your father would fill two pails at the community pump and if I needed more on any day, I had to go for it, and when Rachel was born I had to wash her diapers, two pails weren't enough. He was writing and mustn't be disturbed, or visiting someone in the colony. Who? Where? It wasn't for me to know."

Margi was looking across the kitchen, staring at space, then turned to her son. "How could I step in, Rick, that day in the car, when I'd never done it before? Your father saved me from a dismal, oppressive, colorless existence in a coal-mining town in Germany. I was indebted to him, beholden to him, and in time he became a famous novelist and made up for those early years—"

"Financially, Margi. He made up for them financially, and left you for another woman."

Her eyes clouded over. Margi, the great, uncomplaining bearer of life's burdens, was breaking down. "For a long time I never knew what Chloe was talking about, what she meant by a 'liberated woman,'" she said. "I learned too late. Maybe I never learned at all. I'm sorry, Rick. Forgive me. You're a better man than your father."

CHAPTER
43

On the second day of deliberations, and the next day as well, all was quiet in Judge Wilbur Cruikshank's courtroom. Rick and his lawyers took turns walking about, going outside for breaths of fresh air; they read and re-read the Kingsley-on-Hudson *Daily Freeman* and *The New York Times,* had lunch in the cafeteria, took longer walks outside. At four fifteen on the third full day, the bailiff brought in a message and Judge Cruikshank emerged from his chambers to look it over. Was this it? Had the jury reached a unanimous decision? Clearing his throat, the judge announced that the jurors were calling it a day. Deliberations would resume at nine a.m. tomorrow and all parties would be in attendance.

Rick walked down the broad stone steps with his lawyers, parting with them at the entrance to the courthouse parking lot. They continued to their suite at the Governor Whelan hotel. Rick went to his car and drove south on Rt. 23. When he pulled into his driveway, lights were on in the house and smoke was streaming from the chimney.

He filled in his family on the day's activities: basically another day of waiting, of looking out of windows, of reading about the new Carter administration. Who would be taking what job? Time dragged. That wasn't so bad, Rick said, but always in the back of his mind a jury of his peers was sitting around a table in a little room deciding if he was guilty, beyond a reasonable doubt, of killing Evan Kendrix; or maybe they couldn't decide, someone was holding out; as a body they were hopelessly deadlocked. The jury gave no hint as to how it was leaning. Tomorrow could be the day. Tomorrow his future could be decided.

"I'm sorry you have to be going through all this," Rick told his family. He did not tell them he was scared half to death.

■ ■ ■

They had dinner, a wholesome beef and barley soup with onions and potatoes, perfect for a blustery winter night. No one said very much and at eight o'clock his kids said good night and went up to their rooms and an hour later Margi also went upstairs. Rick put another log on the fire, sat in his chair watching the flames flicker, thinking to read for an hour before turning in. On the little table next to his chair lay a book of Emerson's essays. He opened to one of his favorites, "The American Scholar," and was reading along when the telephone rang.

He walked into the alcove and picked up. "Hello."

"Rick, hi. This is Noreen."

"Noreen. To what do I owe this pleasure?"

"I have evidence, exculpatory evidence."

He pulled out the chair and sat down. "I hate to tell you. The trial is over."

"A trial is never over until the jury comes in."

"The testimony phase is over," he said.

"Listen to me. We have to act quickly on this. Ten days ago there was an obituary in the *Times* on Vincent Ciccarelli—"

"I saw it," Rick said.

"It got me thinking," Noreen said. "At Christine's funeral, I saw a look in Vincent's eye. I didn't understand it at the time but when I saw the article, it came together for me. Vincent must have had it in his mind to kill Evan Kendrix."

"So did one or two other people I know," Rick said.

"He carried through with it."

"The police questioned him," Rick said, "and came up empty. Plus, he didn't know Kendrix; he didn't know that Christine was in therapy—"

"He wrote me a letter," she said.

"Noreen, Vincent is dead."

"He sent it to the White Plains address just before he crashed his car," she said. "My parents were away on a cruise, the post office was holding their mail, and my mother forwarded my mail when they got home. I have an apartment on 11th Street in the city. I walked into my building ten minutes ago and there it was. The envelope has a cancelation stamp on it, November 24, sent from Yonkers. Vincent died the next day."

Rick's heart was beginning to pound. "Will you read it to me?"

"Sure, here goes." She paused for a second, then began. "'Dear Noreen, you are the only person I can write this to and someone has to know. Before she died, Christine called me from California and told me about Dr. Kendrix, crying, apologizing, out of her mind. How she had fallen for him and how he took advantage of her in the name of therapy. Next I heard she had overdosed. I made a vow to kill Kendrix and a month later I carried it out. The Appleton police arrested a professor at the college and are trying him for the murder. Noreen, without Christine, life means nothing to me. When you get this letter, I'll be with her again. So let me set the record straight. I shot Dr. Kendrix on the night of June 11th outside his house. Why should someone else pay? There have been enough injustices already. Do with this as you will. Vincent.'"

She was crying over the phone, and he sat there in agony. He knew what was next, the decision confronting him.

"Rick?"

"Yes."

"Isn't this incredible?"

"It is, and very sad."

"We have to get this to Michael. I can drive to Appleton in the morning," she said, her voice brimming with urgency. "I can be at your house by seven. I'll bring the obit also. They go together."

He didn't respond. He was grimacing, eyes tightly shut.

"Rick?"

"I'm here."

"Did you hear what I said?"

"I heard."

"Are you OK with it?"

And then he said it. Because he had to. "I want you to hold the letter, Noreen."

"Rick, we have to present this now," she came back quickly, "before the verdict. Vincent's letter will bring the trial to a halt. But if we're late with it and you're found guilty, all kinds of complications, legal machinations, and politics come into play. The D.A. of Ulmer County will not give up easily. After winning a conviction in a major case? You could languish in jail for years."

"Hold the letter," he said again.

"It's your pass to freedom, Rick. You're not thinking rationally."

"It's beyond rational."

"What am I missing?" she asked.

"I don't need Vincent Ciccarelli doing this for me."

"He doesn't even know you, Rick," Noreen came back. "I don't understand you. Maybe I never have. Your loyalties, your priorities. There are more people involved here than Rick Forrester! Can't you see that?"

"I see it very well. I don't expect you to understand. I love you, Noreen," he said. "I want to be with you, fully with you. Can you understand that?"

"It's a hell of a way to show it. You're putting me through hell, Rick. *Again.*"

"Don't give up on me."

"I can't talk anymore."

"Please, don't give up on me, Noreen."

She wasn't saying anything. Had she put down the phone? "Noreen?"

"I won't give up on you, Rick. Good night."

CHAPTER
44

No one said very much at breakfast the next morning. His mother, his kids, were all with their own thoughts. Lisa was the first to leave the house and Rick went with her to the front door as the bus was coming down Elting Street. With his handkerchief he dried her eyes, kissed her, and she was down the steps. Rick went upstairs and dressed for his day in court and was ready to leave just when Andrew was.

"I have something for you," the boy said.

"All right."

"You have to promise me you'll wear it today."

"OK," Rick said.

Andrew reached into his pocket; something was in his hand when he took it out. "I want you to have this. It's yours, you won it. I'm sorry for what I said, Dad." He opened his hand.

It was Rick's Navy Cross. "Thank you, Andrew," he said, reaching for it.

"Here's my bus. See you later." He ran out.

Rick looked at the medal, profoundly moved. He took a deep breath. With still a few minutes, he sat with his mother at the kitchen table. "You've been great, Margi. Just wonderful," he said.

"I like being here," she said. "But please win today, Rick, so I can go back to my own house."

■ ■ ■

Both his lawyers commented on the medal pinned to the lapel of Rick's suit jacket. He said his son had requested he wear it. Leonard Cashman seemed particularly impressed; perhaps, he said, Rick should have worn it from day one. Then another day in the courtroom began. Rick and his attorneys took turns walking around in the hall. They went out for lunch in a local restaurant on Pearl Street. All the tables were taken by men in dark suits and their more randomly attired clients. Cashman said he was beginning to think that the jury was at an impasse and he wouldn't be surprised if a message came in to that effect this afternoon. A discussion on deadlocked juries stayed with the three as they ate their BLTs and sipped their coffee. Michael wrapped up by saying with a wry smile that whatever the downside to a hung jury, in capital cases it sure beat a conviction. Rick picked up the check and they made their way back to the courthouse.

At two thirty-five the jowly bailiff handed a note to Judge Cruikshank. He read it, then told the court, "The jury is one vote shy of a unanimous decision." Moans, groans in the courtroom. The judge took his time scribbling a reply and handed it to the bailiff.

The afternoon dragged on. Three ten. Three fifty. Four twenty-five. Outside it was growing dark. All morning and into the afternoon Rick had mulled over his decision not to step forward with Vincent Ciccarelli's letter, wavering but not succumbing. Trusting that he had done the right thing. But now, one vote short, with the clock of justice ticking ever louder, Rick felt himself cracking. He was afraid, and he had nowhere to turn. He found himself turning to Chloe. He recalled how she had spoken to him, as if from the grave, telling him not to clean the barrels. The essence of the blast that had taken her life would be his salvation.

Forgive me, Chloe, he thought, as I forgive you.

Rick's head was bowed, and he felt Michael's hand on his shoulder. The judge was reading a note. The jowly bailiff was standing at the bench. Cruikshank studied the message, then rapped his gavel on the wooden block. "We have a verdict. It will be delivered at six o'clock."

It was the slowest thirty minutes Rick had ever spent, a lifetime—and like a lifetime, the fastest. At the designated hour, the men and women of the jury filed in, eyes straight, seeing no one, sitting in their assigned chairs. The bailiff took a slip of paper from the foreman and delivered it to the judge. Cruikshank read it, nodded at the foreman, then looked at Rick.

"The defendant will stand."

Rick stood.

Cruikshank asked the foreman: "How do you find?"

The tired, slope-shouldered little man who shampooed carpets spoke in a clear but tired voice: "We find the defendant, Roderick John Forrester, *not guilty*."

Clapping, sustained cheering in the crowded gallery. Michael embraced Rick, so did Leonard Cashman. Jurors were polled, and a few minutes later Wilbur Cruikshank was saying, "I want to thank everyone who participated in this trial. Members of the jury, you conducted yourselves with dignity and resolve. The good people of Ulmer County are grateful for your civic duty. My appreciation to the defense and prosecution is very great. It was a hard-fought trial and makes clear it is not always the strength of early evidence that carries a case. Professor Forrester, you leave a free man." The old hand wielded his gavel for the final time. "This trial is over. Court dismissed!"

R. Lincoln Centerwall snapped closed his briefcase and strode from the courtroom, brow leading, lest anyone get in his way.

Reporters barraged Rick and his lawyers with questions in the courthouse, then again on the broad stone steps outside. It had started to snow. A final question to Michael: "Without the appearance of the single size-8 pellet on Kendrix's property, would you have won the case?"

"It was crucial evidence. That's all I can say."

Michael, Cashman, and Rick continued walking. At the

entrance to the courthouse parking lot, they stopped. "Well, we did it," Michael said. "How exactly I'm not sure, but here we are."

"There's a little Davy Crocket in every boy," Rick said.

Michael came out with a big laugh. "We're a good team."

"Thanks, Michael. Send me a bill."

"I was thinking you could pick up our lunch tab in the spring, when we hit the Dunbar."

"Come on. I'm serious."

"Don't kid yourself, the Farlow Diner isn't cheap. Open steak sandwiches, great fries, homemade cherry pie—you'd better have a twenty."

"I'll scrape one up."

They shook hands all around, and the lawyers moved on. Rick stood for a moment, feeling the snow on his face, then walked to his car.

CK2020
10/13